THE ISLAND WITHIN

BY LUDWIG LEWISOHN

A Jewish Legacy Book

BEHRMAN HOUSE, INC. *New York*

A JEWISH LEGACY BOOK

Series Editor: Seymour Rossel

First BEHRMAN HOUSE edition, 1979

Copyright © 1928, 1956 by Harper & Row

Library of Congress Cataloging in Publication Data

Lewisohn, Ludwig, 1882-1955.
    The island within.

    (A Jewish legacy book)
    Reprint of the 1968 ed. published by the Jewish Publi-
cation Society of America, Philadelphia, in series: The
JPS library of contemporary American Jewish fiction.
    Bibliography: p.
    I. Title.
[PZ3.L59lIs 1979]   [PS3523.E96]   813'.5'2   79-14091

ISBN 0-87441-318-4

Published by Behrman House, Inc.
1261 Broadway, New York NY 10001

MANUFACTURED IN THE UNITED STATES OF AMERICA

1 2 3 4 5 6 7 83 82 81 80 79

INTRODUCTION

Today, some years after his death, to think of Ludwig Lewisohn is to think of a writer and teacher whose contribution to the intellectual enlargement of American Jewish life it would be difficult to overstate. One contemplates the eloquent espousal of Jewish traditionalism to be found in THE AMERICAN JEW: CHARACTER AND DESTINY (1950), or the profound analysis of Jewish fate offered in THE ANSWER (1939), or the Jewish messianism which pours forth from the pages of TRUMPET OF JUBILEE (1937). Or one is likely to remember the impassioned Zionist sympathies which compelled attention in THE NEW PALESTINE during the 1940's. In short, one thinks of a man whose attachment to Jews and to Jewish needs was, as Arthur Lelyveld has said, "so fiercely proud as to verge upon chauvinism." Those familiar only with this Lewisohn, the Lewisohn of mature years, cannot be blamed for imagining that so powerful a champion of the Jewish spirit surely fed from his birth on the manna of *Yiddishkeit*. How astonished they must be to discover in this Lewisohn a prodigy of *volte-face*.

The only child of North German Jews to whom Judaism had become scarcely more than an ancestral recollection (and an embarrassing one at that), Ludwig Lewisohn was not yet ten in 1890 when his family quit Berlin for the South Carolina hinterland.[1] Eventually the Lewisohns moved to Charleston where, he tells us in his autobiographical UPSTREAM, they found themselves committed to a life of "utter friendlessness . . . a state of solitariness which would have broken stronger and better-balanced natures." The boy grew up there with a painful sense of gap between himself and his peers. He belonged nowhere, not to the "rather ignorant, semi-orthodox Jews from Posen" for whom his parents had only disdain, and not to his Christian fellow-students at the College of Charleston who "gathered to form the first chapter of a Greek letter fraternity"—and left him out. He had been allowed, even encouraged, to identify himself with the Methodist Church, but this youngster who fancied himself "an American, a Southerner, and a Christian" and felt "a distinct and involuntary hostility to everything either Jewish or German" happened to be possessed of a "name and physiognomy . . . characteristically Jewish." What that meant for him cries out from THE ISLAND WITHIN:

> *Jewishness is like that Hound of Heaven described by the poet. It tracks you through the universe; it lies in ambush from without and from within. You think you have achieved a perfection of protective mimicry and on the lips of your dearest friend you see the unformed syllable, Jew. . . .*

Clearly, the frustrated longings of those years could not but leave permanent scars.

Always Lewisohn would feel himself an exile. Always there would be an incubus of dislocation, estrangement. He put it thus in MID-CHANNEL: "I could not . . . recall a single day of my life since my quite early childhood that had not been tarnished by less or more of moral suffering." Always there would be a yearning for some sure identity, and in time to come he would find that identity, or perhaps it would be truer to say that he would piece an identity together for himself—but what a lengthy, intricate, agonizing process that was to be, how fitful, how lacerating.

Remote from Jews and Jewish faith, Lewisohn would confront rejection as a Jew—so at least it seemed to him—wherever he most craved entry, whether in Charleston, or at Columbia University, or at several other universities where he sought a faculty appointment. Defeat and torment haunted him—a bitter mésalliance with his first wife, a Gentile twenty years his senior; the grief of seeing THE BROKEN SNARE, his first novel, aspersed as subversive of Victorian morality; the need to endure obloquy in World War I America for his exposition of Modern German literature (his probings of French poetry were shunted aside) and his advocacy at the Ohio State University of a pacifist standpoint; the wasting away of his parents and of their hopes for his success; the withdrawal into madness of his soulmate William Ellery Leonard; obstacles of a formidable sort to respectable union with the young woman for whom he had left his wife; a decade-long expatriation in Europe and, in America, the banning of his magnum opus, THE CASE OF MR. CRUMP. One could extend the list, but it is enough to say that, even in subsequent years, fate would play cruel jokes on him: Viereck, one of his closest associates, would achieve notoriety as an apologist for Hitler; Dreiser, who had helped him find a publisher for THE BROKEN SNARE, would turn to Communism and anti-Semitism; the Hauptmann whose dramas had seemed to him so pregnant with the promise of human dignity and liberation would become a Nazi; the German *Kultur* which he had championed with such ardor, and at such cost, would bring forth Auschwitz.

There would be no refuge for him. Even the Jews, with whom he had by then identified himself, would forebear to offer him anything approaching a plenitude of acceptance or appreciation. On the one hand, the Gentile world tended to ignore him as too parochial in his espousal of Jewish values. On the other, his fellow-Jews not infrequently despised him as an exhibitionist or a congenital misfit and refused to look beyond the defects of his personality and the lurid headlines which soiled his name. They forgot, or never knew, what he had written years before of Frenssen's JÖRN UHL:

> *Criticism has pointed out that . . . Frenssen falls at moments into mere fleshliness. The criticism would be unjust even if it corresponded to a fact. Modern man is a moral cripple who is trying to regain the use of his limbs. It is no wonder if he limps a little, if his gait is not at once and altogether graceful and harmonious. . . .*

By the time World War I came to an end, Lewisohn had, of course, long since abandoned any attachment to or connection with the Methodism of his youth, but Judaism had yet to command his attention, much less his allegiance.

Then, during the 1920's, there began growing in him quite unsurely, quite circumspectly at first, a new consciousness, a new self-recognition, a new assessment of what he was and felt. Now, somehow, and with increasing urgency and positiveness, he could discern in himself something Jewish, could answer to some call from the ancestral past of which he had been robbed in his younger years. He had come upon a new direction for his life and new mentors—Judaism, Zionism, Freud, Buber—and the 20's, as they wore on, found him turning to an exploration of these newfound horizons. The result was of far from meager significance for the unfolding of an American Jewish cultural life: the unequivocally Jewish autobiographical volumes ISRAEL (1925) and MID-CHANNEL (1929), and Lewisohn's first Jewish novel, THE ISLAND WITHIN, which is also, in considerable part, an essay in autobiography.

THE ISLAND WITHIN is not lacking in dissonance. Lewisohn was in love when he published it in 1928[2]—he had fallen in love with a woman and with a heritage—but alas, for all his expectations, his love for the woman would pass before long into contention and ruin. His love for the heritage, and the people of the heritage, would live and strengthen itself and become "the ultimate existential reality of [his] life and being." This passionate attachment to Jewishness is not so easily explained—this attachment which had had to contend with a notion of Judaism as an "archaic orientalism." THE ISLAND WITHIN does not completely wipe away the long years when Lewisohn was all but totally incapable of any construction of himself as *homo judaicus*, a man aware, he would say later, that "his ultimate self is Jewish and that his creativity and that deepest self are *one*." No, THE ISLAND WITHIN does not completely wipe away the long years when he had valued nothing Jewish in himself—when to be a "Pan-Angle" or a Southern Methodist or an "Aryan" bespoke the selfhood he had hungered to claim. Always, of course, there had been a Jew in him and a struggle on that score, but he would not know it in its fullness until long after, even long after THE ISLAND WITHIN. For the echoes of the struggle still sound within the pages of his first Jewish novel. The field is not yet cleared of battle; the Jew in him, the particular Jew he would be, has not yet tasted victory entire, only seen it aglimmer in the distance.

As a novel, THE ISLAND WITHIN is scarcely flawless, and I suppose it fair to say that no one who reads it with care can dismiss as entirely groundless Leslie Fiedler's caustic description of it as a "blend of self-pity and editorial." If that were all one could say of it . . . but, *pace* Fiedler, it is an unforgettably beautiful book, one in which Lewisohn's *spiritus rector*, Matthew Arnold, would have recognized a high seriousness, a book rich in melancholic sensibilities and a probing of the tragic dimensions and riddles of the Jewish inheritance. And it is an honest book—is that among its limitations?—making no pretense to ultimate wisdom, offering no fulsome solutions to the heart-wounding fret at its core. For all its air of treatise—a word which Lewisohn himself applies to it—the book is a curiously unideological expression. Certainly Lewisohn is eager to urge on the Jewish reader his conviction as to "the security and, yes, the human dignity, that a tradition lent to the freest minds." Certainly he wants the Jew who denies his Jewishness to "put away a pretense—a stubborn, hard, protective pretense" and to "possess the knowledge that he stood by birth at the human centre of things." Still, Arthur Levy, the novel's protagonist who finds his way back to Jewish pride, "didn't, *of course*, care about myth or ritual or dogma. *He never would.*" I have added the italics and am reminded of that delicate passage in MID-CHANNEL where Lewisohn speaks of his expatriate quarters in Paris as "a Jewish house, wherein appropriate symbolical tokens . . . of our history and its memories and its pieties are plain for all men to see"—and yet, he goes on to say, he is at pains "to avoid over-emphasis and even the shadow of going beyond our needs and convictions. So we have placed no *mezuzah* at our door." Pride, Jewish pride, speaks forth from THE ISLAND WITHIN, but it is a fragile, careful pride, one, still aborning, of touch and discovery. And question. Absent is the assertive religious commitment for which Lewisohn would in later years—depending on the reader's own aspiration—be acclaimed or contemned.

"The concrete, closely considered," Lewisohn had once declared, "is more far-reaching in its significance than the broadest generalization." THE ISLAND WITHIN validates the insight. Sculpted by the experience of the Gilded Age and World War I and the 20's, it addresses itself with undiminished power and relevance to the experience of the 60's. To be sure, such a novel would not be written today. In diction, in structure, in tone, it is at variance with what generally emerges as the temper of contemporary fiction, but these, it seems to me, are matters of technique, not spirit, not meaning. In sensitivity, in ability to move the reader and introduce him to the peculiar ambiguities of American Jewish life, in these respects Lewisohn's novel has lost nothing with age. His own characterization of it holds true: "a story not poor, perhaps, in the significant elements that make up the fate of man." I am tempted to omit the "perhaps," for in essence the experience Lewisohn reveals and reflects upon is not one we of the 60's are entitled to brand alien. THE ISLAND WITHIN stands in a sort of ancestral relationship, it might be said, to the work of later writers, Malamud and Bellow and even Philip Roth and Fiedler.

Mutatis mutandis, Arthur Levy is no stranger to us. Indeed, is it hyperbole to suggest that his tribe has undergone a prodigy of increase? At the least, we American Jews today harbor within our ranks more than a negligible minority of young people—and their elders?—who more or less self-consciously regard their ancestral heritage as something to be treated with as much indifference as boldness or decency will allow. There is, of course, among many of us a current enthusiasm for the State of Israel. I am grateful for this, but I recognize that even this represents something of a turning away from the Jewish past. It is Israel's secular modernity, her military and technological prowess, that feeds our pride and commands our esteem. Israel as a spiritual entity, a projection of Jewish history, a fountainhead of Jewishness, is far less able to excite us. It is with the Army of Israel, and with the Hebrew University, and with the Haifa Technion, that most of us feel connection—but the Hechal Shlomo, Israel's rabbinical establishment, is something else again. I do not cite all this as invidious or blameworthy, but merely to adumbrate the degree to which we continue to inhabit Arthur Levy's world, that world at odds with "myth or ritual or dogma." And do we not also share with Arthur Levy a troubling question: "Where would be the spiritual dwelling-place of his boy?" Where, in truth?

One final and quite personal word. When I knew Ludwig Lewisohn—it was on the Brandeis University campus during the late 40's and early 50's—he was in his last years. He was gentler, sweeter, it is my impression, than he had been at earlier stages of his life. For that, doubtless, age and honors were responsible, and I believe, too, his devoted Louise deserves no small share of credit. I was enormously impressed by him, and inspired by him, and I loved him—for his sadness, his aristocracy, the *m'kor chayyim*, the spring of life, I touched in him. Already there is far too much of myself in this paragraph, but I would have the reader indulge me this once and know my debt to this man. I think I am not the only one to owe him much. He made a Jew of me—he, his work, and particularly this book, THE ISLAND WITHIN. He made me prize what, it is true, was mine by birthright, but it was through my discovery of him that I began to care about that birthright. Even before I knew him in person, he had made a Jew of me, this book his instrument—and it may be, I allow myself to hope, his book will prove as fruitful in the future as it has proven in the past. If the reader takes these words as my *kaddish* for Lewisohn, I shall not complain.

Stanley F. Chyet

Cincinnati, Ohio
November, 1967

NOTES
TO
INTRODUCTION

[1] I have not thought it necessary for the purposes of this introduction to offer the reader any abundance of data about Lewisohn's life and career. The reader who wishes a more detailed account of the man and his work will find the following sources helpful:

"Analyticus" (pseudonym of James W. Wise), *Jews Are Like That!* (N.Y., 1928), pp. 107-26

Louis J. Bragman, "The Case of Ludwig Lewisohn," *American Journal of Psychiatry*, XI (1931), pp. 319-31

Stanley F. Chyet, "Ludwig Lewisohn: The Years of Becoming," *American Jewish Archives*, XI (1959), pp. 125-47; "Lewisohn and Crèvecoeur," *Chicago Jewish Forum*, XXII (Winter, 1963-1964), pp. 130-36; "Ludwig Lewisohn in Charleston (1892-1903)," *American Jewish Historical Quarterly*, LIV (1964-1965), pp. 296-322

Irwin Edman, "Odyssey," *Menorah Journal*, XIV (1928), pp. 508-11

Adolph Gillis, *Ludwig Lewisohn: The Artist and His Message* (N.Y., 1933)

Milton Hindus, "Ludwig Lewisohn: From Assimilation to Zionism," *Jewish Frontier*, February, 1964, pp. 22-30; Introduction to Ludwig Lewisohn, *What Is This Jewish Heritage?* (Revised ed.; N.Y., 1964)

Arthur J. Lelyveld, "Ludwig Lewisohn: In Memoriam," *American Jewish Archives*, XVII (1965), pp. 109-13

James Lewisohn, "My Father, Ludwig Lewisohn," *Midstream*, November, 1966, pp. 48-50

Sol Liptzin, "Lewisohn's Questioning of America," *Congress Weekly*, April 8, 1957, pp. 11-13

New York Times, January 1, 1956, p. 50 (obituary)

Harold Ribalow, "Ludwig Lewisohn's 'The Island Within,'" *Jewish Heritage*, Fall, 1963, pp. 44-48

David F. Singer, "Ludwig Lewisohn: A Paradigm of American-Jewish Return," *Judaism*, XIV (1965), pp. 319-29

Saul S. Spiro, *The Jew as Man of Letters, Being Some Notes on Ludwig Lewisohn* (Burlington, Vt., 1935)

[2] Actually, *The Island Within* first appeared in serial form, under the title *The Defeated*, in the April, 1927, issue of *Transition*.

BOOK I

1

UNTIL the other day we Americans lived as though we had no past. There were old families in Eastern cities who worshipped ancestors and played with heraldic devices in a quiet fashion. But the children of the many millions swept past these into the public schools and began the world all over again with Lexington and Bull Run and Valley Forge and the Declaration of Independence. Would that those happy and innocent days could have endured! We boasted loudly that the enmities and feuds of the Old World had fallen silent here and our boasts offended aristocratic ears on both sides of the Atlantic. No doubt there was a good deal of cant among inferior natures. But even the objectionables of the tobacco-stained whiskers who made the Bird of Freedom scream were the asserters, crude, premature, and doomed, of a better and a friendlier way of human life. Men not yet old can remember barbecues in sunny clearings of a summer forest, and orations, after the beef and beer and whisky, concerning the unexampled freedom of this refuge of the refugeless, this home of the homeless, this haven of the oppressed. We twisted the tail of the British lion, we scoffed at emperors and kings, we called our leaders Nature's noblemen. . . . Cleanse these memories and words of the slime cast over them by the eternal snob. Kings and priests with the inhuman arrogance of their mystical assumptions are in truth unbelievably dangerous and grotesque; Whitman and Lincoln were Nature's noblemen. . . . It is not wholly a delusion that Golden Ages lie always either in the past or in the future. Seen from the frail bridge of the present, evil obscures the good and visible confusion overlays a core of order. If human brotherhood and tolerance and liberty and the aspiration after these be order; if these misused and stained and mangled words are in fact the names of sovereign and saving concepts—then America had her Golden Age, alloyed and faint, but golden, in the past. In that past hard adventurers heaped up unmeasured fortunes. But they had still to use the gesture of democracy and dared

3

not yet display the poisonous disdain and contemptuous aloofness of the oligarch. In that past government was corrupt. But one still hastened to naturalize the alien in order to buy his vote, and by that very act to reaffirm the theory that government depends upon the consent of the governed. There were raw vulgarity and thunderous uproar. But the slave was freed and the oppressed of all the earth came to people the land, and the Know-Nothings and later the A. P. A.'s were defeated and overwhelmed. Democracy lived a feeble life, but it lived. The reflective mind may well look with a wistful tenderness upon those florid orations which, on Fourth of Julys and Washington's birthdays, still celebrated the right of revolution and the duty of civil disobedience. How suddenly those voices died! The Spanish War came, and a weak man, shouting, like all weak and therefore cruel men, for blood and war and dominance and glitter, became the idol of the nation. The World War finished what Roosevelt had begun. The state is an image—brazen, remote, implacable except by stealthy magnates; the augurs, fat-paunched, bellow at each other on the public roads; the gates of the land are sealed; the duped and stupefied populace—no more a people—dances about fundamentalist preachers, baseball pitchers and a Rumanian queen. . . .

2

"BUT we have paid two-and-a-half dollars for a story, not for a treatise!" Have patience, reader; the story is coming—a story not poor, perhaps, in the significant elements that make up the fate of man. But dwell with me for a moment on the question: what, in fact, is a story? Is it a meticulous account of the stream of consciousness as it flows through some carefully isolated mind? Is it an experiment in analysis? Or the symbolical doing of a day? . . . An elegant bed and in it, in silken pajamas, a gentleman who cannot sleep, who takes up one book after another and finds that the books no longer bite into his mind. "The flesh is sad, alas,

4

and all the books are read!" The yellow candleflame with its little orange heart wavers against the dusky hangings. And the reflections, no, not reflections but drifting, simmering, shifting reveries of this gentleman in silken pajamas, run to ten thousand words, words lovely enough in themselves, but without definition or contour quite like the gentleman's reveries, and the sentences steal upon the ear in an endless unmodulated murmur and the story—only, is it a story? —goes on, can go on forever and forever. . . . But beyond the dusky hangings of this room, beyond this house, beyond this carefully draped and cushioned world of the valetudinarian soul, life cries all its old cries, experiences all its old agonies, blazes with all of its old and tragic splendor. Do we know more than the men who came before us? Is our vision more keen and purged? Are we beginning to see the causes of things? Then, in God's name, let us tell wiser, broader, deeper stories—stories with morals more significant and rich. Yes, morals. If a story does not teach by example it is no story; it has no truth. For let men see truth and they will hasten to apply it to themselves. All but the utterly child-minded among them read for such truth as touches them, their lives, their mortal difficulties, their station and their moment amid the sum of things. . . . I am no watcher in another's brain and a day is not time enough for the story I want to tell, and a few rooms not space enough. I have seen and experienced much; I have been told more. I have lived with those who think and meditate and reason pro and con in the difficulties that confront them. It is of such that I would speak. Be a determinist, if you like. I am one, too. The metaphysical truth is irrefutable, but a margin of freedom and responsibility is a fact of human consciousness and human experience. A flat contradiction? But you will find a flat contradiction at the end of every train of human thought. The ultimate wall of mystery is built of antinomies. . . . The people I know, the people whose stories I can tell, are not caught in a web of mere revery. They have the power to bid the stream of perceptions and sensations and images to cease from flowing; they have the power to

5

meditate, to reflect, to reason, to determine. Therefore their stories are stories of thoughts and actions; by their thoughts, more even by their actions, they must be made known to the reader. If the art of fiction is in a state of crisis it is because words, gestures, actions have been blurred and dimmed and the rumor of the world has been shut out and characters, by a false analogy, placed like micro-organisms under a polished lens. . . . Let us recover, if possible, something of an epic note. To do that there is no need of high-flown words or violent actions. Only a constant sense of the streaming generations, of the processes of historic change, of the true character of man's magnificent and tragic adventure between earth and sky. . . .

3

IN the year 1840 there lived in the city of Vilna a Jew whose full name was Reb Mendel ben Reb Jizchack, with his wife and his two children. The man's calling was that of a *melamed*, or teacher of little children, and he was, like all of his kind, indescribably poor. The family lived in a sort of vault, a hollow opening in the ground floor of a house in the Ghetto. The house was old and crooked, and with the other old and crooked houses on either side of it seemed part merely of a great shapeless mass of crumbling brick and mortar that huddled about the courtyard of the ancient and famous synagogue. Near the two steps that led down into the family's single room Braine, the wife of Reb Mendel, would keep a bolt of cloth and a basket of onions. She tried hard to drive a trade, like the wives of other learned men, but little ever came of it. She was the daughter of a good house. For many generations her fathers had been learned men and hence belonged to the *jichess*, or intellectual aristocracy, which is the only class distinction known among Jews. Her father, moreover, had been a rich man at one time and had therefore gladly given her in marriage to the penniless Mendel, then a brilliant *yeshivabocher*, or student at a Talmudic university. But in the Polish uprising of 1830

Braine's father had lost all his worldly goods. The Russians had set fire to his house because they suspected him, correctly enough, of sympathizing with the revolutionary Poles. Mendel and Braine had had to flee from Byalistok and it was the fame of the young wife's house that procured for Mendel the humble employment in a city already overcrowded with the saintly and the learned.

The farther her youth receded from her, the more did Braine dwell upon it as her only romance and as her only dream. She had no hope of any change of worldly fortune. She had long ceased to bewail the catastrophe that had overtaken her family. She echoed with complete conviction the familiar phrase: Well, we are in *goles* (exile); she went to the great synagogue whenever a famous *magid*, or preacher, came thither to exhort the Jews concerning their sins, and wept heartily and felt a moment of inner lift when, at the end of the sermon, the preacher uttered the trumpet-note of his inevitable close: *Uvo leziejn gejel* (May a Redeemer arise for Zion). Since the *Shechinah*, the divine spirit of the Eternal, was itself in exile, what could the people of God expect? She held these beliefs in profound sincerity. But often when the dusk stole into her stony dwelling, and Mendel, his day's work done, had hastened over to one of the many houses of study (*beth hamidrashim*) that dotted the quarter, Braine would gather her little Efraim and Rifke about her and tell them tales of her youth and of her father's house.

From her descriptions there came to the children a vision which was never to fade from their memory or imagination of something glossy and mildly radiant, of a solemn festiveness blended with a great peace. They could see in their minds' eyes their grandfather's long coat of satin and velvet, the deep carpets and brocaded hangings of his house, the *menorahs* (seven-branched candelabra) and *Chanukah* lamps of dimly gleaming brass; they could see the praying-shawls with purple borders and the goblets of silver and the gold threads of heavily embroidered pillows and covers. They could see their tall grandfather in his satin coat going about

7

the house just before the services of *Erev Shabbes* (Eve of the Sabbath), the joy of the coming of the Princess already on his face, teasing his dainty little wife and his children and humming, *Yom Shabbes, yom menucho!* (Sabbath day, day of rest.)

This house and this man, according to Braine, developed on the great feast-days of the years a splendor that was both princely and priestly. Especially on the *Seder*, or great Passover evening. The house had been cleaned and refreshed to its last corner. The rite of burning any crumb of leaven that was left was over. The dishes and utensils used all the year were packed away and replaced by the delicate china and heavy, graven silver dedicated to the yearly feast. The table was set in the large dining room while it was still daylight; it was drawn out to its fullest length and small tables were brought up to its foot to lengthen it still further. For before the first star appeared the children's grandfather would go out into the streets of the city and gather in as many as he could find of poor men and of strangers to share the *Seder* at his house. Her mother, according to Braine, would sometimes gently ask her husband to select people who were clean and seemly in their ways. But her father would frown a little even amid his joy and repeat the saying that was oftenest on his lips: "*Rachmonim bnei rachmonim*—we are the merciful children of merciful parents." And then he would gather in the poorest and neediest and dirtiest. At this point in her narrative Braine's eyes would grow moist. For now she and hers were such poor people as her father used to gather in on the streets of the town.

She would stop for a moment and then describe how, with her father at the head of the table, the company sat down. All were magnificently cushioned in their seats and leaned, in Roman fashion, on their left elbows in sign of the fact that they were free men who had been delivered by the Eternal, blessed be His name, out of the land of Egypt and out of the house of bondage. And out of the old, yellow priceless manuscript *Haggada* her father intoned the begin-

8

ning of the immemorial ritual: Praised beest thou, O Eternal, our God, King of the world, for that Thou hast created the fruit of the vine!

The children knew the ritual perfectly, of course, although they had never seen it performed so beautifully. But they could well imagine how glorious it must have been when, as was often the case, there were learned minds and fine voices among the poor men at grandfather's table and a sonorous chorus answered him when he detailed the abounding mercies of the Eternal. "Had he fed us on manna, but not given us the Sabbath," the grandfather had chanted in his expressive baritone.

And the chorus answered him: *"Dajjenu*—it would have sufficed us!"

"Had he given us the Torah, but not brought us into the land of Israel—*Dajjenu*—it would have sufficed us!" Rifke on her lap, Efraim crouching at her feet there in the twilight in that barren home, Braine would almost forget that she was telling her children a tale out of the past. Tears would come into her eyes and a prayer out of that same majestic ritual rise to her lips, "Almighty God, rebuild Thy Temple soon, oh, soon, in our days!"

Silence and the black shadows creeping higher on the damp walls. A remarkably mature frown would appear on Efraim's face. He was nearly thirteen and ready to celebrate his *bar-mitzvah* and thus become a man among the men of Israel. The frown seemed to say, "What is the use of all this?" But he sat still, partly out of affectionate habit, partly because he knew what was coming and that was something he liked to hear, too. It was Rifke who said, "But you haven't told us about the chest, *Mameleben!*" Yes, even to Efraim this part of the story never lost its thrill. The chest? Ah, the chest. A light came into Braine's face. Yes, under the great *Chanukah* lamp with its scrolls and doves and lions of Judah wrought of brass there stood an old carved wooden chest. No one knew how old the chest was. Not even grandfather who was so learned and so wise that men came for his council from the far Ukrainian marches. It had

always been in the family, long before the days of the Jewish migration to Poland. It came from the west. It was dark
brown and showed cracks in the wood and had an old, old
lock with a huge key. No one dared open it but grandfather, and he opened it only once or twice a year on very
solemn or very joyous occasions. And what was in the
chest? Illuminated *katubahs*, or marriage certificates, gold
and blue and crimson, of grandfather and grandmother and
great-grandfather and great-grandmother and, and—Braine
didn't know how many more. And what else, what else?
Rifke asked. And a marvelous heavy old ring of gold with
the image of a doe wrought upon it, and bundles upon
bundles of parchment exquisitely written by hand in the
square Hebrew letters and illustrated with drawings. One of
these was the priceless manuscript *Haggada*, or Passover
book, from which her father had read, and another very
mysterious one was an account written long and long and
long ago of Jews who died somewhere in the west a death of
martyrdom to sanctify the ineffable Name. Every *Erev
Yom Kippur* grandfather had drawn forth that scroll and
read it to himself, alone, in his study and then come forth to
wash the tear stains from his face. And one more thing
there was in the chest, so far as Braine knew, and that was
the *jichess-brif*, the family-tree of her father's house prov-
ing that it was a noble house—a house of learned and holy
men, some poor, some rich, but all dedicated to study and
good works.

Efraim looked up. "And how far back did you say the
family tree went?"

Braine shook her head with proud mysteriousness. "Who
knows? My mother—*selig*—said it went clear back to King
David. But my father—peace be upon him—said that was
only a story, but that it did in truth go back to the great
Raschi of Worms, the light and guide of Israel."

Efraim got up. "What became of the chest?"

"Woe is me!" said Braine. "It was almost the only thing
saved from the house when the Russians—may their names
be blotted out—set fire to it at all four corners. Grandfather

and grandmother fled and in a village inn grandfather gave the chest to his brother. Why, why? I don't understand."

"His brother, the *Chassid?*" Efraim asked.

Braine nodded. Her voice had a tang of bitterness. "Why a man from such a family should join the *Chassidim*—not of us be it said—that goes beyond my understanding! And why father gave him the chest! But I am only a woman. Let us make an end of talking. It is dark."

4

MENDEL came home from the house of study. In the courtyard of the old synagogue he had stood still for a moment and listened to the wind rustling in the single ragged tree that stood among the cobblestones. He did that nearly every evening and was quite aware of the strangeness of the action. Long ago, at the Talmudic school, he had asked questions to which the teachers had answered: "To what end need a Jewish boy know that?" He had wanted to know something of the world of nature; he had shrunk back into himself at the rebuke and disciplined himself to dwell wholly, as his fellows did, in the world of Israel's thought and history and aspiration. But his dark secret was that, despite his later brilliance as a Talmudist, he was dry of heart. There was no glow in his study and no fervor in his prayers. He was just good enough, he said to himself, being a humble soul, to be a *melamed* and gnaw the crust of poverty.

On the other hand, *l'havdel*, to make a distinction, the Gaon Elia himself, the mightiest of Talmudists, in whose very *klaus* he himself had often studied, had approved the study of geometry. Mendel's father had known the Gaon and knew this to be the truth. Today if you breathed it harsh words were flung at you: "*Goyisher kopp*—head of a heathen!" If such a thing were to be whispered of him, he would lose his wretched position. And there were Braine and the children to be thought of. He must not linger under the tree. Was it the "evil instinct" that often drove him from within—that had driven him on that unbelievable day, two years ago, when he had suddenly left the children whom he was to teach and had run and run out beyond the gates of the Ghetto and found himself in a green, green field under a newly-washed sky? His warning had come to him at once. He had heard a discordant chanting, more like the snorting, it had seemed to him, of unclean animals. There, to his left, stood the synagogue of the Karaites, the accursed heretics who had tried to split the house of Israel a thousand years ago, who repudiated the oral tradition which, no less than the Torah, Moses had brought down from Horeb. The Karaites were in high favor with the Russians. They wore neither beards nor earlocks and were indistinguishable from the heathen.

Mendel had gone home slowly on that day. Braine had seen that he was pale. Yet she had been happy, too. For it had been the eve of the Sabbath and she had—rare treat—a dish of meat for her family, and Mendel had blessed the incoming of the Sabbath over the wine and bread with uncommon fervor, and the voice with which he chanted his prayers had had tears in it.

He had humbled himself for a while thereafter. It was related of the Gaon Elia that he had once stood on a balcony meditating. He had been walking up and down. And so profoundly had he been lost in his thoughts that he had forgotten that the balustrade was broken. He had walked on and on. And the Eternal, blessed be His name, had sustained the feet of His servant in the thin air. And there were men who had seen that. Legend or truth, Mendel had reflected, it was surely not upon the knowledge of the *goyim* that the Gaon had been meditating that day.

But in the two years that had passed since that incident grave things had happened. Shimen the Crooked, whose bitter and equivocal tongue was proverbial, so that pious men said: as crazy as Shimen—this man had first thrown brilliant glances out of his large dwarf's eyes at Mendel in the *shul*. Then he had talked to him in the courtyard, and then, one evening at dusk, he had slipped a book into the teacher's hand. It was a new book in Hebrew, a thing unheard of and strange in those days. By a candle at home Mendel had read the book. He had read on into the night and Braine had not been astonished except at this—he read in silence. He did not intone. But she had not questioned him. And Mendel, with a literally throbbing heart, had read Isaac-Ber Levinsohn's *Beth-Ye-Huda*, in which it was proved from the whole history of Israel that pious and holy Jews had in all other lands and ages cultivated profane science and philosophy and been no less acceptable to God. And Mendel, having finished the book, had gone out into the night and stood in front of his wretched dwelling and looked up at the stars, and tears had rolled down into his beard.

He had met Shimen again and yet again after that, a circumstance that did him no good in the eyes of the *balabatim*, the notables of the community on whom his livelihood depended. Shimen had loaned him the *Teudah be Israel* of Levinsohn and told him the story of Benporath, who, many years ago, had fought for enlightenment and had been defeated again and again and had not given in. And but the other day Shimen had given him Guenzburg's *Kiriath Sefer*, a source book of letters concerning philosophy and literature and life. With a soft fire in his eyes Shimen had said:

"And I will give you to understand another thing, Reb Mendel. Here today in our midst, in our congregation, God has raised up a man who is inditing new songs in the *lashon kodesh*, the holy language. No, he is no *meshumet*, no renegade. He sings even as sang the prophets of Israel."

Thus there had drifted to Mendel news of the doings of the *Maskilim*, the enlightened ones, of his day. And his heart burned and burned. But who was he, a wretched *melamed*, an object of charity, to see the faces or touch the hands of those men? If his completely orthodox piety were to be called into question he could go begging. Tonight, if he lingered much longer on his way home, Braine would say with fear in her eyes: "Where have you been? Talking to Shimen the Crooked? Oh, such craziness!" He must hurry.

But at the corner, near his home, he saw a group of people, of Jews. It was almost dark now and he saw these people, as it were, as black silhouettes against the grayish houses or the bluish air. All the motions and gestures of these people had something tense and rapt, as though they had just completed, or were about to begin a grave and mystical dance. They were poised between ecstasy and ecstasy. "*Chassidim*," Mendel murmured a little contemptuously to himself. But he stopped; he listened. A thin old man was talking to the men and women who crowded about. The old man's face was lifted up. His gray earlocks fell back from his face. "The Holy One, blessed be He, gives us miracles in our day. Yes, my eyes have seen the Gerer Rebbe. And he was sad, sad to death. And a man asked the *Zadik*, the holy man: 'Why are you so sad?' And the *Zadik* made answer: 'I feel the pain and sorrow of every Jew from world's end to world's end in my own heart. That is the cause of my sadness.'" The old man stopped, and Mendel could hear in the gloom that the people were weeping. Then a woman's voice arose:

"Tell us, Reb Menasche, what did the *Zadik* tell Shloime? *Nissim?* Miracles? That was a miracle."

The old man gave a short, hard laugh. "Shloime had a son who, not of our children be it said, would neither pray nor study nor do anything that a Jewish child should do. And the years went on and the shame grew greater and greater and the boy was growing up a heathen. In his despair Reb Shloime took the boy to the *Zadik* and said, 'Rebbe, what shall I do with this child?' The *Zadik* gave the boy one look and said: 'You can do nothing with this child. He is not your child. He is not a Jewish child. Your wife sinned with a *goy*.' And Reb Shloime went home and brought his wife to the *Zadik* and she wept and confessed her sin."

A moan of horror went through the little crowd. A woman wailed. Mendel turned away.

5

ALL day long Mendel sat in his *cheder* teaching the children their Hebrew letters and at most a few chapters of the Pentateuch. Sometimes it seemed to him as though the top of his head were going to fly off. The single dim window of the worn and greasy room gave, beyond a low neighboring roof, on a bit of sky. He did not know whether to bless or curse that patch of blue. Clouds with golden edges would float by. Perhaps it was better when the heavens were gray. At such times Mendel was quieter within. Even while he was going through the mechanical gestures of his task he would be speaking to himself: "What is wrong with me is that I lack humility. I do a work that is pleasing to God. Where is it written that I am to be wiser than others? What is it that I want?" He would grow calmer. But after that a wind would arise and drive the clouds away and the blue would look in upon him again. Lord of the World, why did his thoughts go drifting off? The blue reminded him of the Land of Israel where the sky was eternally blue, and he spoke old words, long grown to be a mere formulary, with a present and aching nostalgia: "This year here, next year in Yerushelayim!" The children tugged at his nerves. Sometimes he thought he was getting childish himself. The Hebrew letters assumed fantastic shapes: the *lamed* looked like a throne and the *tsadhę* like twin towers in a far city, and the *shin* like the harp once smitten by *Dovid hamelec* king and maker of music.

Among his strangest and weakest impulses he accounted this, that he was tempted again and again to share his difficulties with Braine. As the daughter of a learned house she could, of course, read and write Yiddish, and even understood, after a fashion, the Hebrew text of the great prayers and invocations. Nevertheless, she was only a woman and unlearned. But he loved her and he was lonely. When the children were asleep he would, in the fashion of the Jewish intellectual, stride up and down, his hands behind his back, gnawing his beard.

15

"Braine," he had begun the first time, "I'm afraid that Efraim will never be a great scholar."

She had looked up with a conscious terror in her eyes. Plainly she had had the same fear. But womanlike she would not admit it. "Let us cry woe! Why should a father say that of his only son?"

Mendel had stopped in front of her. "I am not blaming him. We bring up our sons to be Talmudists whether they are fit for it or not. In times past it was otherwise. Good Jews acquired the knowledge of the world—"

She had thrown her apron over her head and wailed. "If my father could hear you talk like an *epikauros!* Let us find a good *shidach* (a match) for the boy, so that he can have *kest* (board) and study and grow great in Israel."

Mendel had lifted up his hands. "I don't believe in these marriages of children. They are ruining us physically and mentally as a people."

Braine's eyes had hardened. "I don't understand you. Are we Jews or not? What do you want? That we should be like the *goyim?* I hear of Jews nowadays—may their names be blotted out—who shave their beards and eat unclean food, ay, even the flesh of swine. Is that what you want?"

He had shaken his head in despair. He had tried to get her to understand the distinction between the law, both written and oral, which was eternal on the one hand, and the customs which had arisen in certain lands and periods of the dispersion and which had no binding force. She had seemed to understand the distinction. But her answer had been:

"You and your *chochmeh* (wisdom)! I don't want to talk myself into anger. But my father was a wise man, too, and famed for his wisdom. Men came to consult him from far and near. From Warsaw they came, and Lemberg, and as far as Kishinev. And I have heard him say that it is good for us to be divided from the nation in all our ways. Oh, I can remember him standing up in his long satin coat and looking like a king with his great beard of silver and saying: '*Ato v'chartonu mikol hoamim!*' ('Thou hast chosen us from among all people!') Yes, I remember."

There had been, Mendel could not help thinking, something splendid and prophetic about her. She was still lovely in his eyes. And instead of reasoning with her he had laid his hand upon her head. That night, moreover, against his bosom she had confessed to him that she did not understand Efraim. It was not that the boy was stupid. In that case one would, after his *bar-mitzvah*, simply put him into business, however one hated to do so. No, he "learned" well enough. But it was in a purely mechanical manner. There was no interest in his studies, no piety, no heart.

"It is a new generation," Mendel had said. "He is not the only one. Not all the boys and young men who are drifting west are evil."

Braine had wept herself to sleep. Mendel had lain awake almost all night. He did not think he was a wise man. In worldly station he was the humblest of the humble. But the books he had read and the words of Shimen the Crooked had confirmed him in certain thoughts and perceptions that rose so imperiously within him that he would have laid down his life for their truth. He struggled and he prayed. Curiously enough, it was this futile discussion with Braine that seemed to have crystallized all his spiritual processes. He did not know yet what he was going to do. He felt that a command was upon him, the kind of inner command that no Jew can disobey and live.

6

MONTHS had passed since that night. Winter months. Caps of snow sat awry on the golden cupolas of the Russian monasteries and on clear days glittered in the northern sun. But Jews rarely lifted their faces to look at those symbols of a hostile and impious power. The ancient synagogue had been sunk deep into the earth, for its builders had been commanded to raise it no higher than the insignificant churches of over two centuries ago. Jews looked at the ground or upon the pages of a book. Their faces were not lifted except in prayer.

17

The synagogal library in the basement of the old *shul* was cold as earth and iron. Few came there. In the houses of prayer and study the men had at least the warmth of numbers. But Mendel sometimes sat in the library with a candle he had brought. He did not rock back and forth or intone as a pious man should. He read in silence with lips compressed, except when he was gnawing at his beard. He sat alone, his enormous shadow trembling a little on the wall. There on one evening and later on another Shimen the Crooked, more than ever a gnome or angel of disaster, had slipped into the small circle of the candle's light. The first time Mendel had felt a stab of fear. "*Ovinu malkenu!* Our Father, our King!" he had exclaimed.

Shimen's large eyes had looked at him ironically. "This is a coldness. What are you reading, Reb Mendel?"

"Maimon's *Guide of the Perplexed*." Mendel had pointed to the great folio before him.

Shimen had laughed softly. "The rabbis will put the ban upon you. In any case you will lose your position."

Then, to his own eternal astonishment, Mendel had answered: "I don't want my position. I cannot endure it any longer. If it were not a question of bread!"

Shimen had grown grave. "You are not the only one, Reb Mendel. Many are suffocating. It were better to go into the villages and drink *bromfen* (brandy) with the *Chassidim* and be happy. I will tell you what you must do. Go work with your hands for bread. Then I will take you to a place where other men are planning for a better future not only for us, but for all Israel."

The result of these conferences had been that Shimen had taken Mendel first to the house of the distiller Chaim Bratzlawer, whom the rabbis cursed under their breath but had to endure and even to honor because he was rich and influential and pleaded the cause of his people not only here, but in Saint Petersburg in the house of the Tsar. An eerie feeling had come over Mendel, a feeling of unreality, in that room with its furniture from Germany, before that bald-headed man without earlocks and with a small, clipped beard. And the man was dressed like a *goy*. A heavy watch-chain lay across his paunch. Mendel had kept his eyes cast down. Bratzlawer had smiled.

"A good Jew is not known by his garments, Reb Mendel, nor a *chochem* (wise man) by the length of his beard. Are you good at reckoning?"

Mendel had bowed. "I have studied a little, even geometry, like the Gaon Elia."

Bratzlawer's face had grown red with pleasure. "Such a head! You must come to me. I can get no one to work in the business but these men of the earth. I shall consider it a *koved* (honor) to have you in my house." He ordered a servant to bring in brandy. Mendel was persuaded to sit down. An agreement was made. There was needed a man to explain to the *yishuvniks*, the village Jews who had leased public houses, what they needed and what they owed. Mendel was astonished at the pay he would receive. It seemed sinful. He would be able to give much to the poor, he considered, however, and to have strangers and homeless ones share with him the ushering in of the Sabbath.

Braine had to be told. That was a terrible task. A *melamed*, to be sure, was a humble man. But he belonged definitely to the order of the learned and the holy. Sometime in the past, Mendel knew, Braine's ancestors must have engaged in trade or in money-lending. Else whence that wealth which the Russians had stolen or destroyed? But it was not his desire to quarrel or argue with her. He wanted her to share his feelings and his hopes.

He spoke to her with all gentleness.

Her face hardened.

"They eat *trefe* (unclean and forbidden food) at Bratzlawer's!"

He shook his head. "It is sinful to repeat empty gossip. He had a good Jewish heart."

"And a German teacher for his children!"

"That also is not true. Shimen says the man is a good Jew from Berlin who teaches the children Torah and Talmud but also languages that they may be able to have power and influence not only for themselves, but, like their father, for *klal Yisroel*—for the whole of Israel."

But Braine's eyes blazed more and more. "That this should happen to me. Instead of studying and teaching, my husband must go into the villages and chaffer with low people!"

Mendel smiled timidly. "You will have a dress of satin or of velvet, Braine, and maybe in time a silver *menorah* for the Sabbath!"

"What do I want with those?" She had been implacable. "Woe is me, what do I want with those? I see how it will be! You will count money, and Efraim—may he live in health—will follow your ways and we shall become like the heathen and dishonor the fathers who begat us. Rather would I have rent my garments in sign of your death than to have lived to see this thing."

A chill stole down the spine of Mendel. Braine's tongue was not usually a bitter one. He turned away, saying no more.

7

OFTEN, in the three years that followed, there came to him not so much her words as her passion and her aspect of that day. For Mendel never grew accustomed to his new life. He was not, in fact, working with his hands and letting a new world grow in his soul. Reality had little relation to Shimen's doctrinaire program of how a new Jewish life was to be built up. Mendel sat in Bratzlawer's counting-house or else traveled about from village to village. He traveled with a drunken driver in a rude cart over the mired or dusty roads and put up at brawling filthy inns, and the fumes of brandy often seemed to him the exhalations of hell. He was not overworked, but he was always tired. He had no time to read or study. A nostalgia for books and for the operations of the mind came over him that was so keen and persistent that it brought tears to his eyes. He longed for his little school, for the icy evenings in the library of the synagogue, for the warmer contacts and argumentative exercises of the *beth hamidrash.* He was no longer a rebel or a seeker after forbidden knowledge. He would have returned gladly to the ordinary Talmudic studies. He had moments of an enormous contempt for the active life of the world in which he now had to share. He looked with reverence upon the shabbiest village rabbi. That man, at least, had his mind fixed upon things and issues that did not pass away. He, Mendel, had to discuss the price of brandy.

On quiet Sabbaths at home he had, of course, a clearer vision. He knew that if he returned to his old life the old doubts and hesitations and seekings and rebellions would arise promptly enough. What, then, did he want? Shimen invited him to a meeting of a circle of the "enlighteners." He did not go. He prayed with warm and scrupulous devotion; he gave gifts to the poor. It pleased him quietly that Braine was laying aside money. He became silent and thin. When Efraim, a year after his *bar-mitzvah*, suddenly left the *yeshiva*, the Talmudic university, Mendel merely looked at his son with grave and inquiring eyes. Braine stood beside them, flushed and desperate. Efraim looked a little sullen.

"I had set my hope on him!" Braine cried. She turned to the boy. "What will you do, *shegetz*, worthless one?"

Efraim looked at his father. "Red Bratzlawer sent for me. He heard that I could speak Polish and do sums."

Mendel nodded. He could not command or even advise his own son. The conflict within him had robbed him of certitude and thus of power. Braine turned upon them both.

"Has ever anyone heard of a Jewish father like you? Speak! Are you dumb? Do you think I do not know how little pleasure you have in life? And now you do not command your son to turn aside from the way of the wicked?"

Mendel arose and clasped his hands before him. "I cannot! I cannot!" he cried. "I understand no more what one should do in this world. All that I feel is fear; all that I have is cares!"

Braine grew pale. She said no more. Efraim went to work for Bratzlawer. Dutifully he brought home his wages to his mother. He performed all his devotions correctly as a good Jew should. But he turned up one day with his earlocks clipped off and on another he had discarded his *caftan*, the long coat of the orthodox, and appeared in a German suit of the period. On neither occasion did his mother protest. She was busy saving money, no one knew for what precise purpose. She gave her husband and children the plainest food. Only on the eve of the Sabbath, when a few poor men and strangers were invited in, did she provide meat or cake. There was no open dissension in the family. But there was an understanding between Braine and Rifke, her daughter, from which father and son were shut out. These two, on the contrary, walked and worked side by side and did not speak out. It came to Mendel's knowledge, of course, that Efraim in his quiet way soon made himself indispensable to Bratzlawer. He did not need the distiller's assurance that Efraim had indeed a Jewish head. He could not rejoice at the word. A Jewish head—that used to mean learned and wise. On the lips of Bratzlawer, good man that he was, it seemed to mean cunning and astute. Mendel felt a chill within.

He no longer took pleasure in anything. A great emptiness was all about him. Though he was barely forty, he felt old and worn and came back from the villages thinner and wearier. He had a cough and a perpetual pain in his side. Braine insisted that he must take a rest. He stayed home all during a long and mild Passover week. But though the spring kept faith, his strength did not mend. He went to business one day and remained home another, and then, by an unspoken understanding, went no more. A physician came and spoke of exhaustion and probable sugar in the urine. Bratzlawer had sent the physician—a Jew with a shaved face who had studied in Germany, a man so obviously a renegade that Braine spat out after him and asked Mendel whether he really wanted to take the unclean stuff that the man had left.

Mendel cared little. He lay in bed, and sunlight which he had always loved came in. Peace was upon him now. A conflict had arisen and broken him. It might break many more. Israel was eternal. Perhaps these troublesome and confused days would bring the Messiah and the restoration of the Temple. Who could tell? The ways of the Holy One, blessed be He, were past understanding. For himself he was glad that he would not see another winter and would not have to fare forth into the villages and contaminate his soul with buying and selling. Dreamy visions filled his wavering consciousness. He saw the Rabbi Akiba, once an unlearned man and a shepherd, come home with his twelve thousand pupils streaming behind him over the hills of Judæa; he saw the houses of study beside the dazzling blue of the waters of Lake Kinereth; he saw *Avrom ovenu* (our father Abraham) under a great curved night of stars.

He died, as his son Efraim, who lived to be very old, always remembered with a peculiar emotion, on *Erev Yom Kippur* (the eve of the Day of Atonement). His mind seemed to be clear and he tried, as he felt the wind of the wing of the angel of death, to lift himself up a little and to declare, as a Jew should, the Unity of the Eternal with his last breath. He said in a strong voice: *"Shmah, Yisroel!"* ("Hear, O Israel!") But then he fell back and his son had to finish for him: *"Adonai Elohenu, Adonai echot!"* ("The Lord, our God, the Lord is One!")

8

BRAINE and her children rent their garments and, as the law prescribes, sat for ten days of mourning on the floor with ashes on their heads. Then Efraim went back to business and Braine and Rifke to their household duties, and little seemed to be changed except that Efraim was now the head of the house and blessed the wine and bread on the eve of the Sabbath. He was a very serious young man for his age. He brought back strange-looking books from business and sat studying them in the evening. Braine watched him for a time and then could contain herself no longer.

"What are these heathen books? Was it for this that I prayed over you in your cradle?"

Efraim did not look up. "They are German books," he

answered. "You can't carry on business nowadays without German."

"Business!" she cried in bitter contempt. "You have forgotten God!"

An irritableness seemed to come over the young man. "Let me be, mother. You don't understand."

Braine wept. "*Gewalt!*" ("Horrors!") she cried. "Did a Jewish child ever speak so before? Strike your mother! Why not?"

Efraim's answer was to bend closer over his books. He frowned and his lips were compressed.

Braine sat down. "I want to talk to you!"

He looked up. "Will you see to it that your sister gets a marriage portion and is given in marriage to a pious man of good family?"

"Why do you ask that today, mother?"

She was stern. "Will you, I ask again?"

He looked into her eyes and saw her desperate earnestness. "Yes, mother, I will."

"You swear it by the memory of your father?"

"I swear it."

They both fell silent. Then Efriam, evidently softened, said: "But tell me, *Mameleben*, why you wanted me to promise today?"

Braine lowered her head and spoke.

"The world is growing dark. Maybe a *yom hadin* (a day of judgment) is at hand. You can say *Kadesh* (the prayer for the dead) for your father in *goles* (exile). My heart pants for *Eretz Yisroel* (the Land of Israel). I am going there to die."

Efraim grew pale. "You are not an old woman, mother!"

"I will have the longer time to pray on the blessed earth."

Efraim was only seventeen. Tears came into his eyes. "But, mother, we shall never see you again."

"If not in this world," Braine said, "then in the world to come."

Now they were both weeping, mother and son. Efraim got up.

"And you will not see my children, nor Rifke's."

Braine wiped her tears. "That is the hardest," she said. "Yet I am going for them. I tell you I see signs all about me. Israel is going astray after the gods and manners of the heathens. What joy will I have in your children? Tell me that! You have shaved the corners of your beard and study heathen books. They—God forbid—will eat swine's flesh. I am going to the Land to pray for you and for them."

Efraim looked at his mother as though he saw her for the first time. "You have had this plan in mind long?"

"Ever since my husband, your father, abandoned the God of Israel."

"But he never did!" Efraim exclaimed.

"*Sha!*" she said. "Silence! I have your promise. Now I can prepare."

Efraim ran to Bratzlawer, whose right-hand man he now was. But if he hoped for help in that quarter, he was mistaken. Bratzlawer, who had grown rounder of paunch than ever, clinked the coins in his trousers' pockets and said: "It is a very great *mitzvah* (a holy and deserving deed) and it will be a *mitzvah* to help your mother carry out her pious purpose. What does she need? Money? Advice? Letters to people who can help her on the long journey? Let her come to me!"

To Efraim and Rifke's grief, Bratzlawer's words were echoed by everyone, especially by those who had fallen away from the strictest piety. It was as though these people found a vicarious source of spiritual satisfaction in the decision of the *melamedke* (the teacher's wife), as Braine was suddenly called again by everyone. She sat in her house and people came to give her gifts, to bless her and to receive her blessing. Would she send them, they asked, but a few grains of the sand of the holy earth? A few drops of the water of the Jordan? Would she write to say whether the Turk was bearing hard upon the people of God in the land of the fathers? Would she pray for them?

Efraim had a moment of intellectual clarity in which he saw or thought he saw how her decision and her act ministered to his mother's pride, which had been unfed almost since she had left her father's house. But he put this impious and unfilial thought from him. Rifke clung to her brother as her mother grew sterner, more prophetic, and more detached. Suddenly the noise and the preparations were over and their mother was gone and Efraim and Rifke had their first moment of intimate tenderness each for the other.

9

BRATZLAWER was known to be among the three or four richest Jews in Vilna. To the distilling of brandy he had added the manufacture of *kümmel* and his "genuine Polish *kümmel*" was being more and more esteemed as far west in different directions as the cities of Posen and Königsberg. He owned his house and drove his carriage; he did precisely as he liked because all the Russian officials in the city were in his pay. Yet old women squatting in warm weather at corners of the Ghetto pitied him from their hearts. "*Nebbich* (it is a pity) the poor man hasn't even a *kadesh* (a son to say the prayer for the dead for him)." No, Bratzlawer had no son. He had six daughters, to most of whom he had given elegant Europeanized names, and ever since a jester had run their names together in breathless sarcasm no one spoke of the daughters of Chaim Bratzlawer, but everyone said with a grin, Sarahnatalieberteyettemietehannah. And the old women at the Ghetto corners naturally added to their gossip: "No wonder Reb Chaim has advanced a marriage portion for Rifke, the daughter of Mendel! No wonder! Thus he is sure of Efraim for one of his *mies* (ill-favored) daughters. But what help to him is one son-in-law? Six he needs."

The old women were more malicious than they need have been. The Bratzlawer girls were not ill-favored, though several of them undoubtedly fell below the standard of beauty of the Vilna Ghetto, which has always been high. Moreover they all had excellent minds which had been developed by western tutors, and amiable dispositions. Natalie, for instance, married a young man named Cohn, who had studied medicine at the University of Freiburg. Finding his name a handicap, he adopted that of his wife. Later he was called to a medical position in England, and thus the second daughter of Reb Chaim of Vilna became the progenitrix of the distinguished British family of Ratislaw.

Efraim, with a realization of Bratzlawer's needs which had in it nothing sordid or calculating, felt most strongly drawn to Hannah, the youngest of the six girls. Seeing that among the vast majority of Jews children were still betrothed almost in their cradle, the courtship of these two had both freedom and romance. Hannah's nose might have been more delicately molded. But she had the small full pouting mouth and the lovely oval contour of the face of which the Vilna Jewesses are proud. Hence, when at sixteen, Rifke had safely passed under the marriage canopy with the pious son of a pious father, Reb Jochai Warschauer, who was impressed both by her marriage portion and by her mother's saintliness, Efraim and Hannah saw no reason for not drawing closer and closer to each other. Efraim, who had always worked and studied and hardened himself in the hope of avoiding pain and shown no living creature his grief over either his father's death or his mother's pilgrimage—Efraim found his soul melting and coming to life again at the gentle touch of the girl's hand. Shyly at first, more freely thereafter, he escaped from business in her companionship. They discussed his father and her own. They found that a strange community of ideas existed between them. They wanted in their lives neither Mendel's devotion to mere study nor Reb Chaim's business bustle and superficial piety. Were not new Jewish voices coming out of the west? Could not one be a European *and* a Jew?

Their courtship was cut short. Bratzlawer came to Efraim. He wagged his head. He spoke:

"*Hakodesh borchu m'saveg sivugim!* The Holy One, blessed be He, brings couples together in marriage. When shall we make the *chassene* (wedding)?"

A thrill went through Efraim's pure young body. "Whenever you like, Reb Chaim."

Bratzlawer nodded his fat head. "You know as well as I do, Efraim, that the *kümmel* we sell in Prussia can be made there as easily as here. Thus we shall save the cost of transportation. I have made inquiries. We can manufacture as cheaply in a small Prussian town as here. And Prussia is a free country for Jews. You can buy land. You can own houses. You don't have to waste your substance bribing officials, swine that they are, for the right to breathe. When you and Hannah are married I want you to settle in Insterburg in Prussia and make *kümmel*."

A light seemed to burst upon Efraim.

"You are right in everything you say, Reb Chaim. You can depend on me. Hannah and I have already talked about our wish to go to Germany."

Bratzlawer lifted a finger. "You need a German name to do business in Germany. What will you call yourself? Mendel's sohn?"

"No, no," Efraim protested, "that would be wrong to the great Moishe Mendelssohn and his descendants."

"Well, what then?"

Efraim reflected.

"My father—peace be upon him—was of the tribe of Levi. You have seen the pitcher, the symbol of our tribe, graven upon his headstone, Reb Chaim? I shall call myself Efraim Levy."

It was a very merry and luxurious wedding that Bratzlawer prepared. There were fiddlers and a jester; there was —as was related long afterward—French champagne, although the older people stuck to brandy. There was dancing and merrymaking. Who says that Jews cannot be merry? A group of *Chassidim* came in uninvited. But who would take upon himself the sin of turning away any Jew on such an *unbeschrigen* (absit omen) happy and auspicious occasion. The *Chassidim* danced in the middle of the floor and sang:

"Wos di chassene kost
Wet Hakodesh boruch sain m'male!"
("The cost of the wedding feast
The Holy One, blessed be He, will make up to you.")

The young people took a train on the next day. Efraim had trimmed his beard neatly; the bride was dressed in a traveling dress that had been copied from a Warsaw copy of a Parisian model. They both spoke quite good German and thought it better to speak that language on the German train, even though it seemed affected and even snobbish to them. The year was 1850. They arrived in Insterburg as Herr and Frau Efraim Levy and looked about them for a house in which to establish their business and bring their children into a fairer and a freer world.

BOOK II

1

CIVILIZATIONS, like men, have their moral atmospheres, their affinities, their attractive and repulsive qualities. The bearers of a given civilization, again, have varying powers of resistance to a new cultural environment. The Huguenots became excellent Prussians in Prussia and excellent Americans in South Carolina. Germans tend to merge with Anglo-Saxondom in the United States; they retain their strict cultural identity in Brazil. It is too early to say how the Italian will bear himself in America or the Argentine. There are fortunate peoples like the English who, emigrating to their own colonies, have never been subjected to these strains and tests. The migrations of modern times, whether caused by intolerance or the lack of land and bread, have given rise to problems and to conflicts which were unknown in the earlier periods of an emptier world. And these problems and conflicts, tragic enough to the millions that have to face them, have commonly been regarded with stupid indifference or contempt by those few master-peoples into whose hands historic luck has played the greater part of the earth's surface.

The Jews are not the only migratory folk of modern times, but they furnish the classical example of migration, because nowhere have they yet found the rest of either tolerance or land. They have tested the qualities of all civilizations as well as their own capacities for surrender and self-annihilation. Expelled from Spain with the rigors of the utmost cruelty and contempt, they yet carried with them their Spanish stepmother tongue and have been true to it in Salonika and elsewhere for over four centuries. But Yiddish, the Germano-Judæic speech of thirty generations in Russia and Poland, threatens to disappear in the United States in three. In Germany it disappeared in a single generation. But inferences from these facts are not only dangerous. They are fantastic. Do the Germans retain their identity in Brazil because a Portuguese-American culture is essentially alien from their souls? Did the Jews in Turkey and Africa retain their Spaniolish tongue only because they were cast among comparative barbarians? Do Englishmen retain their identity so well because there is something unbending in their souls or because they are fortified by the consciousness of the power and spaciousness of their empire? Did the Jews cling to Yiddish in Russia for centuries because the Russians were intolerant and the fences about the Law strong? Or were the fences about the Law strengthened by generation after generation because the Russians were cruel and there is no spiritual affinity between the Slav and the Jew? Did the Jews yield so overwhelmingly to German civilization because the Germans loved them? Or was it by cause of an unwilling kinship of the mind? And what of today and of America? Here are Jewish gangsters on the East Side and rabbis who make religion hum with gyms and teams and get-together meetings and business men of the red-blooded, go-getter variety. Were the Jews Germans? Are they Americans? Are the Germans in the United States Americans? And the Swedes? And the Poles? I am not talking about citizenship or passports or external loyalties. What are the inner facts? Enough. Our story may shed some light on them. Or not. . . .

2

GRANDMOTHER Braine died in Jerusalem before even the earlier-born children of Efraim and Hannah Levy were old enough to understand. Her letters had been few and had been exercises in piety rather than the expressions of personal emotion and thought. Whether she found the peace in exaltation which she had sought Efraim never learned. In the freedom and bright bustle of his new life he seemed suddenly divorced from the old hopes and preoccupations. They dropped from him; they faded year by year. He inquired after the cause of his mother's death and received news, after many months, that she had died of a malignant fever. He bowed his head and burned the *yahrzeit* lamp on the anniversary of her death and found the image of her in his soul turning more and more into a legendary one.

34

He built a house; he begot children. Tobias was born in 1851, Samuel in 1853, the two girls, Bertha and Rose, in 1855 and 1858. Hannah expected no more children. It was with more surprise than joy that Jacob was welcomed in 1861. Life became increasingly complicated. The notion of flooding central Europe with Polish *kümmel* had evidently occurred to more than one brain at the same time. And these other brains, trained in the west of Europe, had ideas more practical than Bratzlawer's. Buyers from Berlin bought up the produce of the Polish distilleries on the spot and transported them to their warehouses. There the *kümmel* was bottled in elegant little earthenware jugs with gracefully designed labels. The crude bottles of Efraim Levy & Company never made their way in the great centers of population. The business was sound enough, but it remained small. Bratzlawer, moreover, did not remain the tower of strength he had once seemed. A hard year came and Hannah herself wrote to her father begging a loan for her husband's business. Reb Chaim answered that he was an aging man and in reality not a rich one. He had given dowries to all his daughters—six of them—and ought now to be permitted to spend his "old days" in peace on the little that was left him. He, once the man of advanced thought, added that he wondered whether the blessing of God was on Efraim's business in view of the stories of apostasy and impiety that came to him daily from the west. Thereafter the Levys, having to stand wholly on their own feet in their new world, lost touch more and more with the land of their origin and its customs. One or two letters a year from Poland were all that sustained the frail connection. It was not many years before Efraim and Hannah would smile at each other over the quaint sayings and doings chronicled in these letters. Rifke wrote that the *shochet* (the ritual butcher) of her community had been discovered to be in league with the Gentile butchers and to have passed as *kosher* (clean) both fowls and lambs that were *trefe* (unclean) and that much horror and indignation had been the inevitable result. And Efraim, clean-shaven now except for two small tufts of beard at either end of his chin, had turned

35

to Hannah in her seemly Sabbath "bordeaux"-colored silk and said, wagging his head in good humor: "I wish I had her *zoress* (troubles)." And he had spoken these words, as all words in his house were now spoken, not in Yiddish, but in a German which, though strongly tinctured with Yiddish expressions, was passably correct and pure.

The Levys themselves had not, to be sure, abandoned the observance of the law of Israel in any single respect. Sabbaths and holy days were kept and celebrated. They would not have dreamed of eating *trefe;* they went duly to the synagogue. And it was an orthodox synagogue. A reformed congregation existed in Insterburg, but the Levys had no hankering after that seemly place of worship, nor would they, as *polakim*, have been very heartily welcomed by the little group of intensely German families which constituted that congregation. No, the Levys were good Jews. Only into all their thoughts and observances there had stolen a laxness and a tinge of compromise, and a rigid observer— had there been such a one—would have wondered whether ancestral piety rather than any profound personal conviction were not the force that kept their orthodoxy in its state of decorous correctness.

From the beginning of their sojourn in Prussia on they had had German servants. The growing and primitive household needed both of the ruddy peasant girls who, having the same name but differing luckily in height and girth, were known as Big Trine and Little Trine. Candles were still made at home; so was soap; the flax, above all, was still spun in a big room off the kitchen during the long evenings of the northern winter. So soon as the children could toddle they invaded the spinning-room where Big Trine and Little Trine sang songs and told tales over their work. The tales were the old folk-tales of the Germans, so full of a melancholy magic alternating with a high and gallant energy; the songs were the ineffably sweet folk-songs of faring and parting and longing and love. Little Tobias, a dark curly-head of four with the clear passionate brown eyes of his grandmother Braine, would sit on a low stool in the spinning-room and listen to the songs and tales of the spinsters. Into the waking dream of his impressionable childhood came to echo and to croon forever this speech and these airs and the piercing poetry of this Germanic world. . . . Winter would break and the tardy spring sparingly melt into a northern summer. Big Trine and Little Trinc would go on Sunday mornings out into the open, out across a heath into a fir forest. They were kindly souls and, being gently used by their Jewish master and mistress, they conceived a great affection for the children and would not go on their weekly outings without taking first Tobias, later his brother and his sisters, with them. So landscape blended with speech and song—the unforgettable landscape seen in childhood. There was no fear hovering over these fields and forests for a Jewish child, as there had been for that child's ancestors in Russia; there was no sense that one was out on sufferance and must hasten back into Jewish walls and quarters. Over the heath the maids went singing with the children of their master; they picked wild flowers and wove them into wreaths and taught the children the names of the flowers and trees. They sat down on the edge of the forest and it needed but the beseeching eyes of Tobias to have Big Trine begin to the rustle of the trees above them: *Es war einmal* (once upon a time). . . .

Tobias was four when his parents had a conference. Samuel, a child of two, had just gone to sleep. Efraim and Hannah were in their bedroom. Efraim looked at his wife.

"Hannah, I've talked to Reb Kolnitzer."

Scarcely perceptible was the shrug of Hannah's shoulders and a faint line that deepened between her eyes.

"There is time enough for that," she said.

"No," her husband answered. "Tobias is in his fifth year. He must begin to 'learn.' "

Hannah had let her hair, cut off in the orthodox fashion before her wedding, grow again. She had on a wrapper of velvet. That color of wine trimmed with gold suited her well. The baby being asleep, she wanted to read awhile. She held in her firm white hand a crimson volume heavily gilt. A lady belonging to the Reformed Congregation had loaned it to her. The book was called *Romancero* and was written by a poet named Heinrich Heine. Hannah seemed to draw herself up.

"I want Tobias to go to a *Gymnasium*. Here in Prussia all Jews who want to go can go. You don't have to bribe the director or anything."

Efraim tugged at his tufts of beard. "Good. Maybe. We shall see. Later. But first for a Jewish child comes—"

Hannah interrupted him. She dared not quite say what she wanted to say. Not only her husband, but her own conscience, inhibited her. She drove her impulse into another channel.

"I will not have Kolnitzer beat my child!"

Efraim shook his head. "*Wie heisst?* (What do you mean?) Tobias, you always say, is already a little *chochem* (wise man). Let him be industrious and Kolnitzer won't beat him. I will teach the child his letters tomorrow."

3

TOBIAS thought the enormous Hebrew letters which his father showed him rather fun. He was a bright child and the descendant of innumerable generations of the learned. He picked up the difficult and confusing alphabet in a week. Moreover, his mother seemed sorry for him and gave him bits of sweets and a larger helping of dessert on the Sabbath.

The *cheder* was far less amusing. A barren room with thirty small boys. And many of these small boys came from very poor homes and were ragged and had smudged faces and dirty hands. Reb Kolnitzer was a lean old man with a wiry gray beard and bitter little blue eyes. His strap fell on the just and the unjust. He spoke a mixture of Yiddish and German. A hesitation, a mistake on the part of one of his little pupils, and his face grew red and his little eyes turned cruel. "*Hargenen wer' ich d'r!* (I'll murder you!)" It was with tears and bitterness which he never forgot that Tobias studied the third book of Moses and acquired a knowledge of the laws of priestly sacrifice.

Nor was Efraim wholly comfortable in his mind. He remembered his father. He, too, had whipped his pupils. But Mendel had brought to his teaching a sense of consecration. It had been to him, despite doubts and other aspirations, a holy thing to bring Jewish children into a knowledge of God and His law. Kolnitzer was just a bad-tempered old man. And Efraim also noticed with a sudden quick grief, soon obliterated by the cares and preoccupations of life, that here, too, the lovely old ceremonies by which a child is introduced to the holy learning of his people had fallen into disuse. There was no induction day with its showers of sweets and coins, no little "blesser" and "question-asker." Everything was cold and businesslike and casual.

In the soul of the child Tobias, who grew more and more to resemble his grandmother Braine there was never a moment of conflict. The fields and forests of Prussia, its legends, songs, and speech—these were to him light and home. The *cheder* and its irascible old *rebbe* were a burden and a secret shame. The Gentile children who sometimes assembled to jeer and throw stones at the door of the *cheder* were to him not enemies, but objects of admiration and of longing. He identified them somehow with the boyish heroes of so many of the fairy tales that Big Trine had told him and was now repeating for little Samuel in the spinning-room. The blond girl-children were like fairy-princesses or *Schneewitchen* or *Dornröschen*. When he was seven the sight of them made little shivers run down his spine. Jewish children somehow became tangled up in his imagination and emotions with the dirty *cheder* and Kolnitzer's strap and horrible jargon. He never knew how it came to pass that Little Trine taught him his German letters at this time. Suddenly, so far as his memory went, he knew them and began to read every scrap of printed matter that came his way.

Meantime his mother had been busy. Her ambitions for

her children became intenser from year to year. Stories began to drift to her from friends and acquaintances—stories from the west. In Berlin there was a Jewish aristocracy: Councillor of Commerce So-and-so, Privy Councillor So-and-so. There were merchant princes, bankers, barons even. Great Jews. Where had they come from? Originally all more or less from the same ranks and places. An old highly Germanized lady, all stiff silks and delicate laces, said benevolently to Hannah Levy: "The great-grandfathers of all these people were, so to speak, onion-hucksters. Why don't you send that bright, handsome little boy of yours to school?" It cannot be said that Efraim really resisted. His circumstances were moderate. But his bearing was dignified and his speech had become careful. One evening at the inn of the Black Eagle, whither he had gone to drink a glass of beer, the apothecary and the justice of the peace had been vainly looking for a "third man" for their game of *skat*. They were both of the generation that had brought about the revolutions of 1848; they were liberals and democrats. They asked Herr Levy—a worthy man, why not?—to join them. Thus Efraim began to know Gentiles. When the gentlemen ordered sandwiches, he ordered one, too, though for long he always choked a little over the *trefe* food. But how could he not send his boy to a German school? Once or twice his mother's warning and prophetic despair stole into his mind. With an inner tremor he thrust from him these memories. The strong current of life was not to be resisted. . . .

Tobias Levy entered the preparatory department of the *Gymnasium* at Insterburg in October, 1858. In the entire college there were only eight Jewish boys. Their precocity and their instinctive interest in the things of the mind were like balm to the teachers, who all belonged to the revolutionary generations between 1830 and 1848. Neither the corrosive intellectuality of the Jew nor the naïve creative intuitiveness of the Nordic had yet been heard of. Tobias's career at school was a continuous triumph. And since he was well dressed and modest and mannerly and always will-

ing to be helpful to blond-haired, blue-eyed classmates who
found their studies a grievous burden, he soon had friends
and, if he needed them, protectors, and was invited over
week-ends to the country seats of *Junkers*. None of these
people, to be sure, ever dreamed of paying any attention to
his family or of inviting him on purely social occasions.
This circumstance Tobias strove either to understand or to
forget. He couldn't quite see either his father or his mother
in the drawing-room at Castle Harmsdorff. He knew, having, like all Jews, antennæ of the mind, that the young
baronesses, the sisters of his friend, giggled at his name and
at their brother's friendship for him. But they behaved very
agreeably in his presence and seemed adorable to his adolescent ardor. In secret he wrote poetry to them. Yet whenever he returned from Harmsdorff he was more than ever
the Jewish son in his affection and reverent consideration
for his parents. They, unaware of his discoveries within his
new world, idolized him. He was both brilliant and good.
His success in the Gentile world did not make him less a
Jewish child.

By the time he was sixteen Tobias Levy had grasped the
character of his position with a mature sagacity. His teachers and his Gentile friends were benevolent to him and
secretly proud of the liberality of that unbending. At a
given point, immovable though hard to place, that unbending ceased. Signs to the contrary were deceptive. Young
Wolf von Harmsdorff, walking with Tobias through the
park of the castle, put his arm around the shoulder of his
friend. Frankly he speculated concerning the future. Profession. Marriage. Children. Travel. His instinctive and unspoken assumption—why mention the obvious?—was that
the world of his future was a world which Tobias could
never enter. "I shall travel all over the world before I settle
down. You're going to study law, aren't you, Tobias?
Good. You shall manage the estates from my majority on
until I come back." Wolf glowed with benevolence. Tobias
compressed his lips with a mature bitterness. He had given
his very heart in this friendship. He was to be rewarded

with the post of a confidential upper servant. The young baron would find himself mistaken. He pleaded a headache and was driven home.

He studied with a cold ardor. He was always *primus* of his class. That was the least he owed himself. Gentiles could afford to take things easy. They did not have to achieve one hundred times what was normal in order to conquer a normal position. He somehow dreamed that he would like to be a judge. Any decently intelligent Gentile could enter upon that career in Prussia. A Jew, to hope for appointment even in an inferior court, would have to be a paragon of learning and brilliancy, of suavity and tact, of scrupulousness and devotion. . . . It was like this. Yes. Quite. Life was like a street full of shops. And in order to live you had to buy things. There was no other way. The shopkeepers were honest folk and the prices of things were clearly marked, and for the Gentile customer there was no haggling. But if you entered, *you*—Tobias Levy—the shopkeepers were very courteous and pleasant. But they put up their prices five hundred per cent. And if you objected they thought you were a surly fellow and they called you a lousy Jew. For, after all, it wasn't their duty to trade with you. It was pure kindness of heart. If you paid the five hundred per cent cheerfully, they were good-humored and said you were, for a Jew, not a bad fellow and perhaps it would be good sense as well as profitable and humane to admit you to certain privileges here and there and yon. . . . Tobias remained *primus*. He passed his final examinations at seventeen and a half, *summa cum laude*. He would pay the five hundred per cent. . . .

Before proceeding to the University of Königsberg as a student of *jura* and *cammeralia*, under the softening influence of this first parting from his home, he spoke at length to his father concerning his strange and disheartening discoveries. Efraim, a busy and harassed man now—the family was growing up; a son at the university would be a heavy expense—closed his eyes for a moment as if in weariness. Then he drew himself up. He was profoundly irritated. The

42

eyes that he opened were a little bloodshot. He spread out his hands half in protest, half in beseeching. "What do you want? Are you *meshuga?* How long ago is it that our children were taken away from us by the Russians for twenty-five years of military service and forcible baptism? How long ago is it that we are citizens and subjects even here, in Prussia, in an enlightened country? Do you want them to make you king? We are *yehudim;* we *are* in *goles.* But you have a Jewish head and there is a great God in the world. What more do you want?"

Tobias did not answer. His father had lapsed into his native Yiddish and something in Tobias had winced. He took a long walk and wondered what was the reply to his father's argument. It sounded reasonable enough. Yet with all his soul Tobias rebelled against it. Where was the fallacy? Where? He walked out beyond the little town across a field and came to the woods already touched by autumn. He sat down on a fallen tree and dipped his hands into the leaves upon the ground. He looked down a narrow forest path into the dim, half-green, half-golden glow. "*Deutscher Wald,*" he murmured to himself—"the German forest." He was a Jew. Yes. But he was not in *goles;* he felt no exile. This was his earth and sky and speech. That was it. That was the answer to his father which his father could never comprehend. His father consented with his heart and mind to the fact of exile and was grateful for kindliness and peace. Not he, not Tobias. And there must be many, many more like him. . . .

He matriculated at Königsberg in 1869. At first he was isolated. He looked about him in the lecture-halls. Among the blond East Prussians a few dark heads. Most of these heads were unkempt. Couldn't one almost see where the earlocks had been clipped? These youngsters from the east were dreadfully poor and poverty doesn't make for cleanliness. They talked with a sing-song and a thick Yiddish accent, and when they spoke even the grave professors smiled a little into their golden or gray and golden beards. Tobias felt an acute irritation arise in him at the sight of these

43

young men, at the sound of their voices. He was ashamed of them. He was ashamed for them. His father often talked like that. Was he ashamed of his father, too? Lying to oneself did little good. He would be ashamed of his father here. His fear was that he would be classed and confounded with these young Russians. What chance of a career would he have then? And if he didn't achieve a career as a Prussian, a German, what would become of him? He couldn't, as a spiritual fact, either manufacture *kümmel* or be a rabbi. . . .

Then he met Burghammer. Suddenly, on the promenade made famous by Kant, this elegant young gentleman, whom Tobias had watched in the lecture-halls, came up to him, bowed, clicked his heels, and said: "Hans Burghammer." It was hard to say, "Tobias Levy." The young gentleman raised his eyebrows. A Gentile wouldn't have done so. Tobias understood the eyebrows perfectly. They said: "You'll have to arrange about that, my dear man, if you want a career equal to your personal qualities." The intimacy was swift. Tobias sat in Burghammer's elegant rooms and listened in astonishment, with profound inner pain, with reluctant consent. "Your father's *kümmel* is excellent. It commands respect. Of course it does. My grandfather dealt in junk; he specialized in old iron. *His* father went from house to house with a cart to buy up the metal. His name was Hamburger—Shmuel Hamburger. My grandfather made a great fortune as purveyor to the king during the Napoleonic wars. My father, Commerzienrath Heinrich Burghammer, has increased it. I, my dear fellow, and my brothers and sisters, are *geshmatt* (baptized). When we were infants, of course. No act of hypocrisy was demanded of us. We are Protestants. All doors are open to us. Oh, the *Junkers* cut us socially, unless they want favors. But the state is on our side. Our Jewish brains are needed. Count Bismarck consults my father twice a month. My father raised the money for the Austrian war in sixty-six. If there is another war I shall go as an officer. Why am I not at home in Berlin? Because my social life there interferes with my studies. And I haven't any intention of being a good-for-

44

nothing like so many of the sons of the rich *goyim*. I shall try to be a credit to our house. But your father's *kümmel* is excellent. I must have another glassful."

Tobias stared at the carpet. Something made him say: "My paternal grandmother—I never knew her, of course—went to end her days in Jerusalem."

Burghammer laughed a sympathetic laugh. "How touching! My sister, who is a great reader, tells me that the old customs are being written about very sympathetically by certain historians." He looked at his friend with a slightly superior smile. "But why we should be bound by them any more than enlightened Gentiles are bound by the superstitious notions and ways of their ancestors—that is a question on which you still seem to need to reflect."

Tobias jumped up. The liberating word had been spoken. "You are right," he said, "a thousand times right. I think I see my way now."

4

1870. For king and fatherland. Again and again, the last time within the memory of many men still living, Germany had lain crushed and bleeding under the heels of France. A day of justice was at hand. An uprush of emotion. The students scattered. Blond youths, hearing that Tobias would hasten at once to his native city to join the colors, embraced him on the public streets. Burghammer nodded with a severe air. "I am glad. This will be a great war. Very different from 'Sixty-four or 'Sixty-six. If we bear ourselves faultlessly our position in the new empire that is coming will be unassailable. We are fighting not only for our fatherland, but for our position in the fatherland." Tobias nodded. There was a lump in his throat. Silently the two youths embraced each other. Perhaps they would meet on the field of honor. . . .

On the train to Insterburg young men took Tobias into their midst. They were a little tipsy. They all "drank brotherhood." A young *Korps-student* made a speech which resounded through the compartments. " 'Confessional' differences have ceased to exist—Catholic, Protestant, Mosaic. We are Germans!"

Lieb Vaterland, magst ruhig sein,
Fest steht und treu—und treu
Die Wacht am Rhein . . .

Again and again Tobias had to force back the tears of joy and consecration. . . .

Home. Dear God, was this his home? His mother, usually so seemly and dignified, wept and wailed. Her one comfort was that Samuel, her second son, was too young to be conscripted, and too near-sighted and flat-footed anyhow. Tobias clenched his fists. Thank God, *he* didn't have the flat feet of the *medine-geher* (the peddler). But his father, his father was more disheartening than his mother. Efraim looked sober, thin, angry. A bitter contemptousness was in his eyes. "Must the *goyim* always murder each other?" Tobias bit his lips. In hard, brief words he tried to explain to his father the duty of the German Jew at this historic moment. Efraim stood, lean and black, at the window. He gazed out. He gazed, it seemed to Tobias, into a beyond to which he had no access. He turned to his son at last. "*Shtuss* (nonsense)! All this has happened before. When has war ever brought us anything but evil? I'm going to the *shul*. Will you come with me?" Tobias did not answer. He stood still while his father slowly left the room.

That was their parting. For after that during the few remaining days they hardly spoke. When the regiment entrained, only Tobias's mother was there to weep and say good-by. Desperately clinging to the memory of those marvelous last days in Königsberg, Tobias plunged into the horrors of sickening fear that turned to ferocity, of blood, vermin, strench, typhus. . . . Lost from his company for a minute in an attack through the grass at Gravelotte, he came upon two shivering French boys, as confused and disgusted as himself. Suddenly he remembered Burghammer's words. He drew his rifle to his shoulder and raised himself from the grass. The two young Frenchmen shrugged their shoulders and held up their hands. Both he and they, as appeared soon thereafter, were ill and had to be taken to hospitals. But he had captured two prisoners single-handed. He was cited for gallantry and a colonel came to pin the iron cross on him in his cot in the military hospital at Mainz.

5

HE shared the triumphant entry of the victorious army into Berlin. He wrote his father asking for the same allowance that had been given him in Königsberg. He wrote brief monthly letters to his parents. But he never returned home, and became almost a legend to the mother who bore him. Within two years he announced that he no longer needed financial help from home; within five he began to send generous sums to help in the education or the start in life of his brothers and sisters. In 1880 he informed his family that he was going to marry Else Burghammer, the daughter of his friend and benefactor, the Councillor Heinrich Burghammer and that, for family and financial reasons, he was adopting his wife's name. He did not write that several months before he had undergone Christian baptism at the hands of the later notorious anti-Semite Stoecker. But when that letter came Efraim turned to his wife. He had read it in silence. Now his face was crimson. He raised his arms. He cried in a loud voice: "May his name be blotted out! He is *geshmatt!*" And it was only the long and slow erosion of this once bright and now suddenly hostile world which kept Efraim from rending his garments and strewing ashes on his head as for one who has died. . . .

The anti-Semitic ribaldries of press and pulpit, the growing roar of the race-conscious Nordics—these things did not affect the life of the distinguished jurist, Theodore Burghammer, or of his family. His brother, Samuel Levy, drifted to Berlin and opened a shop on the Moritzplatz. He did not know it until one day Samuel came to his office and with a pain-contorted face asked for help. Burghammer gave his brother more money than he had ever seen before, but had to hurry off for a pressing appointment. He saw Samuel no more. In 1890 he was briefly informed of his mother's death. He drove to the station. He bought a first-class ticket to Insterburg. He walked out on the *perron* and looked long at the black train in the twinkling station. Then he crumpled the ticket in his hand and wandered forth into the streets of the city and caught a late cab home. He wired money to his father. It was returned to him without a word. The next month he was made a *Justizrath*.

His father-in-law died and his wife came into her share of a great fortune. The Burghammers built them a palace in Tiergartenstrasse and all literary and artistic Berlin crowded their drawing-rooms. Burghammer and his wife, Christian and Prussian, conservatives, pillars of the empire, of throne and altar, stood there in those brilliant rooms, and suddenly the eminent jurist not only looked at his guests, but saw— saw for a moment with considering eyes. Musicians, writers, actors, publishers, scientists, jurists. And all were Jews. A handful of Gentiles. Yes, four or five—suppliants or parasites. Theodore Burghammer laughed a loud, harsh, unmotivated laugh. He checked himself at once. He saw his wife's beautiful dark eyes upon him and he loved her. . . .

He loved her and his two boys, his dark handsome sons who had been baptized when they were babies. The boys were growing up. At school they had Gentile friends. But so, their father considered, had Tobias Levy had. He wondered about their future. Would they, like himself, live in a world of ghosts and shams—in a world that pretended with all its might to be one thing but in which there never died the rumor of a strange reality that was like a secret shame yet also like a relief from a tension too great to be borne? Perhaps the boys would be better off than he. They had no troubling memories. No Sabbath candles shone to them across the years, no Jewish words spoken by their mother echoed in their hearts. . . .

Burghammer became a very great man in his later years. He was invited to the table of the king; he was a friend and associate of Walther Rathenau. But for a last-minute intrigue in the dark castle on the *Schlossplatz* he would have been made a minister of state. Dedicated to the service of his country, his day began early and ended late. He saw little of his sons. But again and again he would sit in his study and suddenly let his hands droop to his desk. Then he would lift them to his head. And then a secret agent would find out for him where his brothers and sisters were, and the Levys would get large sums of money from a hand supposedly unknown. . . . They knew, of course, from whom these benefactions came and they wrote him when, in 1910, at the age of eighty-two, his father Efraim, the son of the Vilna *melamed*, joined his fathers. . . . The *Justizrath* did not even tell his wife. His younger son, the well-known sportsman Kurt Burghammer, was about to marry Sybil Ratislaw, the daughter of Lord Ratislaw of Coomb, whom he had met at the great tennis matches in England. This was no time to dig up strange and alien memories. Burghammer looked at the two slim, handsome young Europeans and wondered whether they even knew that they were both descendants of Reb Chaim Bratzlawer, the Vilna distiller. Involuntarily a shadow or irony played over his lips. Why, he asked himself, why?

He was an old man now and the years sped like a vision, like a dream. Once more, as in his early youth, the fatherland was to be defended. Ah, the old emotions were not yet dead even within him. He remembered the year '70; he was a Knight of the Iron Cross. He didn't approve of the policies of his government. But the war having come, he put himself, his fortune, and his sons at the disposal of his country. His older son, Alfred, was safe with the General Staff. But Kurt was a rival of the great Richthofen and had already brought down eighteen enemy planes. . . . There could be only one end to such a career. But the *Justizrath* understood his son's recklessness. Sybil, the Englishwoman, whom her husband adored, had fled to Holland. . . .

It was in the autumn of 1917. *Justizrath* Burghammer was sitting in his study at home. Through the tall window he saw the bronze and yellow and golden leaves of the Tiergarten catch the last glints of a winter sunset. His white almost transparent old head seemed to be listening. Yes, that was more than the ordinary roar of the city. It had all been predicted. How could it be otherwise? Had ever before in history a great people hungered and suffered like this people? And now even its long patience was wearing thin. Mobs from the east of the city were marching toward the west. The government, he knew, had taken its precautions. But he was sorry, sorry to the soul. . . . He sat still. The roar drew nearer. Suddenly like tattered funeral flags in a wind a mob swished around the corner and halted before his house. Something between a murmur and a moan and the growling of angry hounds rose to the ears of the *Justizrath*. And then a woman's shrill, maddened, hysterical shriek: "The accursed Jews feed while our children die of hunger." The *Justizrath* got up slowly and went to the window. He stood upright and stern. A stone crashed through a pane far above his head. Another flew, and another. But the stones were hurled by wild, weak hands and missed their aim. And then came the trampling of iron on asphalt and the mounted police galloped around the corner and rode with drawn sabers into that dark, forlorn, suddenly silent mass of tattered, hungry creatures, and the *Justizrath* hid his face in his hands. . . .

He returned to his mahogany desk and sat down slowly and lit no light. His wife was at the hospital she had founded and endowed, working far beyond the limits of her strength, trying to forget the tragedy of Kurt and Sybil. . . . A faint tap at the door. A footman entered and switched on a dim light and laid a telegram softly on the table in front of his master. He was a German boy who had lost his right arm in the early battles in Flanders. No one else would employ him. He was devoted to Burghammer. He stood for a moment, and the eyes of master and man met. Burghammer knew. He hardly needed to open the telegram and read the dreadfully polite phrases: "Profound sympathy . . . most glorious death upon the field of honor. . . . Twenty-seven planes. . . . Posthumous iron cross of the first class and

. . ." Burghammer let the piece of paper fall from his old
hands. He looked around him. The servant was gone. Yes,
of course; Kurt was dead. He lifted up his face and a dry
sob shook his feeble frame, and from the depth of him came
words, words he had not heard in fifty years, and he
stretched out his arms and cried in a loud voice: "*Shmah
Yisroel!*"

6

I cannot tell in equal detail the stories of the other children
of Efraim Levy, the son of Mendel, the *melamed*. Tobias
was the only one who, according to his father, resembled
Grandmother Braine, and that was strange, seeing that often
enough Efraim could almost have wished his first-born
under the earth. The other children were remarkable for
neither good nor evil, and all but one—not by his own
fault—were a comfort to their father in his old age. Samuel,
who was only two years younger than Tobias, was sent to
the German *Gymnasium* too. But he had what the teachers
called a "heavy head." He worked hard and made little
progress. For a time his mother urged him on. But with the
disappearance of Tobias from his home after the war of
1870, Hannah's ardor and ambition forsook her and she
seemed contented enough when Samuel went to work in a
clothing-shop. Thence the lad drifted to Berlin, married a
woman much older than himself, who was, however, of a
good family and had a dowry of several thousand *thaler,*
and opened a shop of his own. The shop did not do very
well. Samuel was a heavy, vaguely dreamy man oppressed
by his wife's age and homeliness. He loved the three children who came in rapid succession with an eager, pathetic
love. But he could summon neither energy nor real fore-
thought even for their sakes. None of the Levys, in fact,
had much business sagacity. The shop failed. Samuel managed to open another on the *Moritzplatz*, got that one unbelievable cheque from Tobias which he recognized clearly
enough as conscience money and managed to drag along till

51

his children were grown and his wife dead. His daughter and two sons were reasonably competent, unambitious people who married in their own set of Berlin middle-class Jewry, did fairly well, attended a second-rate reform synagogue on New Year and the Day of Atonement, ate *trefe*, as a matter of course cracked Jewish jokes, gave their children excellent educations, and were thoroughly kind to their father in his helpless and obese later years. He lived long enough to see one of his grandsons an eminent violinist and swore that the child was the image of his father, Efraim Levy, *olov hasholem*. . . .

The two sisters of Tobias and Samuel had very unequal fates. Rose, the younger and prettier, fell in love with a young Insterburg clerk named Martin Jüdel. He was blond and thought he was dashing and Nordic-looking. With the modest dowry that Rose brought him he opened a little apron factory in Königsberg. But he neglected both his wife and his business. He tried to emphasize his Germanic appearance and counteract his terrible name by being "horsey" and filling the house with dogs. The unnaturalness of this to his Jewish nature produced a self-tormenting and self-abandoning corruption so poisonous that Rose, with child in the eighth month, threw herself down a flight of stairs and died of the consequent premature birth. . . .

Bertha, the older daughter of Efraim and Hannah, developed a steady and independent judgment almost from her earliest years. She watched the fates of her older brothers with something of sternness in her attitude and speech. She clung to her father, with whom she would take long walks. She talked Yiddish with him and slightly shocked her mother thereby. She did not marry, an unheard-of thing, until she was twenty-six, and then a penniless Talmudic student who had drifted to Insterburg from Warsaw. Her father was divided between spiritual satisfaction and worldly fear. But she explained to him that her dowry would keep her and Benjamin Krakauer, her husband, for six years. By that time she believed that he would have made a career for himself. She proved to be entirely right.

Krakauer had prepared himself to pass all the official German examinations. Within three years he took his doctorate in Semitology at the University of Breslau. Ministering to a small orthodox congregation, he established himself as *Privatdozent* at the same university. Within four more years his publications in his chosen fields practically compelled the university senate to offer him an associate professorship. When Efraim was a very old man he was twice persuaded to visit the Krakauers in Breslau. It was these two visits that made him feel that he would die in peace. His own life, he said, speaking out for the first time, seemed to him a great failure. The terrible defection of Tobias he felt to be a judgment upon him for his sins. But in the old, far days in Vilna he and Hannah, his betrothed, had had a goodly dream and ideal for the future. Here, in the Krakauer house, he saw that that dream was realized beyond anything that he and Hannah had had the knowledge or the wisdom to plan or to hope. The house was full of books in all the languages of Europe. But it was a Jewish house. The kitchen was *kosher* not because Benjamin and Bertha any longer believed that all the six hundred and thirteen commands had been decreed by God, but because they did not think that a day had yet come in which Israel could dispense with any of its methods of spiritual integrity and solidarity. The children went to German schools, but they were taught Hebrew at home by a tutor and could speak Yiddish. And this was, too, as old Efraim did not fail to notice, the only Jewish house of which he had ever heard to which Gentile friends and colleagues came not in condescension or as parasites, but as equals to equals. And seeing all these things, the old man wept. To Benjamin he told the stories of Mendel, his father and of Braine, his mother, and of his maternal grandfather and the mysterious chest. And with a sigh Benjamin heard of the loss of the precious manuscript *Haggada* and of that still more precious historical scroll over which Efraim's grandfather had wept on the eve of every Day of Atonement. It was the Krakauers whom the old man caused to be summoned to his death-bed,

53

which would have been lonely but for them. Bertha closed
her father's eyes; Benjamin Krakauer read the funeral prayers over his grave.

7

I have not mentioned Jacob, the latest-born of Efraim and
Hannah. Why was he not beside the bed of his dying father?
The truth is that little had been heard from him in many
years. That little, a letter and a present every twelvemonth
or so, was well enough. But Efraim, thinking of Tobias,
distrusted these signs of contrition and prosperity that came
out of an alien world. Jacob had been a care and a problem
from the beginning. Alone of all the Levy children he had
been blond. Not strikingly so, but certainly not dark. With
a half-bitter smile his father had said to his mother: "I've
never liked blond Jews." Hannah had gathered the baby the
more tightly to her bosom. But troubles began soon enough.
He simply stayed away from *cheder* and later from school,
and followed the town musicians with a twig held trumpet-
like to his lips. It was with the greatest difficulty that he
could be taught the little he needed for his *bar-mitzvah;* in
school he sat year after year in the same class. A hopeless
shlemihl who, God forbid, would have to submit to three
years of military service with peasants and the riff-raff of
the towns who would jeer at him and torment him. But
Jacob could not be persuaded to regard these things seriously. He got him a cheap fiddle and scraped upon it, and
when, after his *bar-mitzvah,* his father looked around for a
decent merchant to whom to apprentice the boy, Jacob
begged to be apprenticed to the town bandmaster. He went
to the man himself, but the bandmaster would not have him.
So he went to work, with ill-grace enough, in a dry-goods
shop.

He grew up to be a pleasant-looking youth with his gray
eyes and sandy hair and subdued nose and slender figure.
But he had not the slim, scholarly hand, the nervous Oriental hand, of his father or Tobias. He had broad muscular

hands with yellow hairs on them. With these hands he measured cloth for the peasant women and the town women and girls, and the girls, seeing these hands and looking into his gray eyes, took him for one of themselves.

In the spring of his eighteenth year he went out in the milder dusks to meet little Miene under the blossoming linden trees. The girl could neither read nor write. She did not ask his name, and her own was an unpronounceable Lithuanian one. She had long blond braids and sweet lips and breasts. For a month Jacob lived the deep ardor and high poetry of unspoiled instincts, looking neither before nor after. Then came the crash. He went home and saw his suddenly frail and spiritual-looking father hemmed in by two Lithuanian boatmen—great, sweaty, formless giants. They gave Jacob an evil look, but turned back to Efraim: "Money, Jew!" They lifted their red fists that looked like the knee-joints of veal in a butcher's stall. "More money!" Then they deliberately spat on the floor and crossed themselves and tramped out.

Father and son faced each other. Efraim was deathly pale. Jacob suddenly saw a world stripped of glamor. The reaction brought him a great cold disgust. He aged by years in that silent minute. Efraim spoke:

"I gave them a hundred *thaler*. That is nothing. But they say you must leave and be seen no more."

A naked terror that he had long driven from his consciousness by main force leaped up in Jacob's mind.

"I will go. I don't want to serve three years, anyhow, and the time is near. I'll go to America."

Efraim frowned. "If you escape military service you can never come back."

Jacob looked sullen. "I don't want to. We are treated like dogs here. I want to go to a free country."

Efraim shook his head. He remembered the bitter words of Tobias. He had no fault to find with exile in this land. Its burden, if you behaved yourself, was light enough. What business, he asked Jacob, had a Jew not to study long enough to gain his exemption from three years' service or to seduce a *shikse* (Gentile girl) of the lowest class? Such a Jew would come to good in no land. Jacob's face tightened. "You will see, father. Help me to go." He resisted his mother's pleading; he resisted the deeper appeal of his father's wordless sorrow. They equipped him as best they could. "Like a rich man's son," said Hannah amid her flowing tears. They gave him five hundred *thaler* and their blessing. He went to Berlin and looked for Tobias at the last address which his parents had. But it was just a few months before Tobias's marriage to Else Burghammer. He had moved and left no word behind him. Jacob set his teeth. Very well. He would make his way without his brother's help.

He traveled third-class to Hamburg, and two fat men winked at each other when they saw him and began to tell greasy, loathsome, foul stories in each of which a Jew figured as a thief, a coward, a lecher, and a butt. Jacob fled to the next compartment. He did not linger in Hamburg. He took the first ship out. It was a gentle summer crossing and Jacob was not seasick after the first two days. He traveled not steerage, but second class. The fellow passengers were courteous; the stewards respectful. Jacob clenched his hands and squared his shoulders. He was going to a free country where such treatment could always be commanded. He would, God helping him, command it. In Europe the obstacles of prejudice, of military service, of insult and discrimination, were too great. Perhaps he was not such a *shlemihl* as his father feared. He would yet be an honor to his parents, though in a foreign land. . . . They changed his money for him on board. He had $310 when he landed in New York on the 2d of August, 1879. With a sense of release, of hope, almost of consecration he set his foot upon the soil of freedom. . . .

BOOK III

1

THE part played by a feeling of inferiority in the psychical life of man was fittingly discovered and described by a Jewish physician. For though all men can be afflicted with this feeling in consequence of a specific cause, nearly every Jew is thus afflicted without specific and discoverable cause. There is then (granting the incompleteness of all generalizations) another distinction to be made. Where the cause is known the mind consents. Where it is not known the soul rebels. The cashier gambling with his firm's money starts at a shadow. When he sees it is only a shadow he sighs with relief. The Jew, innocent of wrong-doing, starts at a shadow, too. He hates the shadow, himself, the world of shadows; he must transcend it; he becomes arrogant and declares that all things blaze with an unshadowed light. Thence arise intricate maladies of the soul: sudden suspiciousness; fear of fear; propitiation without belief; rage apparently turning against others, actually pointed at the self; sensitiveness in a thousand contorted and contradictory ways. . . . The vulgar reproach of cowardice does not touch the case. A just appreciation of danger is needed if life is to go on at all. Fear and shrinking without immediate cause are symptoms of the fact that unhappy stars watched over the historic experience of one's kind. . . .

One thousand years of intermittent persecution, continued at this very hour by pogroms in Rumania, are enough to account for the Jew's feeling of inferiority and his undying will to compensate. But in truth the causes lie farther back. The Bnei Israel were but a feeble folk from the beginning. What though, at their freshest and fieriest they once wrung a strip of Palestinian hill-lands from scattered and barbarous chiefs! No sooner had they set up their little state than the shadows of Egypt and Babylon fell upon it almost to blotting out. Once they drove back an Assyrian king and attributed the successful defense to their God. Defeat and contrition were their habitual bread. In the early days of David not even all of Jerusalem was in their possession. Solomon, their one brief worldly glory, had to borrow workmen and materials for building from a Tyrian king. They were unapt at all things made with hands. It is doubtful whether they were good fighters at best. They never fought but against overwhelming odds. Then came the Babylonian captivity. It was the end of a people's brief dream of equality with other peoples. The last war-like heroes whom the Jews remember, Judah Makkabi and Bar Kochba, were leaders of forlorn hopes, heroes of defeat, dedicated to disaster before a bow was strung or a spear lifted. . . .

They trembled and sang their penitential psalms and compensated—compensated and liberated themselves by discovering the essence of righteousness: that force is evil, that war is sin, that passive martyrdom is triumph, that victory is defeat and success failure. They transcended the values of a war-like world by denying them. But the process is an infinitely gradual one and comes to completion only in isolated individuals: Jeremiah, Isaiah, Jesus, the martyrs of the Crusades, the early *Chassidic* rabbis, pacifists and lovers of freedom here and there. In a world of force the Jew is still afraid, and Judas betrays Jesus in the same breast. . . .

The Rabbi Jehoshua of Nazareth, even as the late and clouded and confused legend portrays him, had cast out fear. The Law that was the stay of Israel's integrity was to be kept. But to at least an equality with it were to be raised those written and oral precepts, reshaped with the force and poignancy of genius, by which Israel had already from age to age denied hate and force and exalted love and humility and peace. And those precepts were to be deepened and men's actions were to square with them to the uttermost—to complete nonresistance, to faultless charity and loving-kindness. Cæsar was to be given what he demanded, even as the robber on the highway was to be given not only one's cloak, but one's coat. The other cheek was to be turned and the spirit of man to triumph in naked majesty. . . .

Judas heard and believed. But a little pulse of fear kept on beating in his unpurged soul. He saw himself at moments not majestic in the refusal to use force, but craven. He saw himself in the old evil savage sense in the dust. Out of that fear and false humiliation flamed the compensatory vision of a Messiah of the conquering sword. Then this Rabbi could not be He, but rather one to weaken the arm and make soft the marrow of an oppressed people. And in a frenzy of fear Judas brought the torches and spears to the gate of the garden of Gethsemane. . . . But the frenzy and the compensatory vision passed and Judas, a Jew, knowing that he had sinned the unforgivable sin of using force and denying peace, cast from him the thirty pieces of silver and hanged himself. . . .

2

THE terror and the shame of the last episodes of his life in Europe had burned themselves deeply into Jacob Levy's soul. He identified this terror and this shame with Europe; he identified the prudence and the circumspection that arose from that terror and that shame with America. He always insisted in later years that his luck had changed the moment that he set his foot on the soil of the United States. He attributed none of it to the moral shock that contributed to a rather sudden maturing of his character. In spite of such considerations which he would have brushed aside as foolish subtleties, it cannot be said that he was far in the wrong in that favorite discourse of his that he held in early years to newcomers from the old country and in later years to his family circle. In the old country, in Insterburg, say, you had no elbow room. You were So-and-so, the son of So-and-so. What could you do? It was like prison. Oh, there were ways up and out of your original condition. But each way was a prescribed way with special laws and rules and tests and specifications. First you had to pass an examination to avoid three years of military service. One year you had to serve, even then. It was always a matter of examinations. As for business—it didn't seem to him that there was any such thing. His father, an honest man and an able man, if ever there was one, had slaved the whole of his life for a mere living and a few hundred *thaler* to give to each of his children. More he hadn't been able to give to any. He had died a poor man. In America—at this point Jacob Levy would always lift an instructive finger—it was all different. In later years the younger members of the circle would grin a little and Jacob's finger would become sterner in its gesture and his face slightly red. In his time, at least, it had been true. If a man was honest and decent in America it didn't matter what he did. He was respected. And more important even, a man could try one thing and then another and see what he was fit for. He didn't have to become an apprentice for three years. He was no one's slave. Look at his own history. He had landed in '79 with three hundred dollars. He hadn't known a word of English. So he had had to stop the first few days in an immigrants' boarding-house, full of low people and terribly dirty. But it had been for a few days only. He had wandered eastward across town on Fourteenth Street and on a newsstand had found papers printed in German. He had bought one and had walked over to Union Square and sat down on a bench to read it. He could remember that day, he used to say, like today. The heat of the waning American summer was great. Never had he felt such heat. Yet from the whole scene, from the busy people and the many carriages and wagons, there had come to him a feeling of abundant life. There were some terribly ragged poor creatures loitering on the square. Men with paper-white faces except for the bluish-red veins and pimples on their noses. One he remembered especially across all these years—a thin dwarfish man who had on ragged clothes that must once have been a giant's. He would shrug his shoulders in a sickly way and pull up his long tattered sleeves to pick up a cigar stump. And yet, Jacob Levy used to say, although he had never seen such poverty in his part of the old country, either, these loafers and beggars and drunkards didn't depress him. They didn't somehow seem to him a part of this American life into which he was going. . . . Well, he had opened his copy of the *New Yorker Herold* and looked at the employment columns. He thought he had better find work and save his little capital. But even as he was sitting there and wondering whether he could drive any of these many strange trades that were spoken of in the paper, an old gentleman had come and sat down next to him and had asked him in the quaintest anglicized German he had ever heard whether he was a "greener" and how he liked America. The old gentleman had rocked his fat head from side to side in a happy self-satisfied sort of way. Forty years, he had told Jacob Levy, he had already been in America and it was the greatest country on earth. Oh, it was good enough for him. He had come over in the steerage of a sailing-vessel. What did this generation know of hardships! When he left the boat he had had two dollars and a quarter. You have to work in America. That was right. But if you do?—! And the old gentleman had looked fondly at his enormous diamond ring and his enormously thick watch-chain. "And that," Mr. Levy used to say with a smile, turning to his children—"that was old Sol Friedenfeld, the grandfather of the girls." And Arthur and Hazel Levy would giggle when they thought of Ethel and Genevieve Freefield and the house on East Sixty-fourth Street with its formidable footmen, and there as the tiniest bit of malice in their giggle because they really envied the Freefield girls. Not at all on account of the Free-field millions. That would have been vulgar and the Levys were far from poor. But there was the name—Freefield. Hazel could have prayed for such a name. Why, with it you could be taken for 'most anything you liked. And the girls' father, J. Mortimer Freefield, was American born and a Princeton graduate and didn't, like her daddy, who was, of course, the dearest old thing in the world in every other way, say: "Ent det vass de grentfader off de girlss."

Old Friedenfeld had been in his later sixties that summer of '79 when he had entered into a conversation with Jacob Levy on a park bench in Union Square. He was a rich man, though he would have been amazed had he lived to see what his son would make of the original three hundred thousand dollars that it had taken him over forty years to amass. He was a man of the simplest kindness and good will, and the great pleasure of his later years was to pick up young immigrants—"greeners"—especially such as were of decent families and came from somewhere near his old home, and help these young fellows to get on their feet in the new country. He himself had originally come from Bromberg, and West and East Prussia were not so far away from each other. So he warmed to this young man who, moreover, was neatly dressed and spoke very good German and also confided to him that he had a tiny capital. "That's fine," the old man had said. "You must get work where you can learn English. You come to my office tomorrow. Maybe I can do something for you. Maybe." Benevolently he had wagged his head and had left Jacob with the impression that there was something in America that opened the hearts of men.

3

THE small department store of Friedenfeld & Cohn on lower Sixth Avenue was almost obliterated to the casual eye by the enormous establishments that towered on every side above it. It occupied only two floors of a narrow squeezed-in building on the west side of the avenue. But it drove an enormous trade with the poorer Irish of the lower west side, who were shy of entering the more imposing and glittering establishments near at hand. Then poor Italians flooded those streets, and they too came for their underwear and children's clothes and overalls and cheap furniture to Friedenfeld & Cohn's. Furniture was one of the specialties of the house. The whole upper floor was given over to this department. A few parlor sets mouldered there from year to year. The stock that went out and was renewed consisted of bedroom sets, cheap oakwood with imitation marble tops, unpainted kitchen tables, chairs and cabinets, and small rugs of shoddy. The place was so crowded with this merchandise that it was hard for the salesmen to guide a customer through the narrow alleys of its labyrinth. It was dark. It was almost suffocating with its musty odor of wood, varnish, turpentine, oil-cloth and cheap, fuzzy carpet. Yet it seemed not only important, but a citadel and a refuge to Jacob Levy, when, by the favor of the head of the house, he was appointed duster, sweeper, and day caretaker of the furniture department at a salary of eight dollars a week.

Jacob Levy was no self-analyst. He used to say in later years that he was young when he came to America and forgot the old country and its life very quickly. It was, in truth, not an ordinary process of forgetting. His mind expelled with relief the fear and shame from which he had suffered in Europe; it was with the greatest difficulty that he brought himself to write occasionally to his parents. And that was not because he had neither affection nor dutifulness. It was because both glowed in his heart and life had somehow forced him to outrage both. Hence he fled from his frustrate emotions and his old fears. It is questionable whether he was ever aware of the character of this process. Certainly not to the extent of precise memories strong enough to pierce the dust of the obliterating years. So he was quite honest in saying, like many another—since the strong and successful and unblemished rarely emigrate— that he had forgotten the old country. . . . Later, much later, it came to him, slipped into his mind again and again, as a troubling and lovely and pathetic vision, and as his father lived on and on he determined again and again once more to visit the scenes of his youth. But something always kept him from the trip. He alone knew that he was slightly relieved whenever affairs offered a good excuse for delay. A faint sense of woe, of frustration, of estrangement stronger than his longing, kept him clinging without a break to his vigorous, healthy, familiar, unproblematic American world.

That world, even in the beginning, had not consisted wholly, of course, of the furniture loft of Friedenfeld & Cohn. Jacob had found board and lodging at the rate of five dollars a week in the house of Mrs. Bartenwerfer on Third Avenue. Mrs. Bartenwerfer had advertised in the *Staats Zei-*

tung that another respectable young man could be accommodated at her house. Was it so soon a symptom of Americanization through atmosphere that Jacob went to Third Avenue despite the obviously Gentile name of Mrs. Bartenwerfer? The crinkled, short, elderly, self-important woman, widow of a tax-collector in Westphalia, received him kindly and loquaciously. In Minden she had been *Frau Steuerinspektor*. Here she was nobody. But one does anything for one's children. And Hans, her son, had thought there wasn't much of a future for a young man in Germany. He was working in a banking-house; his salary was small; so was her pension. Anyhow, she couldn't just sit still with folded hands. Hence this house and the boarders. She already had one, Herr Mumme, son of a very rich butcher in Minden. The boy was here to study American methods of business. Yes, ach yes! But would he tell her his honored name again? She hadn't quite caught it. Levy? Oh, yes. An Israelite. She knew many fine Israelites. She had had Israelite neighbors in Minden. And the banker for whom Hans worked was one, too. She was an enlightened woman and had no prejudices. Only she must ask him for a reference, though she had no doubt at all of his worthiness. New York was such a big city. Mr. Friedenfeld of Friedenfeld & Cohn. Oh, that was quite enough. Yes, she had heard of Mr. Friedenfeld, a fine man, a benevolent man, as so many Israelites were. . . .

It was, perhaps, this drifting into a German-American environment in the beginning that caused the Jewish habits of his youth to fade more swiftly from Jacob's life. In one of her earlier letters his mother asked him whether he got his food ritually prepared. He did not answer the question. He had already eaten roast pork at the Bartenwerfer table. He played *skat* occasionally in the evening with Hans Bartenwerfer and Wilhelm Mumme; he found himself telling them that he had a brother in Berlin who was a distinguished jurist; the three young men went occasionally to a performance at the old Irving Place Theater. Jacob learned English slowly and spoke it with a heavy German accent to his death. He became more German in America than he had ever been in Insterburg. But this, too, was, though he did not know it, a kind of Americanization. For it was the influence of American ideals, always more closely embraced by the immigrant than the native-born, that caused the old-fashioned Germans in America to disregard the racial prejudices of their fatherland and establish their social groups on the basis of language and personal work. In later years Jacob joined the *Liederkranz;* he entered a synagogue only on official occasions. A dumb instinct kept his closer relations Jewish. He would not have married a Gentile nor perhaps have taken one as a partner in business. But the instinct which guided him was so obscure that he would honestly have denied its existence and explained the nature of his closest alliances upon other grounds. When he himself first became an employer of labor it would never have occurred to him to discriminate in favor of a Jew. He preferred, until life forced him to give up that preference, German-speaking people. He trusted their honesty, believed in their industry, and had a profound sympathy with their love of music. He was approached by Jewish charities as the years went on, and gave freely of his substance. But he disliked people who spoke Yiddish; he felt the immigrants of the later periods to be curiously alien from him. He knew that his own father had come from Poland. But in some inexplicable way this knowledge remained wholly inactive in his consciousness.

4

THERE was a clerk at Friedenfeld & Cohn's named Nathan Goldmann. He was a small, thin, tense young man with very black eyes and very black eyebrows growing together over his long inquisitive nose. He had come over with his parents from Tilsit when he was a boy of fifteen and considered himself an authority on American tastes and habits. He was terribly in earnest and gesticulated violently and found a good listener in Jacob. He said that people in America were growing richer and richer; there was an increasing market for a better grade of goods even among working-people; he had a theory, in addition, that the atrocious taste of the period could be mitigated. On an open bookstall in lower Fourth Avenue he had bought a few second-hand copies of European periodicals devoted to the decorative arts. There was a man in England, named William Morris, who had designed some new types of furniture. If one could manufacture such things here one could make a fortune. Goldmann carried about with him photographs of furniture torn out of the stray copies of periodicals that he had bought. He threw up his arms in hard despair. "But without a capital what can you do? I've talked to the boss. A good man but a *shlemihl*. He said: 'Why should I change my business? It is a good business.' "

Jacob felt a strange quiver in his entrails. "How much capital is needed?"

Goldmann squinted fiercely. He lifted a tense forefinger. "I have a scheme. If I had one thousand dollars—just one thousand dollars!"

Jacob's face fell. "All I have is three hundred."

Goldmann jumped. "I have two hundred, myself. Wait . . . wait . . . wait."

Two days later he came to Mrs. Bartenwerfer's house in the evening and, sitting on the single chair in Jacob's little room, explained. Mr. Friedenfeld had been persuaded to put five hundred dollars into the scheme of the two young men, since they had the other five hundred between them. He liked to help to set up young men in business, though Goldmann's particular scheme still annoyed him a little. If young men had businesses of their own they could marry, and to promote marriages was a good and a Jewish action. Thus the benevolent Friedenfeld argued. With a wave of his hand Goldmann swept him out of existence and explained his scheme to Jacob. They would rent a shop; they would hire a carpenter, a greener, newly from Poland; Goldmann, who could draw fairly well, would design a new type of easy chair from the cuts he had; the rods and cushions for the Morris chairs they could buy ready made.

They would advertise a little. But also they would both canvass from house to house in certain districts. He believed . . . he believed . . . Jacob was swept away by his friend's tense faith. He knew that he would feel rather naked and exposed to the cruelty of the world without either his job or his little capital safe in bank. But there was no backing out now; there was no possibility of risking the reproaches or the despair of Goldmann. The firm of Goldmann & Levy was founded on that evening; it was, of course, not incorporated until several years later. Hazel Levy, as well as the two Goldmann girls, though thoroughly familiar with this whole story, were to be glad enough in their day that no one would have guessed it from the exquisite advertisements of the Phœnix Art Furniture Company, Creators of Beautiful Homes, which graced the pages of their favorite magazines. . . .

Success did not come to the two young men at once. At first the sale of their chair went very slowly. Then when the orders increased they found it difficult to fill them, for they had no money and little credit. If Mrs. Bartenwerfer had not occasionally waited for her board bill and Goldmann's parents supported him and Friedenfeld said a good word for the young men to wholesalers in wood and upholstery, the firm would have collapsed half a dozen times during its first three years. Nathan and Jacob lived frugally and worked hard; Jacob felt guilty when, occasionally, he sneaked off to a concert. Nathan needed nothing for life but his purpose. He was a more typical Jew than Jacob. Had his education and opportunities been higher his purpose would have been higher, too. His children were to illustrate that amply later on. The point is that he knew no drifting, no turning aside, only his purpose. Jacob, the slightly blond with the broad hands, could not so easily curb his hungers and his outgoings. But the example of his partner kept him frugal and definitely at work. By 1888 the worst struggles were over. A tiny factory had been established on the outskirts of Hoboken and a modest showroom opened on Broadway. After that the expansion of the business was rapid, though it was not until 1898 that the great factory at Grand Rapids, Mich., was built and the permanent Phœnix Exhibit of Art Furniture established on East Fiftieth Street.

In the crucial years of expansion of the business both Nathan and Jacob were helped by their marriages. Nathan married Sarah Herz in 1889. She was plump and brown and kind and competent, and her father, an importer of silk ribands, gave her a dowry of $5,000, which promptly went, of course, to strengthen the business of Goldmann & Levy. Thereafter Jacob felt that it was, in a sense, his duty to imitate his partner. But he was in a dilemma. For he was in love with Gertrude Oberwarter and Gertrude was one of the two daughters of a widow who could not touch her small capital without dangerously reducing her income. He had met the Oberwarters through the Bartenwerfers. Fanny Oberwarter, the daughter of a well-known German-American journalist of Jewish extraction named Julius Conheim, had been born in America. Her husband had come from Hamburg in his earliest years. The two girls, though they could speak German if necessary, were very conscious Americans. The family lived in a pleasant house in Mount Vernon and it was on their lawn and under their trees that Jacob Levy first perceived the soft brilliance of an American landscape and in some dim way claimed the earth and country as his own.

Gertrude was a little shocked when she found herself attracted by the young immigrant named Levy. She had liked some of the blond young German-Americans with whom she had gone to school. But in her generation the instinct against intermarriage was still forbidding in its strength. Well, Jacob was blond; he was gentle; he loved music. He seemed less Jewish to her than the swarthy young men with their intense and eager air whom she knew. He seemed less emphatic and so more refined. Her mother liked him, too; spring nights in the little Mount Vernon garden did the rest.

Since Gertrude was younger than her sister Ella there was no hurry about marriage. Also Mrs. Oberwarter wanted to see Jacob's business expand a little more. But early in 1891 old Mrs. Conheim died and left each of the girls $8,000. Jacob looked into the velvety brown eyes of Gertrude; he gazed at her oval face with the burning red lips; he touched her long coils of chestnut hair. She wanted to be a June bride in the American fashion. The minister of a reform congregation read the service over them in Mrs. Oberwarter's parlor. They went to Niagara Falls on their wedding journey....

5

1891. The World Building was the tallest in New York. Weber and Fields were the joy and pride of the town. At her cottage piano in their new apartment on West Eightieth Street Gertrude Levy in a full long skirt and a tight-fitting black silk "jersey" sang and played "Love's Old Sweet Song." The popular songs were becoming less and less refined.

> *It won't be a stylish marriage,*
> *For I can't afford a carriage,*
> *But you'll look sweet*
> *Upon the seat*
> *Of a bicycle built for two.*

The Levy's dining-room was one of the earliest examples of "mission" furniture in weathered oak. Sarah Goldmann thought it terribly plain. She infinitely preferred her own golden-oak set, especially the sideboard with its little protruding, balcony-like shelves on which her cut glass glittered so charmingly, and the bevel-edged mirror in the middle. Her husband, though he was really the firm's innovator in styles of furniture, let Sarah have her way. What he wanted at home was a good bed and good food, good home-cooked food, and peace. In their parlor the Levys had a "set" of silk upholstery and gilt wood that was supposed to be of a certain French "period." It was not clear of which. Their washstands and bureaus were all marble-topped....

The young couple was very happy and very home-loving. Jacob felt that he had come home in every sense. He had long ago taken out his citizenship papers; his wife was native-born. His children, God willing, would be Americans. He still said "God willing." But it was on his lips really equivalent to *"absit omen!"* It was a phrase with which to ward off ill luck. Neither he nor his wife ever debated the question of any religious observance. Gertrude knew, of course, that her husband's parents had been observant Jews; so had her grandparents been. All that lay in a scarcely imaginable past behind her. Here was Broadway, and Lüchow's restaurant on Fourteenth Street, and a delightful little German cellar restaurant on an Eighth Street corner called "Zum Prelaten." Here was John Wanamaker's store. The firm—Goldmann & Levy—was making money. Jacob was very generous. Unconsciously he adopted the whole of his young wife's outlook. It represented peace to him and liberation from fear and prosperity. It represented America. He was a Republican and voted for Benjamin Harrison. He and Goldmann had never raised the question of closing their business on Saturday. It was on Sunday afternoon that they went out walking with their young wives. It was on Sunday that they invited each other to dinner and partook, either at the Goldmann or at the Levy apartment, of roast goose or *schmorbraten* and *lokshen* pudding. They never asked themselves whether *lokshen* and *gefüllte Milz* was all that was left them of the traditions of their race. Well, perhaps it was not quite all. A few words like *mishpoche* (kith and kin) or *mies* (ugly) or *bekoved* (honorable or decent) were still used. And in the earliest days Jacob and Gertrude if they didn't want the Irish maidservant to know that they were talking about her, referred to her as the *shikse*. But even this faint linguistic habit faded. It had never been strong in Gertrude, anyhow.

The Goldmanns were their best friends; they saw a good deal, of course, of Gertrude's mother and sister and a little later of Ella's husband Adams, a very successful drummer in woollens who had had the American *s* added by legalized enactment to his name. They were also, in a quiet, self-respecting way, very proud of their friendship with the Mortimer Freefields, who had, a little to their own surprise, invited them to dinner soon after their marriage. Not that they had not known all about the Freefields. When the expanding firm of Goldmann & Levy found that it had an increasing amount of legal business to transact, it very naturally took that business to the son of its first friend and benefactor. Nathan, to be sure, had said somewhat contemptuously: "Freefield! Why Freefield? A name, too! Is he ashamed of his father?" But he and Jacob were both impressed by the Princeton and Columbia degrees, the somber, solemn office, the superb American speech of the glossy lawyer. The wives of Nathan and Jacob were equally impressed by the fact that Mr. Freefield had married a Miss Ottolengui of Savannah, Georgia, and was thus allied with the aristocratic Sephardic families who had come to America (from North Africa *via* the West Indies) before the American Revolution.

The Freefields were a profound influence in the lives of the Levys. This influence was not very direct; it was never discussed as such; there was no open imitation. What helped to mold the lives of the Levy family were the things which the Freefields took so blandly and unobtrusively for granted. Mr. Freefield never said, "We are Americans." That went without saying. It also went without saying that the religion of the Freefields was Jewish. They, in fact, rented a pew in an old synagogue of the Portuguese tradition and, the Levys believed, attended its services on New Year and the Day of Atonement. This was the one respect in which the Levys did not follow the example of their friends. To them the synagogue still smacked of oppression, commonness, recent immigration, the Ghetto. . . . Gertrude quietly made up her mind that it was Mrs. Freefield who had introduced this factor into the family life. She admired it in a way, but knew that it was not for her and hers. Of the subtlety of this mental process she was wholly unaware. What she quietly watched was the conduct of the Freefield household behind its brownstone front on Fiftieth Street: the refined calm, the excellent management of the servants, the purity of its English speech, the dignity and order. Once or twice a year the Freefields gave parties to which the Levys were invited. There they met the De Leons and the Cohen-Hadrias and the Bolingbroke Sampsons, whose ancestors had been in England since the resettlement under Cromwell, and once a young Baron von Bleichroeder here from Berlin to study American banking methods. Everyone at these parties was subdued and well bred and a little casual. Or did it seem so only to Jacob? Coming from one of these parties, at all events, he and Gertrude had one of their rare quarrels. Gertrude felt both soothed and elated. She loved the atmosphere at the Freefields. She had watched Mrs. Freefield closely. What a hostess! Well, Jacob was doing very well. A few years from now she, too, might give a party which, though more modest, would be equally elegant. This was different from the German-Jewish society of her unmarried days with its foreign speech and interlarded Jewish jokes and sayings, and its eagerness and, as it seemed to her at this moment, its slightly brawling tendency. . . . She wondered why Jacob was so silent. Suddenly he spoke:

"I'm not going to those people again. They're all hypocrites!"

She was shocked and jolted as out of a pleasant dream. "Of course you prefer Nathan Goldmann who takes off his coat and sits in shirt sleeves even in our house, and picks his teeth, or those terrible Libshitzes from Warsaw who smell of garlic a mile off."

Jacob shook his head. "What I don't like is Jews who pretend they're something else."

There Gertrude had him. "Pretend? Why, the Freefields go to *shul!* That's more than we do. And I don't know that I care about the idea. But it's true, isn't it?"

Jacob had a brooding look. "Somehow those people remind me of my brother Theodore. I've told you that story often enough."

"I don't think there's any comparison," Gertrude retorted. "None of these people would dream of joining a Christian church."

She had him again; he was never a subtle man. It irritated him to be so obviously worsted in an argument which involved very strong feelings.

"I don't care what you say," he cried. "These people don't act natural. And they try to make you feel that you're common. Well, maybe I am. But I'm going to stay just that way. I guess Mr. Mortimer Freefield will do our law business without my being insulted in his house! Mortimer Freefield! Moses Friedenfeld is his name. The *ganev!*"

Gertrude wept. Jacob remembered her condition and took her into his arms.

"Never mind, Trudchen. Why should we quarrel over those people? I like refinement, too. But I get too much of it in a lump in that house."

6

THEY were very happy. Of course Jacob went to the Freefields on the next occasion. Why should he disturb the harmony of his home over such a trifle? If his wife enjoyed it, he could stand it. She was as lovely to him as she had been in her girlhood, in spite of the twenty pounds she had taken on. Lovelier maybe. And these were the years, too, during which she merited a special tenderness. Their son Arthur was born in 1893 and their daughter Hazel in 1895. Jacob liked neither of these names particularly. But Gertrude had been reading Tennyson a good deal and had seen the play of "Hazel Kirke," and since her paternal grandfather's name had been Abram and Jacob's mother's name had been Hannah, the children had Jewish names and English names that began with the same letter. So all was well.

During her first pregnancy, reading a book of verses, the thought had suddenly come to Gertrude: why circumcise the boy—she was sure it would be a boy—when he comes? At the thought of an uncircumcised man a little wave of faintness and nausea had swept over her. Perhaps it was only

75

her condition. She did not argue about the matter with herself, but accepted the warning as final. To Jacob it never occurred that his man-child should not be circumcised. He adored the boy with an intensity that surprised himself. He suddenly knew that his life had been empty and meaningless hitherto. Its meaning came to it with that dark baby in its crib. Was it a delusion that almost immediately the baby resembled Theodore? Jacob stood looking at his boy and remembered how, in far years, his mother had told him that Theodore—only she had called him Tobias—had been the image of that grandmother Braine who had died in Jerusalem. And somehow Jacob was strongly tempted to hunt for his old *talith* (it must be somewhere) and go to a temple and pray. . . . But there was so much to be done and Gertrude was in no condition to be left except for the most pressing business engagements. Moreover, he was far away from the old-fashioned *shuls* downtown into which a man could drop informally to pray. The spick and span temples in his neighborhood were open, like Protestant churches, for formal worship on Sabbath eve and morning. . . . So the isolated impulse faded; it did not come again when Hazel was born. . . .

The children did not remember the apartment on West Eightieth Street in which they were both born. In 1896 the Levys bought their house on Ninety-first Street near West End Avenue. Jacob would have preferred one of the newer-styled houses in yellow brick with great bay windows. But Gertrude, who had been born in New York, preferred the unquestionable gentility of a brownstone front with a stoop on which one could sit in the spring evenings. The furniture of the house was in the best taste of the period, still too heavy and somber and cluttering according to the dictates of later fashions, but inoffensive in character and so excellent in quality that it was never changed.

Arthur's earliest recollections were of two illnesses of his childhood. He was in bed in the big rear bedroom on the third floor. He was feverish and restless. Left alone for a moment, he stood up and examined the carvings on the headboard of the bed. He didn't remember why. The whole thing was, in fact, like a remembered dream. Clearest in that dream was the figure of his mother. Not, curiously enough, her face, but her white, cool, plump hand with the ring that she was always wearing—a large amethyst with a tiny gold flower set in the middle of the stone, and a diamond splinter in the center of the little golden flower. Through the dream floated the refreshing, slightly bitter fragrance of eau-de-Cologne. He could not remember which illness was which. The two merged together. Occasionally little Hazel would appear in both, daintily dressed in white and already then, at three, lovely with those burnished golden-brown eyes which, even in their worst quarrels, Arthur could not help liking. . . . It must have been spring, for he remembered that, the first time he went out, the sunshine was very bright and fresh and the trees looked as if they had just had a bath, and yet the wind that blew into the open throat of his little sailor suit had a sting in it. . . .

Next he remembered how, especially in winter, he had played all by himself, and in his mind the game that the house with his father and mother and Hazel and the two maids in it was a fortress in a lonely waste, protected by a moat and a drawbridge and provisioned for months and years, and how, from this imagined situation, there had come to him a lovely feeling both of adventure and of snugness and security. In the early evenings of winter, when the lights had just been lit, he had withdrawn all by himself into a corner of the little playroom between his sister's bedroom and his own and snuggled down there on a cushion and hugged this feeling of security in a menacing world to his childish breast. . . .

More striking, though neither as delightful nor as comforting as this recollection which warmed his heart even in his adolescent years, was the clear memory of a birthday party that his mother had given for him. It had been in April, of course, and a whiff of flowers and cake had been in the house, and in the afternoon he and Hazel had waited, in their best clothes, for their guests. That was, it seemed to

Arthur, his first conscious vision of that familiar group. First had come his cousins, Eugene and Harry Adams; next the Goldmann children, a little boisterous and pell-mell: Sally and Esther and Joe and Victor; and last, in one of the earliest motor-cars seen, accompanied not by their mother, but by their French governess, Ethel and Genevieve Freefield. Bright colors he remembered, and gifts, and the queer smell of the paint on some elaborate wooden toy brought by the Freefield girls, and the terrible painfulness of having to be a little gentleman and thank his guests for their gifts, and a sudden access of rage he had had because Hazel, who hadn't learned her letters yet, was playing roughly and, as it had seemed to him, senselessly, with some books that had been given him. Last, after the chocolate and the cake, as the afternoon was waning, it appears that he and little Esther Goldmann had been found in a corner of the long drawing-room with their arms about each other, and had been pulled out and teased and laughed at for some reason that neither of them understood. Then supper and sleepiness and bed and his mother coming in for a good-night kiss and putting her white, plump hand with the amethyst ring on his forehead and wondering if it didn't feel too hot. . . .

7

HOW was it that, before they went to school, always and always, as far back as the awakening of consciousness, the children knew that they were Jews? This was a subject on which Arthur speculated not a few times in the later years. There was in the house no visible symbol of religion and of race. Had the house been emptied of its inhabitants, to be let furnished, for instance, there would have been nothing in it to differentiate it from the house of Protestant Americans. There were a few German books of Gertrude's. But these, too, had neither Jewish content nor association. Arthur was quite sure on one point, at all events, and that point was the crucial one, that when he was old enough to understand certain definite remarks that betrayed a Jewish consciousness, he already knew, consented, was nowise astonished nor tempted to ask. Such remarks in the household were few enough. They were usually made by his father and usually amounted to this, that one must not expect too much of So-and-so and So-and-so or trust them too completely, as far as one's most intimate affairs were concerned, because the people in question were *goyim*. The corresponding remark was that such and such people could be approached, such and such a physician called in, such and such a merchant trusted because they were *yehudim*. And it was distinctly clear to Arthur, from the beginning of his reasoning life on, that these judgments involved no absolute moral values. They meant that the decentest Gentile was apt to relax his ethical vigilance in dealing with a Jew and that the shabbiest Jew was apt to rise above his lower level when dealing with a fellow Jew. At times Arthur was to repudiate these judgments heartily and even fiercely later on. He was sure that he had made no mistake as to their character and quality from the beginning. He continued to search his memory for other and outward visible methods by which the consciousness of being Jews had crept into his sister's mind and into his own. He found none. Something he had to leave, at his most hostile and rebellious moments, to ancestral memories, to instinct, to the voice of the blood.

Neither was he ever able to estimate how far these early impressions might have been obliterated by life in a various and forgetful world. For on this one point the world was strict and mindful from the moment of one's first contact with it. On his second day in school, from the low form ahead of him, there was suddenly turned a small round screwed-up gargoyle face, red, freckled, pug-nosed, blue-eyed, with crimson tongue stuck far out and hot against the lovely, fair chin. Then the tongue slid, like a quick little round animal, back into its hole and he heard a hot whisper, "Sheenie!" . . . Was it against the voice of the blood? For Arthur was sure that he had never heard that word before. But neither had he any doubt as to its meaning and character. So sure was he, and so hurt, and so rebellious against

79

that hurt which had leaped suddenly at him in a world hitherto all security and tenderness and peace, that, instead of relating the incident at home, he told his mother that there was a nice little boy in his class whose name was Georgie Fleming. . . .

One doesn't reflect at six. But to Arthur the immense value of this incident and this childish reaction lay precisely in their unreflectiveness. The instinctive gesture involved was evidently on the part of the child that he then was a protective and self-protective one. He didn't want this thing with its enormous implications to be true; he wanted to shut it out. He didn't want his mother to heal his hurt, because he didn't want her or, in truth, himself, to know of it. And the reason for this was obviously that it wasn't a quick and fleeting and superficial hurt of childhood. It evidently struck a chord of inconceivably mighty and dolorous ancestral resonances. . . . Or was it too curious to consider so? The fact, the fact remained . . . as well as the indelible memory of that little red gargoyle face and of that hot whispered word. . . .

Yes, that memory clung in spite of the fact that Arthur and George got to know each other very well. And that was possible (as Arthur the child perceived and Arthur the youth recalled) because, while he remembered, little George forgot. George was quite innocent and had a lovable nature. His liking for Arthur was genuine, though casual. He did not speak to him for a whole day at school. Then he would come and kiss him in a strange, bird-like little way. Arthur felt a dim childish passion for George's blithe fairness, and the terror he had at the core of him lest the gargoyle face and the hot whisper return heightened his half-tormented devotion. He asked his mother whether he might ask George Fleming to come over and play with Hazel and himself, and she gave her consent very readily. (Over-readily, Arthur thought in the later years, a little proudly at the first moment that her children were to have a nice little Christian playmate. George's father was an alderman of the city of New York. And Arthur was retrospectively ashamed of that touch of pride in his mother and did not know how many of his own impulses in the matter of human contacts were governed by a similar emotional coloring, a similar hopeless hopefulness of escape from a fate—strange contradiction if one weighs the words!—a fate that seemed, at certain periods, a mere accident, like the blue mark of a bruise received in the dark and unwilling to fade.)

Little George Fleming came to the Levy house and at first seemed shy. He stood there twisting one foot about the other and frankly sniffing the air with uplifted and suspicious little nose. He looked into corners as though he expected something to jump at him. He was extraordinarily polite, as though he had to propitiate somebody by being on his best behavior. He finally followed to the playroom and forgot himself and began to toss the toys about and to romp in a way that made Arthur nervous. Hazel didn't like it, either. But she pretended, and Arthur knew that she pretended, that she did. Georgie wanted to wrestle. He cried: "Gee! but you got a lota books!" He slid along the floor, pretending to make a base. Arthur and Hazel proposed playing their favorite game, in which Hazel was a patient and Arthur a doctor and Hazel's dolls other patients. Georgie looked at them wide-eyed. "Gee! what a funny game!" he cried. Then he said: "Gee! Arthur, I bet I could knock you outa that window!" and came very near succeeding. Then, red and panting a little from the struggle, he announced: "Gee! I guess pretty soon I'm goin' to be as strong as my Dad! I bet I will." At this point—Arthur and Hazel were beginning to feel sleepy and a little forlorn here in their own home—Mrs. Levy came in and asked the children to come downstairs for some chocolate and cake. George twisted one foot about the other again. Mrs. Levy put her white hand with the amethyst ring on the little boy's shoulder, an action which, for a moment, infuriated Arthur. . . . They all went downstairs and sat about the table in the dining-room. At first Georgie seemed afraid to touch anything. At last he took a crumb of cake—it was a home-made

Marzipantorte—and then a mouthful, and then drank his chocolate, too. Enjoyment and elation sparkled in his beautiful blue eyes. A piece of cake in his hand, his mouth almost too full for utterance, he leaned back and kicked his boots against the table and said with deep conviction: "My Dad says theyah lotsa nice Jewish people. He did so!"

8

HOW swiftly Arthur's childhood fled! His age of innocence, at least, was brief. He never remembered later what hints dropped by a teacher in the schoolroom warmed the eternal zeal of learning in his soul. He knew that by the time he was ten years old he drew books out of the Ninety-sixth Street branch of the Public Library that made the librarians look at each other with smiles, half wondering, half approving. He understood very little of what he read in these books of history and science and poetry. But from a popular text-book on astronomy he got a vision of infinite distances and dazzling globes, and from repeated dips into Gibbon a vision of marble and purple and glittering cohorts under African suns and small dark masses of riders riding as through a dream over plain and mountain toward something that filled them with a nostalgia that he shared even unto childish tears. And the name of that something was Rome. . . .

He loved the books he did not understand. But sometimes he took out volumes wholly unreadable. That was on account of the youngest of the librarians, Miss Fergusson. She reminded him, he never knew why, of lime-drops. She was dark. But she was so sweet, and so severe in her sweetness. And her eyes had a golden-greenish glimmer. And she admired the small boy because he was so grave and able to read such hard books. She would go with him to the shelves and sometimes put a hand on his shoulder, or even, ever so lightly, on the back of his neck, and then thrills would run down his spine and, though he was selecting a book of history or science, he would daydream that Miss Fergusson was being assailed or affronted and that he was her knight whose strong sword smote and whose unfailing lance drove true in her defense. . . .

The library was his place of romance. Alas! like many places of romance, it was hard to get to. There were no lions in the path. But at a certain corner, which was hard to avoid, there lay in wait, quite regularly after school hours, a group of boys who lived on Amsterdam Avenue. He didn't suppose that he ever saw the boys as they really were. To him they seemed raw-boned, stinking, and malignant devils. They never actually did him any harm. Once only they tripped him up and scattered his armful of books in the street. And even then he heard one of them say: "Aw, bo, why don't you pick a feller your own size." But they would say: "Pipe the sheenie! Gee! lookat dem books, will yer?" And they would make dashes at him and scare him and tell him to run. There was no room for resistance. Each of the boys was bigger than he and there were always at least five. . . . And so Arthur would be utterly blinded by his passionate, impotent rage and hatred. He had, unluckily for himself, a keen insight into the contrasts of the situation. His mind was filled with poetry and learning; he had the appreciation of the lovely Miss Fergusson. And these beasts, these animals, had the power to frighten and humiliate and chase him. . . . He wept on his way home after such an incident. But the tears were followed by accesses of arrogance. He would be a great man, a learned man. People would come to speak with him and take council with him from far countries, from Rome itself, and these hoodlums would be sweepers of barrooms and diggers of mud. . . .

There was, of course, a way of avoiding that corner. But it was long and inconvenient and Arthur disdained to take that additional trouble on account of those despicable brutes. But one autumn he felt tired and dreamy and walked the longer way around through Amsterdam Avenue with his books. He loitered peacefully, and somehow—he did not remember later on the precise beginning—scraped acquaintance with a small, fat Jewish shopkeeper named Lesser who used to sit on a camp stool in the afternoon sun just outside of his squeezed-in little notion shop. Lesser had a round black beard and a round fat face and very thick lenses in front of kind, intelligent brown eyes. He shook his head in a knowing, pleasant fashion and said: "Like a little *melamed*." Arthur asked at home what a *melamed* was. Both his father and his mother laughed a little at the question, and he thought that his father's laugh was somehow touched by pain. "A teacher," he was told. . . .

He couldn't remember later on what he and Mr. Lesser found to discuss. But he could see himself standing in front of that shop on Amsterdam Avenue in the blue and bronze afternoon sunshine and could see the admiration in Mr. Lesser's eyes at his own maturity and knowledge and Mr. Lesser's wagging head and thick, short, demonstrative forefinger. And one scene, at which there was a third person, imprinted itself indelibly upon his memory. The third person was a tall, broad, bony man in a long black coat and a large hard derby who had small watery blue eyes and a great red beard that spread out and covered nearly his whole chest. The man was a city missionary, whether self-appointed or not Arthur never knew, and he went about in a sweet, persistent, feeble way, trying to argue Jewish shop-keepers into an acceptance of Jesus Christ as their personal Saviour. It amused Lesser to talk to the man, and he had told him that it needed only a Jewish child to confute him. So Arthur found the red-bearded missionary at Mr. Lesser's shop one afternoon and argued with him. He knew retrospectively that he didn't argue as a Jew at all, but as a rationalist who had dipped into Gibbon. But he remembered how proud Mr. Lesser had been of him and how horrified the missionary had been to hear such arguments on the lips of a boy.

As winter came this strange friendship faded. The afternoons were dark, the rough boys were gone, and Mr. Lesser retired into his narrow shop. Moreover, Arthur and Hazel were sent to dancing-school and Arthur fell in love with Eleanor Kahn. . . . He was thirteen; he was to enter high school the following year. . . . Twice a week he saw Eleanor at dancing-school and occasionally met her in the street. . . . Once or twice she stopped before dancing-school for him and Hazel. . . . She was small for her age, but her lovely form was already rounded; she had eyes like midnight pools in a forest brimming with stars and a dimple in each creamy cheek. Arthur avoided dancing with her. The ecstasy would have been more than he could bear. But the torment of seeing her dance with other boys was dreadful, too. Only this torment was passive. And when occasionally he danced with Eleanor, she had a way of softly snuggling close to him that made him so dizzy that he was mortally afraid that he would fall and shamefully drag her down with him on the polished floor. . . . No, the rapture of his love was most bearable when the boys and girls had returned from dancing-school to their homes and he let Hazel stroll ahead with some girl friends and himself walked through the streets in which the lights were slowly blooming through a dim winter afterglow. . . . During that hour he meditated over the perfections of his beloved and imagined almost unimaginable scenes in which, by some exquisite and unheard-of miracle, it would be seemly for him to kiss her, kiss her long and deep, and see her yielding almost unto swooning under his kiss. . . . Tears would come into his eyes. . . . He would stand in the dark beside the stoop of his father's house and linger before going in, stand in the snow and snatch another minute of undisturbed dreaming before facing the brightness and talk of the house and dinner and lessons and bed . . . linger there in the star-dark and snow as though a watcher within him bade him drink in every moment of the irrecoverable magic of adolescent love. . . .

9

HE did four years' high school work in three. Harsh years full of pains and headaches and nightmares, waking and sleeping. Strange, irritable years. His mind hungered for knowledge, but his nerves were unreliable and his body was feverish. He watched George Fleming, still in his class, though barely scraping through from semester to semester, lithe, happy, care-free, active in gymnasium practice, member of a neighborhood baseball team, untroubled, though a bit given to smutty remarks that apparently meant nothing to him but that filled Arthur with a sudden gloom cracked as by zigzag lightning. . . . Arthur tried to force himself not to cut gym. But the naked brown boards and the smell of naked bodies and the excremental jokes of boys standing under shower-baths made him literally ill. . . . Then came a fatal hour. . . . Boys stood there stripped, waiting for shower-baths to be free. . . . A large fellow whom Arthur scarcely knew pointed a thick thumb over his white pimply shoulder and guffawed aloud. Wasn't it funny how those sheenies. . . . He insisted, without giving a reason, that he would leave school unless he were permanently excused from gymnasium. His father said: "All the other boys go. Why not you?" Arthur, red and furious, shrugged his shoulders. "I'm not going, papa." His mother had a troubled look. "I'll send him to Watermann, Jake." Dr. Watermann gave Arthur a long lecture on the benefits of physical exercise precisely at his age and in his general nervous condition. Arthur kept his eyes on the floor. "I'll leave school rather." He was sullen. Dr. Watermann then gave him another little lecture on sex hygiene and prescribed a nerve tonic and wrote out the excuse from gymnasium for him. . . . Arthur plunged into his studies and into discussions on socialism with Joe Goldmann and joined the debating society. Henry Loring, the big senior of the fatal scene in gym., was the president of the society. Arthur attacked him with a dull, nagging ferocity. He found Joe's golden-brown, twinkling, scared, astute eyes on him. "Why do you bother with that stupid *goy?*" Arthur attacked Loring no more. He didn't argue with Joe, either. But he felt profoundly that Joe's solution of the problem was no solution at all. And what, in fact, was the problem precisely? Or was there simply none? Did Joe never suffer? Was he himself an exception and a freak? . . . He became morbidly aware of the sound of his name. When a teacher or a fellow pupil said, "Levy," something within him contracted, grew tense, was ready for resistance. . . . He discovered now that his father talked with a foreign accent, as did his grandmother Oberwarter and Joe's father. . . . In a way he had always known it, of course. Now his awareness became acute and painful. He sat at table at home and bit his lip in terrible irritation as his father talked, and was ashamed of that irritation and utterly powerless to restrain it. . . . Then came a day and a moment memorable to Arthur forever afterward. His father was discussing certain of his employees and wondering whether he had not better investigate definite conditions that seemed to be telling unfavorably on his business. Arthur understood little of the matter. His father's accent and uncertain grammar had put his nerves on edge. He must, he said to himself later, have been reading some silly pseudo-idealistic stuff. He cried out: "Oh, always this Jewish suspiciousness!" His father laid down his napkin and turned to him, and the eyes that Arthur saw were reproachful and hurt and sorrowful: "Vell, ve are Jews, you know, my son. . . ." Arthur rushed out of the dining-room and locked himself into the little playroom that had been given him as a study, and threw himself on the floor and lay there in desperate, grim, blind misery for hours. . . .

BOOK IV

1

THE Pharisees have a bad name in history. According to the Christian legend and tradition they were leathery formalists and hypocrites who voluntarily shut out a dawning light and delivered unto death a king of glory. They were, as a matter of plain fact, patriots and hundred-per-centers of a nation in bondage, comparable to Italians under Austrian rule or to the South Tyrolese under the Fascist boot. They were not insurgents because they had no hope, nor did the concept of the right of a nation to be free yet exist in the world. But the passion and the impulse existed. Their aim was to preserve Jewish nationality, to substitute religious and cultural solidarity for political independence, to preserve Israel from being nibbled away and destroyed as a people by emigration, by intermixing, by Romanization, by Hellenization. How right they were as practical politicians! There came, as every school child knows, the year 70 when the Temple was destroyed; there came the even more terrible repressive laws and massacres under Hadrian. . . . Today oppressed national minorities survive by the preservation of their language, literature, and schools. The Jews survived by the preservation of their national religion and its sternly intricate law. . . . The Pharisees were preservers. . . . They didn't object in the least to the ethical or purely spiritual aspects of the teachings of Jesus, who said nothing of this kind which had not previously been said by sage and prophet and duly embodied as law or Jewish aspiration in some sacred book or accepted tradition. What they objected to even in the first faint stirrings of what was later to become Christianity was its universalism, its anti-nationalism, its supposedly disintegrating power. . . . And this fear of theirs is, in view of the fierce and militant nationalism of every so-called Christian nation throughout the Christian centuries, one of the great ironic jokes of history. . . . As for the Crucifixion, we may, accepting the legend, leave the responsibility for that safely to Pontius Pilate, who was a Roman patriot, imperialist, and hundred-per-center, intent, like the general who ordered the firing on the defenseless at Amritsar, on preserving the empire that he served. Crucifixion was a habit with him just as the use of machine-guns is with modern imperialist administrators. He had a hundred Samaritans crucified because they made a religious pilgrimage to a certain hill which may still be seen as the dwelling-place of their feeble remnant near the Arab city of Jellin. A crucifixion more or less meant very little to him. Only the cross is more picturesque than the machine-gun and was used in a still mythopœic age.

Do I, then, pacifist, internationalist, uncompromising libertarian, suddenly defend—riding my own Jewish hobby —the Pharisees' hostility to Jesus and to the doctrine of universal brotherhood, and range myself against him who is the eternal symbol, sacred even to those who question his very historicity, of the lonely might of the spirit opposing itself to the confederated forces of the world? No. My place is forever with the outcast, the resister, the despised and rejected, the Jeremiah or the Jesus of his hour in history. . . . Only, only as I warned you in the beginning, at the end of every train of human thought there is a flat contradiction. In an ambitious empire flinging its millions into war, the defeatist is the righteous man and the absolute pacifist the only friend of mankind left. But in an oppressed and decimated and tormented national minority—the Jews under Rome, the South Tyrolese under Fascism—is there not something, is there not much to be said for those who are anxious that no jot or tittle of the cultural or religious heritage that makes that minority a people be abandoned or be lost? For a people has the will to survive just as a man has. And that will to mere existence, mere continuity, forever to be distinguished from a will to power or dominance, is a sacred thing. . . . Power, in brief, is the distinguishing mark. The same action which is right for a weak or defeated people is wrong for a mighty and victorious one. The mystery at the core of conduct is this mystery of defeat being victory and victory being defeat, of defenselessness being the strongest shield and mighty battalions but so many broken reeds. . . . Ghandi will be a voice in the councils of men and a living vision at their hearthstones, when all the powers and principalities that opposed him are but dust blown by the random winds. . . . But observe, please, that Ghandi, in this respect more like the Pharisees, wants home-weaving and home-speech and home-thought and the preservation of his people's peculiar spiritual and even material life. . . . Before there can be an internation there must be nations. And we must not let the strong nations stamp out the weak before the days of the internation. For the sake of the strong we must preserve the weak; only through the fellowship of the weak can the strong be saved from the sins of their strength. . . .

Under the aspect of a little time it is easy and seems profitable to merge oneself with the strong and victorious, especially since the strong and victorious, opposed to their own breaking and salvation, demand it. . . . Many Jews tried to forget themselves and their people in the Hellenizing time and in the Germanizing time and again today in the Americanizing time. . . . But most Jews do not succeed. . . . Something draws them back to stand by weakness against strength and by defeat against victory. . . . And even when they cannot recover the weakness and defeat of their own folk to stand by, they will range themselves, like Marx or Lasalle or a hundred others, by the side of the weak and the oppressed and the defeated of the whole earth. . . . That is probably why the Jews have persisted. . . . Those who "don't know when they're beaten," the blindly and brutishly belligerent, will one day be dashed into dust. . . . Those who accept defeat with all its spiritual implications have a chance of lasting forever. . . .

2

ARTHUR entered Columbia University in the fall of 1910. The new buildings on Morningside Heights had been opened for a few years only and still gleamed and glittered in their efficient newness and splendor. The stuffiness and the cares and torments of the crowded high school seemed to drop away literally like an old and irksome garment. One walked on this quadrangle with the erectness of a man. One sat in a capacious chair in that great domed library and had attendants bring one books and partook somehow of the dignity of learning. One had a considerable freedom in the choice of courses and studies; one could leave the campus between classes and loiter by the brilliant gold-flecked river under the yellowing poplars. The world became spacious and soothing. All of one's hurt susceptibilities seemed suddenly to be healed and one's secret torments to be quieted. . . . Arthur could walk to college from home and even go home for luncheon, though after a while he preferred to take his luncheon at the commons in University Hall. Yet this closeness and compactness of his life, blended with the spaciousness of the university itself, gave him an indefinable feeling of comfort, of being at home in the world. Or, rather, of that bit of the city that lies between Ninetieth Street and the northern edge of the campus and between West End Avenue and the North River, Arthur made himself a world that was, spiritually, an extension of his home and to which he transferred that feeling of snugness and security which had led him all through his childhood to dream the waking dream of his father's house as a fortress. . . . He didn't at this time analyze his feeling which was so strong that it irritated him slightly to go downtown at all, even on an agreeable errand or to a concert or a theatrical performance. He let his instincts guide him rather unreflectively at this period. Later on he was to examine their guidance in this matter with amazement and a kind of awe. . . .

So delightful was the new life that Arthur would have been satisfied for a period without any companionship at all. But the older of his two cousins, Eugene Adams, was already a sophomore and Harry Adams and Joe Goldmann entered Columbia with him. Eugene, thickly immersed in college life and college politics, made sudden dash-like appearances, taking pride in what he considered a duty, to guide and advise the younger boys. He had already at this time a hard, cool elegance of appearance. His father had long given up traveling for his woolen house and had become a real-estate broker. He had built one of the enormous seven-story red-and-white elevator apartment houses on lower Morningside Avenue which were then considered the last word in New York and now occupied one of the first-floor apartments. He wanted one of the boys to study medicine, because the location was excellent for a doctor. In the meantime he refused to lease an apartment in his house to any physician. It was on this subject that Eugene unbosomed himself to his cousin Arthur and to Joe Goldmann in one of those dashes of his in their direction. His voice was suave and yet had a suppressed harshness in it. He carefully nursed a glossy small moustache. His physiognomy was unmistakably Jewish when observed by a Jew. But his straight nose, slender figure, carefully impassive bearing, coupled with the *s* at the end of his name, might easily have deceived a Gentile. He strolled with Joe and Arthur on the campus.

"Between you and me, I haven't the least intention of studying medicine. Harry can, if he likes. Or you, Arthur. Father could let you have the office. But people seem to think that there are no professions but law or medicine." He lowered his voice. "The town is already overcrowded with Jewish doctors and lawyers. And now the East-Siders are beginning to go to college, too. We have to break into other professions."

Arthur listened solemnly and with admiration. He always received the words of men exactly as they were meant to be received. He never assumed guile, impure motives, imperfect sincerity. He could understand a lie concerning a matter of fact; a distortion or veiling or prudential repression of opinion or conviction lay wholly beyond his grasp. He wondered at Joe's knowing grin.

"Well, what are you going to do?" Joe asked. "Be an engineer?"

Eugene smiled a little abrupt, superior smile. "Not on your life! I like literature and Odell tells me I have an instinct for it. I'm going to be a publisher."

Suddenly Arthur visualized Professor Odell with his

95

prematurely white hair and his impassive Roman face. He was more impressed by his cousin than ever.

"That's a fine idea, 'Gene," he said.

Eugene nodded at the tribute due him and darted off.

Joe laughed a little, though his golden-brown eyes remained sad. He had frightened eyes. To strangers they seemed furtive. But Arthur knew better and always felt a little sorry for Joe, though his friend was so much more mature and sagacious than himself.

"A fine scheme," Joe said with that indefinable Jewish undertone—the speech rhythm of Yiddish—which no member of the Goldmann family ever lost. "Sure he likes literature. So do I. So do you. But why does he want to be a publisher? Because it will give him a position. The authors will be Christians, most of them. They'll be under obligations to him; they'll come to his house. Whom does a Jewish doctor treat? Jews. Who are the clients of a Jewish lawyer? Mostly Jews. But a publisher—that's something else. He's a snob."

Something in Arthur rebelled hotly against Joe's interpretation of Eugene's motives. Not because 'Gene was his cousin. He felt quite as close to Joe. He reflected on Joe's words. Yes, he thought he had hit on the fallacy hidden in them.

"Listen, Joe," he said. "That's ridiculous. If every time a Jew goes into a profession that brings him in touch with Christians, you're going to make *that* the motive, why, why"—he got tangled—"well, isn't that what they call in logic a reduction to the absurd? Does a Jew have to do nothing but what will keep him among Jews? I don't see that at all. What's Jewishness, anyhow?"

Joe's sad eyes were fixed on the ground.

"Jewishness is a curse. But the way to do is not to try to run away from it, but to destroy it."

Arthur's heart suddenly beat in a strange excitement.

"How?"

"By working for the proletarian revolution and the real brotherhood of man. Karl Marx explained. . . ."

96

Arthur stopped listening. His excitement had faded. He had no mind for economic facts. They bored him. How excited in a taut, still way Joe could get. And always his eyes retained that scared look. Arthur suddenly wanted to leave Joe and go home. These long, eager arguments made him feel tired and forlorn. . . .

3

THERE was Hollsworthy Brown. Joe, affectionately mimicking his own father, said: "Hollsworthy—a name, too!" The young man in question was blond and blue-eyed. But his blond hair had a peculiar reddish tinge and a tendency to curl tightly; behind the apparently clear and innocent gaze of his eyes there lay something immemorial. His nose was straight, though a bit long. He went in for sports and college spirit and associated exclusively with Christians.

"What have you against Brown?" Arthur asked Joe.

"He's the son of H., that is to say Hyman, B-r-a-u-n, millionaire cloak and suit manufacturer, one of the rottenest sweat-shop bosses in New York. And here he tries to act the *goy*."

Arthur was weary of Joe's injection of this question into every discussion and every human judgment.

"Well, why shouldn't he, if he likes?" Irritably he flung the words at Joe. "We don't believe in the Jewish religion, do we? Gosh! we don't even know anything about it. In America all men are equal, anyhow—"

Joe sniggered. "Then why pass off as something that you're not to prove it? Why change your name? Would you change yours?"

Arthur flushed. "No."

"Why not?"

Dully Arthur answered: "I don't know."

Joe sniggered again. "I don't give a damn about my name. But I wouldn't play into the hands of anti-Semitism, which is a purely capitalistic phenomenon, by changing it. But Brown's getting along. He's made a fraternity. I bet he won't take any of his frat brothers home. There's a *mezuzah* over H. Braun's door."

"What's that?" Arthur asked.

Joe writhed a little with interior chuckles. "Never mind. Why spoil your innocence?"

At luncheon Arthur suddenly asked his mother what a *mezuzah* was. His mother thought a little. "I believe, sonny, that it was a sort of a little metal case with the Ten Commandments in it that old-fashioned people used to nail to their doors and kiss when they entered the house."

Unmotivatedly Hazel, tall for her age, slender, pretty as a dark sword-blade with deep glints of light in it, burst into choked sobs and rushed from the dining-room. Arthur looked at his mother.

"What's the matter with the kid, Mamma?"

Mrs. Levy frowned. "She was crazy to enter the Bretherton School. Very fashionable, you know. I've kept it all quiet because I had an unhappy feeling about it. But the child persisted. So I applied for her and they turned her down."

The sunny room seemed for a moment to Arthur to become small and remote, to float away from him and to leave him, as it were, in an outer darkness beyond life. He shivered with sudden loneliness and fear. Then by some half-conscious process he forced himself back into an imperfect contact with reality and saw his mother's white hand with its amethyst ring toying with a silver spoon.

"What reason did they give?" he heard himself ask, "and how about the Freefield girls?"

His mother's eyes were not lifted from the silver spoon with which she continued to toy.

"Miss Bretherton was lovely to me personally. She said she hadn't herself the slightest prejudice. She said she was proud of the Freefield girls and of Marjorie Brown and of other Jewish girls in her school."

"Yes, well?"

"But she said that if she took more Jewish girls than, say, one tenth of the whole number of her pupils, the school would get the reputation of being filled with Jews and the Christian girls would stay away. She said that very thing had happened to a fashionable boys' school in town and that owner had lost all he had in the world. She didn't dare take any more Jewish girls till some had graduated."

A sadness overcame Arthur. From these early years on he was always accessible to what seemed the voice of reason. He was about to answer when Hazel rushed back into the room. Her thin, graceful body was trembling. Sobs still broke her voice.

"Please, Mamma, *please* don't discuss it! It's just because our name is Levy."

Mrs. Levy looked up. "How about Helen Cone?"

Hazel gave an hysterical, ironic little laugh. "Yes, C-o-n-e!"

"But, look here, kid," Arthur said, "if conditions are as Miss Bretherton describes them, what can she do?"

Hazel lifted her dainty chin and her eyes blazed. "I just hate you sometimes, Arthur. You always take everybody's part against us."

Mrs. Levy got up. "To tell you the truth, sonny, I don't believe that Miss Bretherton, either. The Freefields and the Browns and the Cones are much richer than we are and I guess there are other reasons."

"For instance?" Arthur asked.

But Mrs. Levy shook her head in a melancholy way and would say no more.

At dinner that night, as though impelled to probe her own wound, Hazel said suddenly: "Well, what am I to do now?"

Quickly Arthur looked up at his father, who usually limited his words to the discussion of purely practical things or to the playful expression of his intense love for his family. Jacob Levy was quite gray now. But his face had few lines and his head and hands had acquired an aspect of solidity and force. His blondish gray moustache drooped to his chin. His eyes were calm. He lifted his eyebrows now and compressed his lips and wagged his head in a manner that

99

Arthur perceived, with a faint hostility, to be inimitably Jewish, from side to side. He bent over and took a spoonful of soup with a little sucking noise that increased the tension of Arthur's nerves. Then he spoke.

"Vy do you hef to go to a fashionable school like det? A goot school? Yess. I don't obchect to expense, neider. Vat for foolishness! A frient of mine, Warschauer—you know, Trudchen—Warschauer ent Sonss—he tolt me vile ve vere lunchink today—det he sent his daughters to a vonderful school vere dere vere only Chewish girls ent det dey got a magnificent education dere. Vy can't Hazel go dere?"

Hazel's face flamed. "I won't, I won't, I won't!"

Jacob Levy's calm eyes hardened a little. "Vy? Are you ashamed of being Chewish?"

A liberating cry came from the adolescent girl's heart and nerves. "Yes, I am! I'm just as good as anybody else and I'm just like everybody else—like all the Christian girls I know—and I can't go to a nice school and people grin in shops when I give my name—"

"Oh no, they don't, kid," Arthur interrupted her.

Hazel looked at him squarely. "Well, they'd like to often and often and you can just feel it!"

Mrs. Levy shook her head. "That's hysterical, Hazel."

Jacob Levy brought the palm of his hand sharply down on the table. He looked from Hazel to Arthur.

"You don't know how goot you heve it in America. You are citizens de same as everybody; dere iss no militery service. Now in de olt country in my time—"

Arthur was suddenly infuriated. "That has nothing to do with it, Papa. Conditions have changed in Europe, too. Nobody pretends today that they have any right to discriminate. Well, they may go on doing it in Europe. They can't do it in America!"

Jacob Levy smiled. "No? Dey cen't? Vell, dey vill. But vy shoult ve care? Vy go vere you're not vanted? My business frients are all Chews. Maybe a few Chermans. Ent det's goot. I understent dem; dey understent me. Ve like de same t'ings. Ve look at t'ings in de same vay. Stay wit your own kint!"

Arthur's anger faded. He felt tired. He knew of no reply to make to his father and yet he felt himself to be profoundly at variance with his father's words. Were Jews his own kind? Were they his sister's? And even if, by and large, that were true, should one be restrained from making other and wider choices or, if one pleased, altogether different choices because one had—whatever the inner being might be like—a certain kind of physiognomy and a certain kind of name? No, it didn't seem to him that his father's words so much as touched Hazel's problem or his own.

He asked tentatively, almost dreamily: "Who *are* our own kind?"

But pursuing an argument from ramification to ramification was not his father's strong point. All that he heard from under the drooping grayish-blond moustache was a word that sounded like "*Meshugas!*"

4

AT the beginning of his sophomore year Arthur made the acquaintance of Charles Dawson, his neighbor in psychology class. Dawson was long, large, whitish blond, and lethargic; his pale eyes had a quietly intent, cool, abstract look. His voice was level and his words a little morose. He was two years older than Arthur. The acquaintance had begun by Dawson's saying to Arthur in class that there was no use taking notes, since the instructor didn't know what the hell he was talking about because the poor fool was ten years behind the times. They left Philosophy Hall together on that day and, lighting their cigarettes, strolled across the quadrangle. "Here you have," Dawson explained, "one of the results of academic inbreeding. That young man took his degree at Columbia. Doesn't think much of Münsterberg because he's at Harvard; never heard of Freud. Probably can't even read German decently."

Something clicked in Arthur's mind. He determined at

once to study German. He knew that both his father and his mother knew the language, that it was, in fact, his father's native tongue. Was it his father's English accent that had led him to elect Latin and French in high school? Was it some dim sense that German belonged to that past of his family from which, consciously or not, he wanted to flee that had kept him from studying it? Hazel, too, it suddenly occurred to him, had shied quite irrationally at the notion of studying German and had taken up both French and Spanish. From Dawson he got an entirely new attitude. Dawson's father, he learned, was a Brooklyn neurologist who had studied for several years at Leipzig and Berlin; there, studying music at the Leipzig conservatory, Dr. Dawson had met the American girl whom he later married. Charles's American parents had brought him up to speak and read German from babyhood. "Why," Dawson said to Arthur, "it's damn' foolishness to think you can go in for philosophy or for any science without German. French is an all-right accomplishment for the young female of the species. If you want to go in for psychology or biology seriously, you'd better hustle."

Psychology class was thrice a week, from twelve to one. Charles and Arthur got into the habit of going to luncheon together. "Ready to feed?" Charles had asked the first time. Arthur had nodded. "Awful grub," Charles had added. They had gone into the clattering huge dining-room. Two other students drifted to their table, a tall red-headed chap and a small brownish gentle fellow. Dawson had introduced, curtly: "Levy, that's Heller—the red-top, I mean—and that's Goddard. We used to call him Mouse at prep school." This kind of cool unemotional "kidding" was new to Arthur. Equally new to him was the way in which these young men could slide conversationally from philosophy to football and from literature to campus gossip without any shift or change of emphasis. It was new to him and strangely refreshing. It made Joe Goldmann's conversation seem naggy and over-eager and disingenuous. And this impression became temporarily fixed one day when Joe, having watched these luncheons in the commons with his half-frightened, half-ironic eyes, spoke to Arthur with his mumuring, internal snicker: "Joining the Hollsworthy Brown class, eh?"

Arthur choked a little. He felt that he was profoundly within his rights, radiantly decent. Yet he did not know how to combat Joe's insinuation. That made him angry.

"I don't know but what I understand Brown."

He didn't mean it; Joe, as his next words showed, saw that he didn't.

"Well, at least they have to accept you for what you really are. You're not blond and your name isn't A. Hollsworthy Brown."

Arthur felt profoundly relieved. "Exactly. Then why do you blame me? They're awfully nice fellows. Damned intelligent, too. Join us some day and you'll see."

Joe shook his head. He grinned, but with those still sorrowful eyes of his. "That's nothing for me. They'd soon see the hoof and smell the sulphur."

Arthur shrugged his shoulders. "Dawson is as radical-minded as you are. He was just saying the other day what a farce and disgrace it was in this age of science to spend twenty-five millions of dollars on an Episcopal cathedral."

"Very good for him," Joe said. "But I bet he believes in the institution of private property to the jumping-off place."

"Well, I think I do, too," Arthur answered. He wasn't, in fact, interested in that sort of thing at all. But he felt that he wanted to establish a reasonable solidarity with his new friends. They didn't talk economics at all and treated politics as rather a joke. Heller was a great reader and a good student, but he was from "up state" and interested in farming; Goddard, to whom Arthur's heart warmed more and more, was curiously divided between poetry and pure mathematics; Dawson was driving straight for the equipment wherewith to follow his father's profession. Their talk was rarely intellectual. Arthur had gathered these various facts about their mental lives almost by the way. He didn't even know that Goddard wrote verse until he had heard Dawson kidding him one day about a sonnet of his in the *Literary Monthly*. It was not until Goddard had rushed off to his next class that Dawson had remarked casually: "Damned good stuff, too. I believe the Mouse has the makings of a poet in him."

Unconsciously Arthur took color from his new friends. Their ways answered a deep-seated reticence in his own nature. It was difficult for him later on to estimate the measure of their influence. But he took on something of their coolness of demeanor, their casualness of speech, their habit of being unemphatic or jocular about the things that were closest to their hearts. He had, in relation to these friendships, his dimly troubled moments. The three young men all spontaneously took to calling him Arthur and he, after some hesitation, began to call them by their Christian names. They spent many hours together on the campus, at luncheon, on walks; occasionally they met downtown and saw a play together. Once in a while they would foregather in Goddard's room opposite the garden at the foot of University Hall. Heller and Dawson lived in Brooklyn, where Dawson was at home and Heller had a married sister. What Arthur remarked hesitatingly and unwillingly was that he was never invited to Brooklyn; next he discovered, from something that Goddard had said, that Goddard had been. To this he replied, in the inward debate which followed, that he had not invited his friends to his home, either. He had thought of doing so and had not done so. And he asked himself precisely why. An obscure tangle of feeling was all the answer that came to him from within. Perhaps it reduced itself to this: that he was unwilling to expose his home and his family to the possible criticism of hostile eyes. But why hostile? Were not these fellows his friends? Yes, he believed they were sincerely his friends; he believed profoundly that they would defend him from the criticism of others of their own kind warmly on the ground of their personal knowledge and appreciation of him; yet he knew with a fatality of knowledge deep within him that their eyes, so far as his home and his family were concerned, would be cool and slightly hostile and detachedly smiling eyes. And this conviction which, in these early years, he could not yet account for or ground saddened him. He had hours in which he was ready to dismiss the whole thing as a delusion. He was ready to put it to the test of experience. Only he never did. . . .

5

JOE Goldmann, whom he saw more rarely now, came to him and said: "Listen. Victor is here. He can't get along at Harvard. Wasn't kicked out, exactly. But, well, I'm not saying. You've got to help me with him." Joe grinned in his melancholy way. "Your father promised my father" —deliberately he mimicked the Yiddish sing-song—"et cetera."

Arthur winced. "Thought he was doing such brilliant work in architecture?"

Joe's head gave a Jewish wag. "Perfectly wonderful. The kid has genius. But he's so damned disputatious."

"He always was a little," Arthur said, mildly.

"Well, it isn't a little now. He's a terror."

Arthur half-heartedly promised to do what he could. Next day Victor Goldmann, whom he hadn't seen for nearly two years, burst in upon him. The room blazed and boomed. Victor's brilliant black eyes seemed to be about to start out of his olive face. Not only the nose, the whole head was aquiline. It flew at you. The heavy, well-modeled lips were like poppies. The voice heard only itself. It roared at the top of a world fallen silent. Victor stood and talked. And his talk was immensely intelligent. Only it was tireless, tense with a half-mad intensity. Occasionally he feigned to listen for a moment. Actually the words of others obviously came to him faintly across great distances. He went on with his tremendous monologue. He talked about the academic feebleness of his teachers, about his own notion of an American city that should soar strangely up hills into a burning sky. He took out a pencil and with ten lines on the blotter of Arthur's desk evoked a shadow of his vision. And talked and talked. And his talk was I . . . I . . . I.

Arthur shuddered at the thought of introducing Victor to Dawson or Heller or, above all, the gentle Goddard. They would be appalled and flee. He himself, curiously enough, understood Victor. He loathed him. But he understood him. Had he not, at least once or twice, with a touch of immediate terror and shame, found himself talking and not listening, over-eager for the moment to project his inner world, to emphasize the ego which created that world? Was not some, at least, of the well-bred quietude which commended him to his Gentile friends the result of a definite discipline and the shadow of a hidden shame?

Victor stayed to dinner. He talked. Hazel almost became hysterical and had to leave the table. Mrs. Levy was the only one to whom he listened for an occasional moment. Arthur's father watched him with eyes half amused and half regretful. After dinner Victor proposed to Arthur that they go downtown. It was just as well, Arthur thought, to get him into the open.

Victor talked in the streets; he shouted above the roar of the subway.

"Where are we going?" Arthur asked, feebly.

Victor did not answer. He led.

Somewhere on Sixth Avenue, in the thirties, they entered a huge dance-hall. Around the polished quadrangle of wood, at small, beer-splashed tables, sat men and women or women alone. The women were hard-faced or melancholy and gaudily dressed. They were all heavily rouged and their eyes seemed to be of glass. A spear seemed to go through Arthur's vitals. He touched Victor's arm. Was this to be the end of his long, severe inner discipline? He had bitten his lips and not asked Joe, who was knowing on all subjects, where such places were. He had tried hard not to overhear student gossip. A fear had held him back, a fear that with him, if once a dike were broken, an irresistible sea would roll overwhelmingly in. . . . He was swept on now. He was lost. Soon he and Victor were sitting at a small table with two women—a large and gorgeous creature in a glittering crimson cape, and a small, pale blonde from whose low-cut frock emerged forms still adolescent. . . . They drank beer, which quickly went to Arthur's head and released him from his habitual inhibitions. He was glad that Victor talked interminably in a hoarse whisper now to the large gorgeous woman. . . . It left the girl to him. . . . In the midst of the haze and the excitement, tense and vibrant as a string upon an instrument, he remembered with infinite gratitude that he had more money in his pocket than usual. . . . Fate, evidently. . . . He drank another glass of beer. . . . Beautifully and slightly the world swayed. . . . A golden haze covered it. . . . He touched the arm of the girl beside him. . . . They got up and danced to the clashing, pulsing music. . . . After that Victor and the large woman were lost and Arthur followed the blonde, slim girl. . . .

6

ARTHUR woke up into a clearer world, a world more precisely defined and more intelligible. He cut a ten-o'clock class with an unwonted lightness of conscience, made the eleven-o'clock, and joined his friends at the accustomed luncheon table. The steamy air in the great, rude dining-room had a crystalline quality to his eyes; the faces of his companions seemed clear and burnished; the sunlight flooded in in golden streams and pools. . . . Arthur talked and jested vivaciously beyond his wont. Dawson, in one of his slightly morose moods, commented: "Aren't you chipper today?" At once the light was sucked out of the air and the faces that Arthur saw became dull and hostile. He felt his friend's casual words to be a rebuke. From this feeling proceeded at once a consciousness of the fragility which, without admitting it to himself, he found these friendships to possess. It did not lighten his depression that Heller and Goddard chatted as usual and even asked Dawson why he was so glum. . . . He suddenly felt alone and disgusted at the thought of last night. He felt unfriended and somehow ridiculous. But a degree of the mental clarity with which he had started the day remained with him on the solitary walk that he took on Riverside Drive after luncheon, and he told himself that it was absurd, that it was monstrous, to be so dependent in mood and spirits on the light words of an equal. . . .

It was a clear day of winter waning into afternoon. The stripped branches of the trees were black against a hard blue sky. The sun was already dipping toward the Palisades. Here and there arose a curling line of dark brown smoke from the red smokestack of a tug. In the distance appeared the dead whiteness of the Soldiers' and Sailors' Monument. Arthur gazed down at the river, which was free of ice, and watched the slow, great rolling onward of its voluminous flood. He experienced a deep dispiritedness. He was poised here, not placed. This sky, this river, these trees, this monument in the distance, this boom and roar of life that came to him faintly from far away—all these things that he loved and with which he lived were in some fashion that he did not understand divided from his soul. He remembered an autumn trip that he had taken up the river to Dobbs Ferry. He had stood in deep, still, blazing woods—bronze, golden, crimson—and watched the river like a blue pool beneath him and heard the soft crackle and whisper of the rain of the falling leaves. He had, that day, been able to wrap the beauty of the scene about him like a garment sheltering him from the cold shorelessness of space and time. Now that autumn scene came back to him in an aspect almost as forlorn as this scene of the city winter presented to his eyes. He told himself that he was a sentimentalist, that neither Charles Dawson, on the one hand, nor Joe Goldmann, on the other, probably yielded to such vague and poignant and irrational moods and ended by attributing the whole thing to his adventure of last night.

These reflections were very well, but they helped little. He found himself after a little and actually to his own surprise, walking in the direction of the Goldmann house. He knew that Mrs. Goldmann always served coffee and cake in the afternoon in the old German-Jewish fashion; he had not been near the house for months. He could hear the voice of Mrs. Goldmann while she was calling on his mother one day: "Arthur don't come around any more, Gertrude. Except that I hear about him from Joe now and then, I wouldn't know he was in town." Why was he going to the Goldmanns'? Not, Heaven knew, on account of the girls. They were thin and dark and hardly past their adolescence, and not the type that his inevitable dreams presented to him at all. His childish fondness for Esther was a thing forgotten. He told himself that he was going because he wanted to talk to Joe. He tried to persuade himself that he had an errand; that he would tell Joe that Victor was too much for him. He knew beneath these operations of the superficial mind that he was going out of a deep and pain-stricken instinct. To find what? Ground under his feet. At the Goldmanns? Absurd. Yet he shivered with a strange expectancy of peace and good as he entered the house.

In the dining-room, just ready to sit down to their coffee, he found Mrs. Goldmann and Joe and Esther. Neither Sally nor Victor. He was glad of that. Mrs. Goldmann stretched out a welcoming hand. "*Nu*, that's nice that you remember us again. Sit down, sit down!" She turned to Esther. "Never mind ringing for Mary. I see enough of that *shikse* already. Get a cup and saucer and plate for Arthur."

Esther got up, tossing her chestnut head a little.

Joe grinned. "You and Victor saw life, eh?"

Arthur didn't know what to answer.

"Victor is a strong character," Joe continued. "He takes the lead, doesn't he?"

"The trouble we have with that boy!" Mrs. Goldmann exclaimed. "And he's a gifted boy, too. But nobody knows what to do with him."

Joe was serious, which was rare. "Never mind, little Mamma," he said. "Victor will come out very much on top. He's unbalanced. But he has ability enough for anything."

"But look how he acts!"

109

Esther looked sullen. "I just hate him!"

Joe laughed. He turned to Arthur. "You go in for psychology. You ought to be able to understand all this."

Arthur thought he did, but he shook his head. He wanted to hear what Joe had to say in the presence of his mother and sister.

"Why, don't you see"—Joe's sad and yet smiling brown eyes were raised—"Jews have the reputation of being loud and vulgar. Generally speaking, it's not true, not at least in the sense in which it's usually taken. Now when a Jew is loud—I wouldn't admit, in fact, that Victor is vulgar—but when a Jew is loud, all the other Jews tremble in their boots for fear that he'll be taken as a confirmation of the general prejudice. And especially those members of his own family who want to be regarded as refined in a *goyish* way. And that's why Esther—"

He was cut short by a momentary hubbub. Both Esther and Mrs. Goldmann protested. In a moment Esther's voice emerged.

"I don't agree with you at all. Refinement is the same for Jews and Christians. Victor is simply impossible. I just won't associate with him."

Mrs. Goldmann's face was stern. "Such nonsense! What I don't like is that Victor won't take any advice and you never can tell what he's going to do. I don't think he knows himself. And of course he ought to be more respectful to his father and me. But the other thing! I agree with Papa. When did the *goyim* ever like us and since when do we have to act the way *they* like? We pay our way, don't we? We don't drink or gamble or commit crimes. If all people behaved the way the Jews do, the country would need no jails and no penitentiaries and no prohibiton agitation." She folded her hands in a satisfied manner. "Have another piece of coffee-cake, Arthur. I notice you haven't said anything. What do you think?"

"I don't know what to think," Arthur said, slowly. "Honestly, I don't. Only—" he hesitated.

"Come on, Arthur," Joe said. "I want to hear what you really have the impulse to say. Don't rationalize it first."

"Well, I wonder if we ought to relate everything, every single problem of life, to our Jewishness? Isn't that the mistake? Aren't we much more *like* other people than we are *unlike* them?"

This was evidently too subtle for Mrs. Goldmann. "Don't you want to be a Jew?" she asked, a little blankly.

"That's not the question, little Mamma," Joe cut in. "There's a good deal to be said for your point of view, Arthur. You know, of course, what my opinion is: we ought to work for the international communist-anarchist state in which, by the nature of things, there will arise a standard of values, and of manners, too, by which the present racial and social prejudices will inevitably disappear. In the meantime, however—and this touches all our points —we ought to be far less Jewish than we are or far more so. Our present condition is either one of nervous snobbishness, like Esther's, or one of protective self-satisfaction on a low plane, like little Mamma's."

Mrs. Goldmann sighed and got up.

"I'll let you boys go on talking. Jews always have been Jews and they always will be. I can tell you that."

She went out, and Esther followed her with a last, indignant glance at her brother. Joe looked at Arthur.

"Well?"

"Can we be less Jewish than we are?" Arthur asked. "Isn't it only that we're not honest about it? What is specifically Jewish about you and me?"

Joe's eyes were suddenly veiled by their deepest melancholy.

"I don't know. I'll be damned if I know. And yet. . . . Oh, for Christ's sake let's talk about something else. I'm sick of it."

"So am I," Arthur agreed, heartily.

He left the house. It was dark now. The same homeless feeling that had subtly driven him thither was still upon him. It seemed to him suddenly as though all he had heard was irrelevant and yet somehow wounding hubbub, and as though all he wanted now was to be alone in his room, in the dark, and in that darkness to sit and lay the palms of his hands upon silent, unresisting, familiar objects.

7

HE heard voices from the front room as he let himself into the dim hall. The voices belonged to his family and quivered with suppressed hysteria—his mother's voice, his sister's, his father's. Father must have just come home and been caught up into a discussion that was already raging. He hoped they had not heard him. His foot was already carefully on the stairs when a door opened and he saw his father's head. So sudden must have been the assault that his father had forgotten to take off his large derby hat, which now sat, pushed agitatedly back, ill-balanced on the grayish blond hair. His father's profile under the hat, pale and unwontedly sorrowful, looked immemorially Jewish in the sharp light that now streamed into the hall. Arthur realized instantly that this perception of his was itself an un-Jewish one and showed how he had grown up to view his very parents slightly from without and how, indeed, in all thoughts and discussions, he treated the Jews as objects of his discourse. Fancy an Irish-American boy saying to himself: How Irish my father looks! . . . Hesitatingly he responded to a gesture of his father's and entered the room. . . .

The quarrel or discussion, whatever it was, had evidently begun above stairs. For Hazel crouched gracefully and yet in the very abandon of grief on an armchair, clad in a blue velvet dressing-gown, and her rich lovely hair wrapped her girlish torso above it. Her head was bent down until her face nearly touched the tips of her blue mules. Her legs were folded under her. She had apparently wept until she was weary of weeping and only now and then uttered a desperate little moan. Arthur's father, having summoned him in, took up an interrupted striding up and down the room. His hands were behind him, the left clasping the wrist of the right, and that right hand, loose beyond the spanned wrist, rose and fell with a fluttering motion. Arthur's mother sat erect in a straight-backed chair, clasping her hands upon her lap. She was the calmest of the three. It was she who lifted her face a little higher as Arthur entered and greeted him with a hovering little shadow of a smile; it was she who offered her son an explanation.

"Listen, sonny," she said. "I blamed Hazel for always forgetting everything this afternoon, and she told me that she wouldn't be in this horrid house much longer, anyhow. I asked her why and she said because she was engaged to Henry Fleming and they were going to get married as soon as possible. You know Henry, George's older brother, He's just been promoted to assistant treasurer of the Hibernian Trust Company. What do you say to that?"

Arthur sat down. His father stopped before him in his walk and bent down to him a gray face drawn in indescribable misery.

"Yes, my son, vat do you say to det?"

Arthur put his hands to his head. "I don't know," he said, slowly. "I really don't, Papa."

His father's face bent closer, almost touching his; his father's soul tugged at his own. "Do you like it, my son?"

Relief and liberation came to Arthur. He could answer that question honestly. "No, I don't."

Hazel jumped up. She drew her blue dressing-gown about her with a slim, pale hand. Her head was uplifted; her dark eyes glowed. "Why don't you like it, Arthur? Aren't all your best friends Gentiles? Do you *like Jews?* Honestly, now, do you? Do you feel very Jewish inside of you? I've never liked a Jewish boy in my life. Papa always says that America is a free country where anybody can do as he likes. And now look at him!" She gave an hysterical, ironical laugh. Then her eyes grew lustrous with tears. "Aren't you going to help me, Arthur? Are you such a hypocrite?"

Her father, who had resumed his walk, stopped and regarded her sternly yet appeasedly. "Arthur is no hypocrite. He is a goot Chewish son!"

Something began to burn in Arthur's chest. This wouldn't do; this wouldn't do at all. To assent to this would be hypocritical. He strained his mind to the utmost. Yes, yes, he thought he had found the truth to which he must bear witness. He addressed himself with eyes and tone to his mother. She seemed the sanest person here. What he had to say would hurt himself terribly. But it was his duty now; there was no room for hesitation.

"I think I ought to say, Mamma, that I don't feel very Jewish, either. And I admit that I know some very nice Gentile fellows at college and that we're very good friends. That is, we seem to be very good friends. But when it comes to the real test, to their asking me to their houses and introducing me to their families or showing any real desire to know my family—why, well, I don't know. Joe Goldmann was teasing me one day. He called these friendships 'street friendships.' "

He stopped; he felt that he had said too much, that by putting this matter into words he had coarsened it, falsified it, betrayed himself and his friends. His mother nodded affirmatively. "It's an old story," she said. He couldn't retract now. Besides, what in truth was there to retract? He hastened on, knowing that what he had to say next expressed a deep, almost a passionate, feeling.

"Anyhow," he said, "if that weren't the case and if Dawson or Goddard had fallen in love with Hazel, I'd be on her side with all my heart."

"Snob!" Hazel almost hissed at him.

"I don't know," he said, slowly. "It's all right in America to become American and to marry an American gentleman. But an Irish Catholic, the son of an immigrant, of a ward heeler—I don't see the sense of that. I can't help feeling that way, kid."

Mrs. Levy drew herself up. "I've told Hazel that exactly. No, not exactly. But I have known a few marriages between really nice German people and Jews that turned out very successfully. At least they seemed to. But this is too different. And, anyhow, Hazel says that she'll have to become a Catholic."

"Why shouldn't I?" Hazel flared up. "Henry loves me and I love him, and I feel the need of a religion. I do so. Well, no one ever taught me any here. You ought to know Father Finnegan, how wise and cultured and lovely he is!"

Arthur's father stopped in his walk with a jerk. His face was scarlet; he trembled from head to foot. His eyes were preternaturally large. He shook his fists above his head.

"Has it come to det? Den it stops now, today, in dis hour. Ent if not, den you cen leave dis house and your fadder and your mudder det bore you forever. Uch! I'd radder see you under de eart'!"

Silence, ominous, dreadful, deep. Arthur pulled himself together. He went over to his mother.

"Do you feel that way, too, Mamma?"

She lifted eyes to her son, that were full of tears now, too.

"No, sonny. And Papa doesn't mean all he says, either. If we can't prevent it, we'll be good to the poor child, of course. But I agree with him that I'd rather see her dead."

Arthur drew himself up. He looked from his mother to his father and back again. "Good heavens!" he said. "I don't like it, either. But that's going too far. Would you feel the same way, father, if it were one of my friends?"

His father's eyes still blazed. "Exectly de same vay, my son, exectly!"

Again Arthur's glance sought first his mother and then his father. Something weird and eternal and remote seemed now to have come over them both.

"Why?" he asked, and then, raising his voice almost to a cry: "Why?"

His words fell into the silence like stones. There was no echo and no answer.

8

GLOOM that brightened but slowly lay over the house. The tragedy itself—why tragedy? why? kept humming in Arthur's head—was easily averted. After a sleepless night

Mr. Levy had gone to the ever more magnificent and magisterial J. Mortimer Freefield. The latter had reassured him at once. Mr. Alderman Fleming had many Jews in his district; he wanted their votes; it would be most inconvenient for him to have known that a member of his family was a party to the proselytizing of a Jewish minor against the wishes of the aforesaid minor's parents. Mr. Freefield would communicate with the alderman through a common political friend; he would send him the assurance that no one concerned was opposed on principle to such a marriage, and that, if Miss Hazel Levy desired to take up her religious instruction again at the age of twenty-one, nearly three years from now, no obstacle would be placed in her path. Everything, Mr. Freefield assured Mr. Levy, would be seemly and dignified. His last words were: "They wouldn't like it any more than you and your wife."

To which Mr. Levy had replied: "I'm glet dey heve so much sense."

Poor Hazel! Arthur was immensely sorry for her. She had to send back the few gifts that Henry Fleming had given her. She was caught weeping over a withered flower. Simple-hearted but touching. Arthur offered to take her out. Dumbly she shook her head. Her father gave her a new piano, a baby grand. She didn't open it. Gradually Arthur perceived that she was having an exquisitely luxurious time, being quiet, reading poetry, dramatizing herself as one in that long line of women, fair and intrepid, who had suffered greatly for the sake of love. . . .

He plunged into his studies and plunged, though only from time to time and restrainedly enough, into a friendship with a certain Miss Lucy Treat, whom he had met one night loitering provocatively in the neighborhood of a student tavern. Miss Treat was chubby and young and blonde and vague-eyed, with very full lips, almost negroid in formation. A gay drummer had brought her to New York from her home town upstate, and then left her with a few hundred dollars in New York. She liked Arthur and signed her notes making appointments: "Your loving friend, Miss Treat."

He grew much cooler and more self-collected and found that his chief interests lay more and more in psychology and biology. He took up anthropology at Dawson's suggestion, under the guidance of a famous professor of Jewish origin, and was icily sustained by the study of the variableness of racial types. It was perfectly clear that no existent racial strains were pure. All men, if you wanted to put it so, were inextricably mixed mongrels. Hence the application of the term mongrel in a deprecatory sense to man was a flagrant absurdity and all pride in purity of blood an equally flagrant one. There were, it appeared, certain large divisions into type. But these types were anything but coincident with the conventional races or nations. Jews, for instance, except where older or later Slavic or Germanic admixture was obvious, were, generally speaking, a Mediterranean type, like Spaniards, Italians, Portuguese. From the start they were, like every so-called race, a mixture: Israelitish, Canaanite, probably Phœnician. They had in all likelihood absorbed the non-Semitic Philistines in the course of time. All this before the Babylonian captivity. They must have mixed with Semitic Babylonians and Aryan Persians and Romans and Greeks and mixed breeds of a hundred kinds in the cauldron of Alexandria. And since, in their long wanderings over the face of the earth, blood must have trickled into theirs from ten-thousand streams. . . . Generally ·Mediterranean then. A very loose concept—even that. Very loose. . . . Science was salvation. So much was clear. To know the causes of things, to know things undeludedly and in their true character. Thus one transcended the follies and prejudices and superstitions of the herd. . . . Arthur grew literally more erect, more certain of himself, even more sparing, but more precise of speech. He saw more than ever in classroom, laboratory, at luncheon, and on walks, Charles Dawson. He saw Joe Goldmann as often as ever. He sedulously avoided any discussion of the Jewish problem. In the cold light of science there was no problem. To admit it on the usual plane was in itself unscientific. Herd prejudices of this as of every other kind would have to be lived down in the slow, laborious, but certain process of enlightenment through knowledge. One didn't, after all, burn witches any more, nor wage wars over the question whether Christ were coeternal with the Godhead or not. One didn't. . . . He worked with a cold ferocity; he had to put on glasses and was not displeased at the necessity. His junior and senior years were given over almost wholly to scientific pursuits. It was perfectly understood that he was going to study medicine and specialize in diseases of the nervous system. His father and mother were enormously proud of him. The house revolved about him. His father regarded him with an adoring look. "More ent more you look like my brudder Teodore. Ent fadder alvays saitt det *he* favored exectly our grentmudder Braine who vent to die in Cherusalem. . . ."

BOOK V

1

UNDER your eye the grasshopper turns from leaf green to earth gray. At foaling-time the spidery-legged young camels between the palms of Jericho and the hard glitter of the Dead Sea need but lean against the tan hills to be invisible to any hostile eye. The lion is gone from the Libyan desert, and except for the sandstorms in which men flutter like flags the caravans fare on in peace. But the eye recognizes the tawny color of the sand-dunes from the morose beasts seen in the circuses and zoos of childhood. . . . Natural history has much to say of the phenomena of protective mimicry in respect of color; the dead statement of the printed page leaps into life in the desert lands where the eye always reaches to the horizon and where there is no escape or shelter. There man builds brief huts of desert-colored mud and thatches them with desert-colored straw; there the camel and the lion are indistinguishable from the sands. . . .

Not to be seen; not to be spied out; to merge with nature or a group of creatures like oneself—to disappear as an individual, to be conventional—how profoundly does this universal urge point to the terror that is at the core of all mortal life! . . . The modern woman, following a fashion comfortless and unbecoming to herself, puts on her lion's skin in the desert of her social life. She thinks she is doing so to be agreeably visible; her real motive is to be invisible, to be inconspicuous, to avoid singularity and merge herself with a plural. . . . War is at the heart of nature, war at the heart of society. To be conspicuous is to be a mark for arrows; the moral quality of the conspicuousness matters little. . . . The arrows fly. . . .

In primitive and literal-minded societies there was no pretense concerning this fact. By a law violently enforced the Jew was ordered to wear a yellow cap or gabardine in Europe and a black turban in Africa. He was to be made conspicuous and therefore shelterless. But there was another motive. Malignity was tempered by a genuine fear, at least in Christian countries. If the Jew could assume no protective coloring nor merge with the surrounding social scene, one could be materially on one's guard against his supposed astuteness and spiritually against his inexorable refusal of the Christian faith. . . . Had conspicuousness not involved physical danger to the point of the constant imminence of martyrdom, it is doubtful whether the Jews would have objected to special garb or ensign. Many thousands in Poland still cling to *caftan* and even *streimlach;* I have seen beautiful old men in North Africa wear with a quiet dignity the black turban that was once a mark of degradation and of danger. For it never until at most a century ago, occurred to Jews that they were not different from other men—different in religion, in character, in historic experience. And the millennial persecution had bred in them a high degree of stoicism in the endurance of that public proof of a private fact which no one sought to deny. . . .

The badges of shame were removed; the ghettos were opened; the Jews flooded into the desert of the world. The long strain was broken, at least in the west of Europe and America, and the old stoicism faded through disuse. The nations said: Be like us and we shall be brothers and at peace! Then began the Jewish practice of protective mimicry; and it was practised then and has been practised since in a myriad of cases, not consciously to escape difference, conspicuousness, and hence danger, but in a spirit of devotion, love, loyalty, fellowship. The Jews have wanted profoundly to be Americans, Englishmen, Germans, even Poles. . . . Can such things be done? Can they be done without inflicting an inner hurt, a wound to the moral fiber? Can people, in masses, as groups, repudiate their ancestry and its experiences? Can the Jewish imagination live permanently and gladly as though it had shared in historic experiences which, in fact, Jews watched from without as outcasts and martyrs? . . . Also, this mimicry through devotion and the desire for union has not always remained pure, but has merged, has had to merge, in nearly every case—at moments, hours, days—into mimicry for protection. For do what he would, the Jew remained conspicuous if only subtly, because he remained different if only indefinably and hence, despite gentler manners and sincere protestations, a target and a creature without shelter. And from this blending of mimicry through devotion with mimicry for protection has arisen that intricate, sick, subtly tormented, gifted but rarely creative, sensitive, arrogant, cringing, sentimental, hard, patriotic, revolutionary modern Jewish soul, of which all qualities can be predicated and all heroisms and all treacheries and all confusions, and whose very being is a cruelty and a cross. . . . For Jewishness is like that Hound of Heaven described by the poet. It tracks you through the universe; it lies in ambush from without and from within. you think you have achieved a perfection of protective mimicry and on the lips of your dearest friend you see the unformed syllable, Jew. . . . You have stylized your very face and reconstructed the impulse of your gestures, and in the street boys are jeering at a peddler with a push-cart—a dirty old man in a long coat and flat feet and a long beard and a thousand wrinkles and you—you pass by and feign not to notice. . . . And what is there left then but that complete coarsening of the inner man which is more terrible than degradation and despair? . . . Or war comes. And you hasten to the so-called defense of your country with an ardor in which you cannot, once more, distinguish the element of volitional from that of protective mimicry. For you can't help seeing the other side and the same roguery and barbarism on all sides, and you do, from the depth of your soul, despise physical courage of the aggressive type. Your horror at the unreason and dirt and unveracity of it all is unmeasured. But you have practised protective mimicry so long, you have so carefully built up the seeming of a Gentile character, that you cannot with decency slough off that character at such a moment. You are no coward. You are a Jew. But having lived as though you were not a Jew, you have given your fellow citizens the right to call you a coward and a traitor if, at the moment of danger, you were to try to run to the cover of your Jewishness. . . . And you go forth and suffer and perhaps die the death of a mimic, of a clown. . . .

2

ARTHUR Levy graduated from Columbia College in 1914. He had become increasingly absorbed in his studies. He no longer felt that his father's house was a refuge and a fortress; he had long ceased to feel the comfort and home-likeness of the nearness of the college to the house or his old intimate delight in the portion of the city that circumscribed both. He dwelt increasingly in a cold world of reason, of scientific hypothesis and proof, upon a height from which, though it meant a degree of isolation, one could at least look down with equanimity upon the irrational welter of human experience. From that welter he sought deliberately to withdraw himself more and more. Joe Goldmann had begged him to come downtown with him and to associate himself with certain half-revolutionary or humanitarian or artistic movements. He had refused curtly. He had said that knowledge must come before action and that he, for his part, felt sure he didn't know enough. Joe had grinned and snorted and observed Arthur's small, unobtrusive moustache and his quietly elegant clothes and said: "The perfect American scientist. All you've got to do now is to cultivate a refined bedside manner. But maybe you won't have to make it too damned refined. Your patients will be Yids, anyhow." Arthur had let the sting as well as his sense of Joe's self-torment in inflicting it drop without reverberation into a dark hidden chamber of his mind. He had answered, coolly: "I'm not going into general practice." He felt the loss of Joe, whom he saw more rarely again. Occasionally a melancholy would overcome him, a curious nostalgia, young as he was, for still earlier years. He conquered these attacks by intensive work, especially in the laboratory. Even during the summer following his graduation and preceding his entry into medical school he took a few heavy courses that involved seven to nine periods of laboratory work a week.

It was a wretched summer, anyhow. His mother and Hazel had gone to Far Rockaway, to a large hotel near

Hamel station. His father and himself joined them there over the week-end. The guests at the hotel were all Jews, and it seemed to Arthur that there was something graceless and uncurbed about the demeanor of these people. They were letting themselves go. And in this abandon, which never, he admitted most willingly, involved anything that one could really criticize (there was no insobriety or gambling or sexual unseemliness), there was a note of excess that annoyed him more than restraint punctuated by outbursts of rowdiness would have done. His father and his mother both seemed to enjoy the psychical atmosphere immensely. He saw from Hazel's somber expression that she felt less at home. But when she tried to make common cause with him she was so violent that he evaded a discussion and told her not to be a little snob. He knew enough to perceive that these people lived all the year according to dictates of behavior imposed upon them by a Gentile environment. Now they could be themselves. They were, by reaction, more themselves than their normal selves would have demanded. He saw that. Only, since he thought that he felt neither their winter restraint nor their summer relief, he could not help being irritated and annoyed. To these discomforts was added, toward the end of summer, the outbreak of the European war. Arthur felt it to be something irrational—a hiatus in the march of civilization. He wanted to think about it as little as possible. He was a little angry at the Germans, who seemed to be doing about two-thirds of all creative scientific work—at least in his line—for turning aside to so barbarous an adventure. Toward England he found himself, to his own mild wonder, in a state of slight hostility, and promptly dismissed as morbid the thought that it was because the American of more or less pure English descent was most coolly contemptuous of Jews. In regard to France he had no emotional reaction at all. But he tried to avoid all discussion of the war since, one day, he had found himself furiously telling Dawson that the Russian alliance invalidated all the moral claims of the Western powers, and had been shocked to the marrow by the careless arrogance of Dawson's reply: "Of course now you're arguing as a Jew, not as an American." His cheeks still burned at the memory. It was the first time that the word Jew had been uttered between them in the three years of their companionship. It came quietly now; it came courteously. But Arthur could not deceive himself as to the complete and intricate and precise implications of Dawson's words and glance. And the implications were these: We—not you and ourselves—but we as subject and you as object —*we* have permitted you Jews to come to America; we have permitted you, Arthur Levy, to attend Columbia University, we have even treated you—as far as can be expected —as a friend and an equal. We have done so on the assumption that you had identified yourself wholly with us, shared our thoughts, hopes, ideals. And now, at the first great test, you intrude into a vital question a set of hopes and fears and loves and hates with which we can necessarily have nothing to do. We have been deceived in you. We must watch you from now on. . . .

He had had an almost sleepless night. He was an American certainly. There was no doubt about that. But he was, as everyone had a right to be, an American, so to speak, on his own, not by virtue of a rubber stamp of approval granted him by someone named Dawson. He wasn't here on sufferance, to be approved or disapproved by a self-constituted authority. His father was an immigrant. Well, so was Dawson's grandfather. He was supposed to be a little ashamed of Insterburg; Dawson was always quietly mentioning his people in Inverness. The devil of it was that he was, if he looked sincerely into himself, a little ashamed of Insterburg and had tried to dismiss his family's past—the shadowy little that he knew—from his mind. He thought suddenly of poor little Hazel. She fairly squirmed when their father talked of his father or of the old country. He had, in fact, done so very little in recent years. Arthur sat up in bed and held his aching head. Something was wrong here—something. The Dawsons didn't only want the Levys to be loyal to their common present; the Dawsons wanted the Levys to give up imaginatively the Levy past and adopt the Dawson past. And the Levys did it; they did it. Look at Hazel. Look at himself. Look at the Freefields. Wouldn't they all hock their shirts for ancestors and cousins in Inverness? Christ, what a mess! But even this very fury of self-destructive loyalty to others—even this wasn't enough. You mustn't have any sentiment which wouldn't be yours if your people had in fact come from Inverness. As if there weren't other plague spots on Tsarist Russia outside of her treatment of the Jews. But wasn't her treatment of the Jews a matter that not only a Jew, but any decent and humane man, might well take into account? Jews . . . Jews . . . Jews. . . . He loathed the very word. And as for the Jews from Russia. . . . He had seen them on Grand Street and Norfolk Street and once in a Yiddish theater to which Joe had dragged him. Utter aliens to himself, these people—repulsive, in fact: dirty, sunk in superstition, loud, Oriental without being picturesque, jabbering in a mongrel jargon, smelling of garlic. . . . Why he should take their part, why he, in considering Russia, should instinctively think of Kichinev—he didn't know . . . he simply didn't know. But the point was, as far as Dawson was concerned, that he had a right to do so—a literally perfect right. He'd like to see Dawson—supposing an almost impossible eventuality: Scotland conquered by a foreign power, kirks closed, civilians shot—he'd like to see Dawson not triumphantly and passionately making that an American issue. And everybody would applaud Dawson. So that—argue it any way you liked—Dawson really fundamentally meant something quite brutal and coarse that he simply had had no occasion to express before. He meant this: there *are* fixed qualitative racial differences. Jews are, of their very nature, inferior beings to Englishmen or Scotchmen. They are tolerated among us so long and in so far as they become, to the full measure of their ability, like Englishmen and Scotchmen. . . . Of course Dawson, who was already a rather brilliant scientist, would not admit that he meant quite this. . . . But he wouldn't admit it only because he knew that it was sci-

entifically bosh. . . . He would act on this hypothesis because it was in his blood. . . . Well, Arthur supposed wearily, in *his* blood was the protest about Kichinev. . . . And
the prime difference, then, between himself and Dawson
was that Dawson consented to his instincts and was quietly
proud of them, and that he was filled with dislike and shame
of his own. . . . And maybe—he was beginning to get
drowsy at this point—it all amounted to this, that Dawson
was the upper dog. . . . What a vulgar phrase—the upper
dog. . . . His poor father seemed to have a hankering for
these crass phrases. . . . He slept. . . .

After the declarations of war he passed only a single
week-end with his family at Far Rockaway. His father
hummed:

> *"Ich hat einen Kameraden,*
> *Einen bessern gibt es nicht. . . ."*

At table he said, testily: "Dis talk about atrocities already
makes me sick. I know de Cherman people. Dey have deir
faults. But dey are de most civilized people in Europe. Vy, I
got nephews who may be in Belchum now. Atrocities.
Ridic'lous."

"Why, Papa," Hazel exclaimed, "how can you say that?
Why, it's been proved in hundreds of cases. Don't you read
the papers?"

Mr. Levy smiled grimly. "Yes, I read de papers. Vall
Street is betting on de Allies. Det's shameful enough ven
you consider Russia. I also read de *Staats-Zeitung* and de
Herold."

"Why, I wouldn't touch those disloyal sheets!" Hazel
exclaimed.

Mr. Levy shrugged his shoulders. "Don't talk foolishness.
Vy disloyal? Dis iss a nootral country."

"Mr. Freefield says we're sure to get into the war before
it's over," Hazel announced.

"Gott forbit!" said Mr. Levy. "It voult be a disgrace."
Suddenly he looked at his son. "I hope de papers don't take
you in, Arthur?"

"No," Arthur said, hesitatingly, "not entirely. But look here, Papa, I feel about the alliance with Russia very much as you do. On the other hand, I think I've heard you say many a time that Germany was a very anti-Semitic country as compared with America, too."

His father's face darkened. "All *goyim* are *reshoim*, my son. Dey all dislike us. But you don't hear about pogroms in Chermany, and t'ings have chanched since my time. Dis Dr. Dernburg, for instance, he's a Staatsminister ent a Chew ent he isn't *geshmatt*."

"Ge—what, Papa?"

"Baptized."

"Well," said Mrs. Levy, "no one did ever have to get baptized in America to get along."

To which, to his mother's and to his own surprise, Arthur answered: "There are baptisms and baptisms, Mamma. Perhaps the requirement of lying about religion and being sprinkled with a little water isn't the worst kind."

"Arthur," she cried in sudden alarm, "you're not thinking of—"

"Of course not. I was thinking of an argument I had the other day. That's all."

But these discussions and similar ones that he overheard made him nervous and unhappy. He excused himself during the brief remainder of the summer and spent endless hours in absorbed laboratory work.

3

ALWAYS, later on, Arthur was glad that the war years coincided with his medical studies. He had increasingly the power of becoming absorbed in the pure life of the mind. He hardly observed the loneliness of his own existence; he was able, if necessary, to reply conventionally enough to whatever was said to him of the catastrophe. He tried unobtrusively to avoid the newspapers and only now and then awoke with a sudden sensation of pure horror to the facts of the maniacal world. He had gradually the sense that the horror was creeping nearer and nearer to himself and, in self-protection, shut it out the more sedulously.

His barometer of the war was his father. By 1916 Jacob Levy's mild neutrality with its pro-German dash had faded. He looked worn and harassed. He never spoke of the war at home. He sat after dinner with sorrowful eyes, reading the evening paper. His German papers had disappeared. He had either canceled or not renewed his subscription and Arthur was certain that he had done so out of fear. Arthur was also certain that his father had not changed his sentiments at all; they were deep-rooted. But over Jacob Levy hung a shadow. He was sucked into this shadow more and more. Arthur refrained from asking by what subtle insults and threatening slights and direct pressure from larger houses, from political bosses, from banks, his father and his father's friends and associates were gradually "brought into line." He could follow the process almost from day to day. His father grew grayer; the moustaches drooped in a careless and defeated way; the pride that the man had taken in building up his life and his prosperity was gone. He muttered over his soup: "Damned *goyim.*" He complained for the first time in the family's memory that the expenses of the household were too high. Arthur immediately offered to get along with a smaller allowance. His father's eyes filled with tears. His nerves were evidently thread-thin. "You are a goot Chewish son? Never mint! Ve vill pull t'rough."

Arthur telephoned to Joe Goldmann and made a luncheon appointment. Joe was more melancholy of eye and more cynical of speech than ever. He listened to Arthur's questions. "Father's in the same fix, only he argues at home and shouts. Poor old boys! Did they think that the political capitalistic state had changed its heart or its manners? Because, mind you, it isn't that they care so much about Germany. What makes them sore is that, having escaped one kind of conscription in Europe, they now find another kind of conscription here. Conscription first of sentiments, habits, loyalties. The conscription of life and money will come soon enough. By the way, your eyes will let you out, eh?"

Arthur started. "If it actually comes to this country's going to war, I don't think I'll be able to take that attitude—"

"Noble to the last!" Joe jeered. "So you want to get maimed or killed over this little argument about export markets for overpopulated areas? This is the first of a series of explosions due to the mechanization of industry and the prolongation of human life. In about a hundred years, unless this civilization is destroyed, we'll go in for birth-control and the pooling and coöperative distribution of the earth's food-supply. Meantime, ain't I glad that I've got a nice little purely functional cardiac disturbance *plus* the flat feet of my venerated ancestors? Oh, boy!"

Arthur suddenly felt glances upon them from the neighboring tables. He looked around. Joe laughed softly.

"Don't mind. These are my fellow students of the law. I've got a devil of a reputation among them already. They look at me sternly. Sternly. Disapprovingly. They babble stuff about the war that bears the same relation to the facts as witch-burning bears to the scientific observation and treatment of hysteria. It's funny, very funny."

Arthur leaned his head upon his hand. "I haven't a doubt that you're right, Joe. But does it make you feel as depressed and forlorn as it does me?"

Joe's brown eyes were suddenly tragic. "It does. God! wouldn't it be delicious to be able to be a damned fool and a patriot and to take orders and plunge? You lose yourself then. And the self is a ticklish customer. You can lose it in religion, too. Or in booze. But the so-called corrosive Jewish mind can't go in much for patriotism or religion or booze. So there you are. Your emotions are unsatisfied and your mind won't be fooled. It's a mess, I admit."

"You think it's specifically the Jewish mind?"

"Looks like it. If the same proportion of Gentiles kept their heads as Jews do, could the present situation have come about?"

"But do so many Jews keep their heads?"

Joe nodded. "Even the Hollsworthy Browns are not fundamentally fooled. D'you know why he rushed to France and volunteered? Because he's got such a Jewish inferiority complex that he feels he can't go on living unless he's really accepted as a simon-pure American. So he's gone a-soldiering. If he's killed—not that he likes the thought—his troubles will be over. He'll be a dead Jew. If he lives—aha, can you see any social or professional discrimination used against Lieutenant or maybe Captain Hollsworthy Brown who volunteered in the great cause of civilization and democracy? Well, at least he thinks he can't. I can."

Arthur laughed wryly. "You lay the black on thick."

"I do not. Wait and see."

Arthur saw. The fury began to blow like a hot wind. America entered the war. Conscription of life and property followed. Jacob Levy, suspected of German sympathies, was brutally informed what amount of bonds he had to buy. He came home one day beside himself. "I made my money in dis country. De government vants to borrow. Goot! Goot! But dis vort 'liberty' is to me already an emetic—an emetic!" . . . He stopped protesting; he grew gray and cracked like an ancient wall when conscription came. He muttered the polite name, selective draft, and then cried: "My son, my son!" Luckily, they were alone together. Arthur reassured him. In the first place, he wore glasses number so-and-so; in the second place, he had already been unofficially informed that he could make himself useful as assistant to the psychological expert—an extremely ignorant young man named Smith—at Camp Ticonderoga. Binet tests. His father breathed again. He himself felt a hidden and cloudy shame as though they had both been conspiring. He didn't see why. He agreed thoroughly with Joe Goldmann. Perhaps it was the spectacle of Goddard. Goddard had wanted to volunteer ever since 1914. Only the plea of his widowed mother had kept him back. Yet he had been moderate in speech about the war and had not been an atrocity-monger. But Arthur always remembered the white

expression on that purely modeled face with which Goddard had once said: "I simply feel an element of great moral
evil that must be combated." Now in his uniform he was
very serene; happiness, good will, consecration radiated
from him. He wrote some charming verses—not of hate,
but of knightly comradeship and courage. A pure soul, a
lofty soul. Like his New England ancestors who set out to
free the poor slaves. Like Robert Gould Shaw. Like the
Englishman, Rupert Brooke. Arthur felt grimy and depressed. He knew himself, of course, that moral fervor had
nothing to do with wisdom or even rationality of action. He
was able, himself, to analyze Goddard's state as one of those
varieties of religious experience to which youth is prone.
He knew a great deal more. For he had privately, precisely
because his professors pooh-poohed them, bought and read
and reread the works of Sigmund Freud. He knew. Yet an
element of idealism—imitative American idealism—which
had soaked into him early and gone deep always kept him a
little from facing what he himself called the ultimate music.
Half-jestingly he painted the portrait of Goddard going to
war to Joe Goldmann. And Joe, to his astonishment, was
great.

"Trouble with you, Arthur, is that you don't know
enough history. Now the majority of your so-called knights
have always been indifferents or thieves and scoundrels. But
there have always been fine souls like your Goddard. Lots
of them. I wouldn't even dispute about the proportions.
The Crusaders who burnt whole synagogues full of men
and women and children—hell, don't you suppose that
many of the younger ones felt what your Goddard calls 'an
element of great moral evil there'? There were young aris-
tocrats in the Tsar's cadet corps who believed with all their
hearts that they were on God's side. And how about the
Prussian *Junkers*, Nordics and Protestants, like Goddard,
who are gladly laying down their lives for their ancestral
king and who feel 'an element of great moral evil' in the
policy of encirclement that goaded their country into war?
You're a hell of a little psychologist. Whenever anybody

feels an 'element of great moral evil that must be combated' in anybody else, that's the time to shut him up as an edifying spectacle for his pastor and his maiden aunts. Because, if you let him loose he'll become a murderer. And that's flat."

Yes, Joe was great. And he was no empty babbler. He took risks for the sake of his convictions. He confided to Arthur that he was helping Hindu revolutionaries get out of the country.

"Good Heavens!" Arthur said. "Suppose it's discovered?"

Joe tittered and rubbed the back of his neck nervously. "Oh, mamma, wouldn't they pile on the sentences! Thirty years would be nothing."

Arthur saw that there were knights and knights and retired to his Binet tests in peace. In camp the officers were coolly polite to him; Smith made him do all the work; the doughboys good-naturedly took the attitude that the Yid doc knew his business. . . . Running home on a week-end leave, he found a soldier hugging Hazel in the downstairs hall. He slipped quietly past and ran into his father. Jacob Levy had recovered a measure of inner comfort recently. He smiled at Arthur's question and said: "Dat's Hazel's reel American hero. She's engaged to him. She's a reel American now. Who is he? Young Sinzheimer. Sinzheimer Brudders and Company. Boston. Shoes. Fine rating. If Gott villing, de boy isn't killed, it vill be a fine metch."

4

ARTHUR took his doctorate in medicine in June, 1918, very near the head of his class. The armies were of course still in Europe. His cousin Harry Adams had just been killed in an obscure skirmish. Eli Sinzheimer, on the other hand, was still in America, buying leather for the government. Young Adams's death welded not only the family, but the family's friends, closer together. In a business conference with Mr. Freefield, dollar-a-year man, high in the councils of the government at Washington, record-breaking

Liberty-bond salesman to all the esteemed Jewish fellow citizens who were his clients—to this eminent person Jacob Levy could not help bragging a little of the brilliant degree his son had just taken.

"Now vat he needs, he says," Mr. Levy explained, "is a position in a hospital for de insane. You see, det's his specialty. But I say, vill dey appoint a Chew?"

Mr. Freefield drew himself up. "You're entirely wrong, Levy, in thinking that there is any prejudice—any whatsoever. But at this time competition at home is undoubtedly less great in any profession than at ordinary periods. We have given our sons to the defense of our country. There should be no difficulty at all. I—uh—have very pleasant relations with the commissioners in question. I may say that the secretary of the State Board is under some obligation to me. Would you like me to inquire?"

Five weeks later Dr. Arthur Levy was appointed interne at the Hospital for the Insane on Drew's Point, Women's Department, and with his trunkful of books and clothes was duly installed. He was assigned a large, pleasant, though rather barren room in the cottage in which lived the five members of the medical staff; the superintendent's house was across the road. Beyond, farther back from the river, stretched the long, three-story hospital buildings.

He had been perfunctorily introduced to his colleagues on a visit the week before. He now met them at luncheon: Dr. Duval, a swarthy, sleepy-eyed man of thirty-five; Dr. Kirke, young, thin, short, with bright gray eyes and an extremely inquisitive nose; Dr. Lowden, a crushed, emaciated, golden-bearded person of at least forty; and a thin, worn, straight-lined, mouse-colored spinster, Dr. Hopkins, who must have been pretty in a cool, precise, eternally virginal way twenty years ago. They all greeted him cordially enough. "Glad to see you, Doctor." They called each other "doctor" with an amusing frequency and persistence. It was evidently a comfort to them.

"Room all right?"

"Very nice," Arthur said.

135

"Grub's not so good recently," Dr. Lowden grumbled through his beard. "But you're new to it. Lemme give you a bit of advice right now, Doctor. Don't stay too long in institutional practice. It ruins a man."

"Listen to the old sour-ball," Duval shouted. "You oughta been stuck away upstate like me. That's no fun, sure. But here with two nights off a week in li'l' ol' New York—I'm not complaining."

Little Kirke expanded suddenly like a bathing sparrow. "If you fellows spent more of your evenings studying you'd get ahead both scientifically and professionally. Do you read German, Dr. Levy? I'm just working through Kraepelin. Tough, all right. But that Hun knows his stuff."

Arthur admitted that he read scientific German and knew Kraepelin thoroughly. He added that he was a little disillusioned with all the descriptive and diagnostic stuff. He felt sure that future research lay in a different direction.

Kirke fluffed himself out a little more. "What do you mean exactly, Doctor?"

"I mean preventive therapeutics partly through educational direction and partly through psychoanalysis!"

"Hot dog!" Duval shouted, and laughed.

Dr. Hopkins, who was sitting next to Arthur, murmured: "I don't see how you can go in for that disgusting stuff, Doctor. Why, it's positively immoral!" Her lips tightened.

But Kirke's nose was high. "I'd like to discuss that at length with you some time, Doctor. But we'd better visit the wards now."

Arthur was, of course, thoroughly familiar with hospital architecture of this type. The attendant's key clanked behind them; the heavy door slammed. Before them lay the long circularly running hallway carpeted with hideous, sickly brown linoleum, imperfectly lit by heavily barred windows. Off this hallway lay the bedrooms of the patients. But these were locked by day. The patients loitered or walked or crouched or lay on benches of wood in these halls and in the occasional window niches in which on a

136

small table stood a rusty artificial palm. The hospital was evidently crowded to its utmost capacity. There were women of all ages and all types, from wild-eyed adolescents to ancient crinkled crones. A few mumbled or hummed; a very few walked agitatedly up and down. But the great majority were apathetic with a hopeless, horrible empty apathy which changed, if only by a glance, to swift animal suspicion and fear as the doctors with the attendant behind them came in sight. The place was clean; it was, in fact, almost too obviously scrubbed; no doubt it represented a vast advancement in both humanity and comfort over the institutions of even a few years ago. And yet it was indescribably unhuman, fetid despite its cleanliness, sordid with an overwhelming sordidness that went beyond anything physical, tangible, describable, but hovered in the air like a great foul bird with bitter eyes. . . . They met female attendants—untrained, cheaply gay young women who smirked at the doctors and, seeing a new one, laid obviously hypocritical hands of kindness on this patient or on that. Fear leaped into the eyes of the patients thus touched. Here and there Arthur saw blotches and discolorations around the eyes and on the cheeks of the younger and probably more troublesome patients. . . . He looked at them; he looked at the attendants; he looked at the cool, self-important face of Kirke. What a seemly sort of a hell this was! . . . Kirke talked:

"You observe, Doctor, how very crowded we are. The war has caused an immense increase in insanity, especially among the foreign element. And you see that most of these women are foreigners. That complicates our problem. Half of them don't know any English. I sometimes wonder why we should take care of them at all. Still, you can't I suppose deport them all."

Arthur didn't look up. But he asked: "Are there attendants belonging to the various nationalities who can interpret for the patients?" He caught Kirke's sidelong suspicious glance.

"Well, hardly, Doctor. You're a New Yorker; you ought

to know. These jobs are within the gift of state and city politicians. The attendants are mostly Irish."

Arthur walked more slowly. His instinctively diagnostic eyes were absorbing more and more. He could tell the specific malady of nerves or mind from the *Krankheitsbild* of each of these patients: from motions, gestures, colorings, eyes, nails. From the atmosphere that hovered over each. Also, of course, he distinguished the human elements. Poles, Italians, Germans, Jewesses, Jewesses, Jewesses. . . . More and more and more. . . . His heart contracted. . . . Suddenly he was afraid. Afraid for these women of his people in the hands of the contemptuous doctors and attendants. . . . Good God! what nonsense! He was a scientist. An American. The Poles and Italians and Germans were in no better case. . . . Yes, they are, something within him said, yes they are. . . . He stopped. An emaciated, middle-aged woman with ragged blond hair and high, Slavic cheek-bones was walking up and down. She turned her head incessantly to look behind her; she swung her long arms back and forth. She stooped suddenly and whirled around and pointed an outstretched arm and finger at an old woman crouched on a bench and whispered, as her pupils expanded unnaturally: "Yid!" . . . Arthur's mind kept stupidly repeating the phrase: Yes, they are. . . . He stopped before the old woman at whom the Pole had pointed. She was a small old woman very neatly dressed in black, with white hair parted in the middle, clasping a clean white kerchief. She did not move; she did not raise her eyes. A mountainous dejection seemed to drag her down into the very earth. Arthur looked up. Kirke nodded.

"Sure, involutional melancholia. Arteriosclerosis, of course." He bent forward a little. "How are you, Mrs. Rosenberg?"

A pair of dark eyes in which all the sorrows of all the earth seemed to be concentrated. "Vy can't I die, Doctor? Vy don't you give me somet'ing to make me die? I'm such a burden." It was a weary thread of a voice.

Kirke exchanged a glance with Arthur. "The reason I know her name is because her family are perfect pests. Two sons and their wives. I've told them and the superintendent has told them that these senile cases are always hopeless. They don't seem to believe us. They come running here on visiting days and try to get extra privileges and extra food and bribe the nurses. We have similar cases, but none quite so bad. But then all these uh—uh—these people are neurasthenic themselves."

A curious thing happened. Arthur heard himself say: "Why didn't you say 'Jews,' Doctor? I wouldn't have been offended. There *is* a high percentage of nervous and mental disorder among Jews."

Kirke gave a little relieved laugh. "Right you are, Doctor, we're fellow-scientists. Yes, the percentage is high. And, understand, I don't blame the sons of the old lady for their feeling. Only they don't do her or anybody else any good."

They made the rest of the rounds rapidly. Kirke admitted voluntarily that the cottage system ought to be introduced and that this herding of innumerable patients of all types in a single building was rotten and thoroughly out of date. The one thing he was proud of was the room with the three continuous baths for "violently disturbed patients." Here, in three bathtubs, with white pilloried heads in clamped boards, three young women were immersed in tepid water.

"Manic-depressive cases, as you see, Doctor. It weakens them. But raving weakens them even more."

Arthur assented. He assented outwardly to everything. Privately his opinion that average neurologists knew nothing but words and that hospital treatment of the insane hadn't even begun to be studied, was depressingly and overwhelmingly confirmed. . . .

5

HE plunged into his work with a feverishness that he had not known before. He could not dawdle in his barren room. On his nights off in New York he was restive and ill-at-ease. The conversations of his colleagues on Drew's Point after dinner annoyed him. Duval chattered like a horrible overgrown adolescent. Lowden told smutty stories whenever Dr. Hopkins wasn't in hearing distance. That lady herself usually announced that she was going to her room to read her chapter in the Bible and pray and retire. Kirke seemed to be the only rational creature. He invited Arthur to his room and the two talked shop. Only it soon became clear to Arthur that Kirke, perfectly honorable and straightforward in the matter, was not interested in the study and cure of disease, but in his career. If he prepared case histories it was for his career; if he plugged away at scientific German, it was for that. He was going in, he informed Arthur, for hospital management. He realized that he didn't have, perhaps, the personality to become a metropolitan specialist. He would try for the superintendency of some great state institution.

"Look at Foster," he said.

Foster was the superintendent on Drew's Point. Arthur didn't want, heaven knows, to look at him—the exquisitely garbed, cool-faced, calculating diplomat who impressed politicians as the very ideal of a scientist and had long forgotten the little he ever knew. Arthur had been duly invited to dine with the Fosters. Dr. Foster's single scientific observation had been to the effect that as Americans we couldn't possibly go in for that degenerate, dirty Freudian stuff. . . . "It revolts every decent instinct in one," Dr. Bryant Foster had remarked with that heavy British accent which he cultivated despite his vaunted Americanism. . . .

Arthur spent much time with his patients. He talked to them; he watched them; he brooded over them. He found that he had a calming influence over them. Faint, faint shadows of smiles would sometimes arise in his presence. And that was remarkable. For the insane laugh wildly or despairingly. But they do not smile. He persuaded some of his patients who were capable at intervals of attention, however ill-sustained, to try to tell him about themselves. When, during their outdoor hours, the older women would be sitting on benches under the trees of the island, he would sometimes sit down quietly beside them and talk to them quite as though they were normal. His retentive memory made it possible for him to note down their words immediately afterward. He wrote out, for his own benefit, case histories which were like human stories. He became more and more convinced that wherever the hypothesis of alcoholism or luetic infection was definitely excluded, insanity meant a breakdown under the too heavy pressure of life, a cracking of the psyche under moral suffering, a flight from a world grown intolerable. There were, to be sure, the physical parallel phenomena, like old Mrs. Rosenberg's arteriosclerosis. But since no one had ever been able to establish the slightest casual nexus between these parallel phenomena, on the one hand, and the psychic disturbance, on the other, and since practically all these diseased states were known to exist without the accompanying insanity, Arthur came thus early to the conclusion that the future of at least preventive medicine in his field lay, with whatever developments and modifications, in the direction pointed out by Freud. . . . Meditating upon these matters at his desk, late at night, beside his green-shaded lamp, smoking a last cigar, he found his thoughts drifting in directions familiar and yet strange. He wondered suddenly whether Hazel was happy, as happy as his mother said. . . . He had a strong visual image of Hazel during bright, fiery, unhappy moments of her adolescence. . . . The delicate, sensitive girl had felt the disadvantage of being a Jewess just the one added burden that seemed too much. . . . She had made little attempts to escape into unrealities: little falsenesses, snobbishnesses, flirtations with an alien religion, foolish little denials and suppressions. . . . Escape into the fanciful and unreal, into a world unlike the world of experience as given. . . . Flight from experience. . . . Yes, the mechanism of the Jewish anti-Jewish complex was precisely analogous to the mechanism of insanity. . . . He had felt this urge toward flight himself, flight away from a reality that had no inner meaning, from a burden that seemed irrational. . . . The Freefields, Eugene Adams, Joe Goldmann, his brother

Victor—they were all in flight from a disagreeable reality whether their flight was toward pomp and patriotism or toward a technique of life which would insure Gentile society or toward dreams of a world-revolution that would set the crooked straight, or merely toward a cloud of arrogant disputatiousness in which all voices were silenced save one's own. . . . He got up. His cigar was finished. Determinedly he put aside these reflections for some vague future. . . . Analogies were notoriously deceptive. . . . Yet *if* insanity were in many cases merely a violent exaggeration under excessive pressure of processes and techniques of the so-called normal psyche—then . . . then. . . . He was sleepy. What was certain was again that your conventional neurologist was a wretched empiric, a shallow scientific opportunist who hadn't even established a connection with the causes of things. . . .

He didn't know, he hadn't considered whether his studying of the patients had been noticed. He came into the dining-room rather suddenly for luncheon a few days later and saw the bent and intimate backs of Lowden and Duval as they sat together—the inimitable posture of men gossiping or telling dirty stories—and caught the coarse though softened voice of Duval: "That Yid is certainly nuts on nuts." He sat down heavily and took up a magazine. Lowden and Duval shot up, came over, were oily in politeness. He acted as though he had heard nothing; the two men exchanged a comforted glance and sat down to their meal. . . .

It was a pity that these two were such coarse and trivial souls. Kirke at least was an honest man and a gentleman. It was a great comfort to Arthur to be able to make that reflection because he had a very special matter on his mind. He knew that he wouldn't be able to hold in much longer. Vague suspicions of his had long solidified into facts. There was cruelty in the hospital. The nurses beat the patients, Now he was very well aware that this was a charge that could not be lightly brought. In the present hospital system a certain amount of physical coercion was sometimes wholly unavoidable. Patients who had agoraphobia might yet benefit by the open air. . . . A slight manic disturbance might pass over if the patient had to adjust herself to hospital routine. . . . Women patients were notoriously harder to manage than men. . . . Also the attendants were uneducated women working for a pittance at a hateful job. . . . To be too critical was to wipe out the system, and that wasn't the job of a young interne. . . . But Arthur had found bloody welts on the bodies of young women, swollen eyes, ghastly bruises, arms almost wrenched out of their sockets. . . . Then he had come into the ward unexpectedly and found Miss Donovan dragging an elderly Jewess down by her hair and saying: "I'll beat you into a pulp. . . ." He had no rest or peace any more. He jumped up in the middle of the night. He curbed his imagination not to torment him with more than he knew and could establish. That was enough. . . .

He asked Kirke to spend the evening in his room and very calmly and objectively, with almost exaggerated casualness, introduced the subject.

Kirke nodded. "You're right, Doctor, it's a problem. I myself slip into the wards now and then when I'm not expected. I guess that's the best we can do. I wish we could have a better class of attendants. But how are you going to get that?"

"Perfectly true," Arthur agreed. "And I'm not asking the impossible. But I've got the goods on that Donovan woman to such an extent that it might clear the air for some time to come to fire her. What do you say?"

Kirke looked about him with a wandering gaze. Then he drew circles on the table between them with his inverted thumb. Finally he half-met Arthur's eyes.

"Fact is, Doctor, that we're up against a difficulty there."

"What difficulty?"

"Well, you see, Donovan is Duval's sweetie. They beat it off to New York together and raise the devil, and it's my private belief that she slips over into his room right here."

"Well," said Arthur, "I'm not supposed to know that. I'm rather sorry you told me."

143

Kirke got up. Whenever he wanted to be impressive he stood. "All right, Doctor. But look here: Donovan's a political appointee, isn't she? Can't be exactly fired without cause. Duval is the regular doctor on her ward. He'll give her a clean bill of health. It'll be his word against yours; he'll be raving mad. And if there's one thing that old man Foster won't stand for it's any aspersion on conditions here. If you think you'd have him with us—you're dead wrong."

The blood rose into Arthur's head. "In other words—anything short of murder goes?"

"No, Doctor, you're too pessimistic. We have fired attendants for cruelty and drunkenness and misbehavior. It just happens that Donovan has a drag with the State Commission and so has Duval. The consequence is that they'd fight. I'll be frank with you. If Duval didn't have a pull, would he be here? Oh, he's a good fellow and all that, but you'd hardly call him a—Well, never mind."

Arthur controlled himself. "Suppose you and I quietly lay the case before Foster and ask him to transfer Donovan to the men's side?"

Kirke started slowly toward the door. "Do as you like, Doctor. I must say that I certainly admire your spirit. But, for God's sake, leave me out. You can take risks that I can't. Your father is a rich manufacturer in New York City. Well, mine is a Methodist minister in the North Carolina mountains. I can't afford a professional black eye. Foster welcomes what he calls constructive criticism, anything that'll tend to make this a bigger and a better and a more Christian place for the unfortunate. He doesn't like a knocker. And, when you get right down to it, nobody does, do they? So give me your word that you'll leave me out of it." He held out his hand.

Arthur took it. "I give you my word."

The little man was gone.

Arthur sat down at his desk and wrote his formal letter of resignation in duplicate: one copy for the State Commission, one for Dr. Foster. He stated briefly as his reason that he had discovered abuses which his conscience could not overlook and had been convinced at the same time that, under existing conditions, these abuses were not capable of being remedied. Next day he confronted Miss Donovan. He characterized her practices in a few stinging words, admitted his own powerlessness, and commended her to her conscience and that of her friend, Dr. Duval. She looked sleepy and sullen and made no reply. He turned back once more and saw the virago's muscular arm and threatening, upraised, menacing fist. His heart fell. She would take out her rage on the Jewish patients. He had been an utter fool. . . .

Late that night he was awakened by a tumult in the hall. Duval had been to town. His tread was heavy; now and then he lurched against a wall or a door. In front of Arthur's door he stopped. "Yah!" he yelled. "Goddam foreigners—ought be Goddam deported. All of 'em! Look at these Goddam foreigners—God, this country's gettin' so lousy with 'em—it stinks. Yah, it stinks! Guineys, waps, kikes! Jesus! Especially kikes. God damn interfering kikes! Yuh hear me? I say God—damn—interfering—KIKES!"

6

ARTHUR'S father said: "You heve done right, my son. But do me a favor, vill you? Tell Freefield ent rub it in a little. Ent don't vorry. Business is vonderful since some mont's. I'm prouder of you den if you het made a million."

Mr. Freefield's offices were now in a building on Broad Street that had a magnificent Roman portico with sixteen stories dwarfing the portico. Mr. Freefield sat in a huge luxurious room. His secretary's secretary took your name. You entered and walked through what seemed brilliant space to the gigantic mahogany desk and saw the glossy, heavy figure with its impassive, utterly weary, boundlessly disillusioned features.

"Sit down, young man."

Arthur said what he had to say with the most careful restraint and objectivity. Mr. Freefield sat impassive with closed, wrinkled eyes. He continued to sit thus for a full minute after Arthur had finished. Then he opened his eyes. They were wearier than ever.

"Ethically you are in the right. Practically I consider it a grave error, especially at this time in our country's history, for Jews to put themselves forward in any way that might be interpreted as a criticism of the existing order or its institutions. We have been, however wrongly, implicated with the Bolshevik crime. We should be conspicuous for law-abiding and constructive endeavor."

At certain moments Arthur could never keep from a touch of fury. "And we should let Jewish as well as other indigent patients be beaten."

Perceptibly Mr. Freefield turned toward Arthur; perceptibly the weary, impassive, official voice was lowered. "I am personally of the opinion that we should take care of our own sick of all kinds in Jewish institutions. But the calls upon our charities, especially today, are so vast, that that plan cannot be realized for some time to come."

"Why should we have to do that?" Arthur blurted out. "We pay taxes. Why should we exclude ourselves from any of the benefits of the government we help to support? Why shouldn't we clean up the institutions which are ours as much as anybody's?"

Mr. Freefield slightly raised a white, feeble, but still unwrinkled hand.

"Our religion teaches us that we are in exile."

"Oh, does it?" Arthur said. "You combine one-hundred-per-cent Americanism with the concept of exile. And you consider that a tenable position, Mr. Freefield?"

A faint note of exasperation crept into the voice.

"I used the word exile in a purely religious sense. When you have done as much for your country as well as for the Jewish community and over as many years as I have, young man, we can discuss this matter again. Remember me to your father."

The thing gnawed at Arthur. He was idle and hated it. Joe Goldmann laughed at him. Dawson's comment was:

"The asylums are all rotten. You're well rid of the place. At the same time most private institutions are worse. What you might have done was to have stayed and tried to get that fellow Duval to break his own neck. Give that type rope enough and—you understand."

He was not yet quieted. It was the first severe outer conflict of his life. He went to a noted Jewish neurologist whom he knew slightly and told the story as an anecdote. Dr. Dresdener played with his soft, short gray beard. "Hum, yes. Great pity. Conditions are especially bad in our large cities. I always feel a pang when I have to commit any patient of mine to a public institution. There should be Jewish institutions, whether state or private. You see man is rather a loathsome brute and you get the minimum of cruelty only where there is racial and religious solidarity; in other words, where the innate callousness of people is not aggravated by what I'm fond of calling secondary planes of psychical friction, such as racial and religious and political prejudices, both conscious and unconscious. I wouldn't worry over the whole thing if I were you. You can build up a decent practice in time in New York, especially if you go in for psychoanalysis. I dabble in it myself. But it came too late in my professional life."

Arthur was immensely grateful for the good sense and good feeling shown by Dr. Dresdener. At last something that sounded like the voice of reason. He ought, of course, to study for another year with Freud or Adler. But Central Europe was in a hopeless plight at present. One would only be wrung by sufferings that one could not assuage. Also, Arthur had a deep feeling that what he needed, if only he could get it, was direct activity. He knew that, in a sense, his uncle Adams, first almost broken, then much softened, by the death of Harry, was lying in wait for him. If he could not have a son who was a doctor in his house, a nephew would do. Eugene was beginning to make a brilliant success of his publishing business. Mr. Adams had no one to take care of. It didn't matter whether the boy paid rent or not. There was the apartment which so many doctors had coveted and which he had let none have. So Arthur's father furnished the apartment for him—bedroom, study, reception-room, a small laboratory with all the latest instruments from Germany, and Arthur sat in his charming, empty, cool place—half proud, half scared of it and of himself. Eugene called up. Would Arthur come to his house for an informal gathering of literary people that night? They were all tremendously keen on the new psychology. And he had just waked up to the fact—would Arthur forgive him for his tardiness—that he had an expert in the family. Arthur went and saw many things that he had not seen before, and saw, above all else, the face of Elizabeth Knight.

BOOK VI

1

PROGRESS is no word that has an agreeable sound to civilized ears. The Latin verb from which it is derived means "to stride forward" and the reflective mind at once asks: whither? The tiger in his cage strides forward. But his path is a vicious circle within a world of a few squalid square yards. Has man made progress? He has undoubtedly stridden prodigiously in the past century. But forward? Does the airplane carry him on nobler and more profitable errands than the ox-cart and the chariot did his ancestors? The airplane, marvel of gods and men, deals death in battle and writes a cigarette advertisement across the noonday sky. Morally, then, it is obviously on the level of the spear and the wooden Indian. Purpose and direction are the test of whether our striding has been forward. . . . Amusing little writers and painters vociferate that this is the machine age, the age of speed. They write in the style of badly composed cablegrams and paint pictures of steel circles and gutted skyscrapers. . . . The age, in fact, is relatively a creeping one. The gentleman, flask on hip, tearing along in his Cadillac at sixty miles an hour, has a sluggish mind. He sees so much and so fast that he sees nothing; the thoughts of his really great contemporaries are so infinitely beyond his grasp that his mind is a storehouse of moldy fallacies. A filthy monk in the Libyan desert who really understood his Augustine was a much nimbler-minded person, far more progressive, far more contemporaneous with his age, than he. . . . Our friend in the Cadillac probably believes in his muddled way in Nordic superiority, America for Americans, Preparedness, Clean Books and Plays, and the sagacity of Calvin Coolidge. The deceptive mastery of physical speed and mechanical short-cuts serves only to confirm him in his grovelling superstitions. . . .

And yet progress has been enormous, has been unimaginable—strictly unimaginable to the average man. He does not share in it; he revels in its base, mechanical by-products. These make his savagery in war and competition more effi-

cient. They have left his mind and his instincts untouched.
. . . What does he know of that complete change, that divine
enlargement of all fundamental concepts concerning man
and nature and human life that may be symbolized by such
names as Darwin, Einstein, Russell, Freud? He accepts the
marvels of medicine and chemistry as modern improve-
ments, like oil-burning steamers or the ice-chest that manu-
factures its own ice. He sees that his children are saved
from diphtheria and small-pox. He will even babble about
serums. But the minds from which these benefits spring are
wholly inaccessible to his understanding, and as a two-fisted
and patriotic citizen he would have to persecute such minds
if ever he saw them at close range and in action. . . .

Progress since 1859 has been so vast that it has left the
enormous majority of mankind hopelessly behind. Tiny
groups of scientists and thinkers here and there are the only
human creatures who are the spiritual contemporaries of
their age. . . . Therefore we have Russell and Einstein, on
the one hand, and War, Fascism, Fundamentalism, on the
other. Between these two extremes wander the semi or
quarter educated—lovers of peace who go to war when the
trumpets blow, lip-liberals who flee when anyone practises a
rational liberty of action, unprejudiced souls who think the
Negro ought to be treated justly if only he will keep to
himself, and that the Jewish fellow citizen ought to be respected if only he will obliterate within himself all that
makes him a Jew; religionists who have given up the virgin
birth but damn all *mores* differing from their own—people
of kindly feelings but pulpy minds, hearers of echoes of the
great thoughts of modernity, a little troubled, a little scared,
easily driven back into the ranks. . . .

A figure and a symbol: Mankind travels along the road of
civilization not only by a few steps a millennium, but in
triangular formation. Let the mind once grasp the immea-
surable human triangle at whose acute apex march a handful
of solitary thinkers. The two sides are heart-breakingly
long, long as the unimaginable distances of interstellar space.
. . . There, at the base, crouch slothfully and dully the

thousand millions who have changed a little, but only a little, since the days of the Cro-Magnon man. . . . Keep your vision on the apex—there is progress; on the base—there is none. . . . At the apex war and race prejudice and sex slavery are things forgotten. Those few who march there do not ask after each other's ancestry or color or love life. Peace, knowledge, and compassion are theirs. . . . But a few, only a few, ranks below, the old savage diseases of the soul, not yet truly a soul, emerge and darken the faces and darken the very light of the sun. And soon you come upon hate and the cries after war and force and uniformity, and knotted, ape-like creatures, whether from the plains of Kansas or the Ukraine, grasp in their claw-like hands the sword, the lash, the fagot, and the stake. . . .

So there is confusion. How shall a young man facing the world bear himself? As though there were progress or none? As though the apex were the norm of human life or the base? And if that young man be a Jew, shall he say: "At the apex there are Gentiles and Jews only as there are poets and philosophers, equi-valent souls functioning in a different but complementary fashion; there is no Jewish problem; I shall at least live as though there were none"? But can he guard that isolated and precarious station of his against the cries of hate and pain that come inevitably to his ears? Shall his heart not speak? Will he not be forced to take into account the various coexistent realities of the historic process and live and act *as though* there were progress and he could contribute to it, *as though,* on a day a thousand years hence, the tears were truly to be wiped from all eyes, and he could hasten the coming of that day if but by one twinkling of the eye or one beat of the heart?

2

ARTHUR Levy had met his cousin by marriage, Mrs. Eugene Adams, once or twice only. She was a golden-haired Jewess with fine gray eyes and transparent skin. But she had no freckles and she had soft, round lines. His mother had told him that Joanna Kohn belonged to a notable family that had run to blondness for generations. Joanna was a Barnard graduate and reputed to be brilliant. Arthur turned these facts vaguely over in his mind on his way to the Adams house in West End Avenue. Eugene had, undoubtedly, even to minute details, a talent for success. Oh, on a fairly high level, no doubt. But to be apparently incapable of a wrong move—that somehow alienated Arthur's feelings.

He found the two longish drawing-rooms already crowded. People were still being admitted with the utmost informality. They did not necessarily seek out their host and hostess. They drifted brightly about or snuggled on seats or even on the floor or slowly made their way into the dining-room beyond, where a long table was laden with sandwiches and bottles and glasses. From what one heard superficially one couldn't possibly tell who anyone was. Only first names, preferably abbreviations or diminutives, were used. The gathering was like an enormous happy family. Arthur stood for a few minutes squeezed in a corner near the door. He saw a tall ravaged keen-looking woman in deep slouchy decolletage; a small, round, eager chirpy man with heavy lenses and the quick coy movements of the homosexual; a tall, pale, golden-bearded man with a deep bass voice who was talking to a slim, dark, detached, elegant one who said nothing but smoked a cigar and kept his fawn-brown eyes staring into vacancy. A dazzling lovely young person with wide eyes, rather high cheek-bones, exquisite subtly shameless shoulders, brushed against Arthur, gazed into his eyes, smiled, and passed on. Through a rift in the crowd he saw Victor Goldmann sitting in a far corner, brooding, sultry, sullen-eyed. . . . Suddenly then, having caught sight of him, Eugene Adams hastened in his direction. He was delighted to see Arthur. Had he seen Joanna? Had he just come? He probably didn't know many of the people. Eugene was immensely self-possessed, radiantly successful without undue emphasis. He drew him into the inner room and introduced him, his cousin, Dr. Levy, a distinguished young psychoanalyst, to a famous novelist, thick, sleepy, over-dressed as an aging woman; to a columnist who was steadily the talk of the town, a tall, angular Jew with a deeply lined face and an entirely Gentile name; to another famous novelist, a woman this time, who looked thirty years younger than her age, but gave the impression of having been preserved in formaldehyde; to a theatrical manager and a playwright, both Jews; to a famous critic, a large, beaming, enormously intelligent and kindly Gentile; to poets, story-writers, editors, men and women, Jews and Gentiles inextricably mixed, all still calling one another by their first names, all teasing and kidding one another, all slightly drunk, all giving a little start of pleasurable surprise and next a little start of fear and withdrawal in the face of a psycho-analyst, as though he could see into them all and they were first subtly glad and then a little sorry to have anyone gain a glimpse into their secret difficulties and vices. . . . Joanna came up and put an arm, a lovely, bare, dimpled arm, around Arthur and took him into the dining-room and gave him a tall, strong, stinging high-ball and said he must be tired of standing, and over there, on the divan, there was a place for him to sit down next to her dear friend and former class-mate. She steered him thither and introduced him to Elizabeth Knight. He sat down. Joanna was already gone. He looked at the woman beside him. Pale arms and throat against a simple black frock, a head held straight and a little proudly, a profile half boyish, yet with something of a little girl it, an adorable little girl who had been naughty and was sorry. The hair, brown and straight, was bobbed to just below the ears and swayed backward or forward with Elizabeth Knight's motions like a bell. . . . She turned to Arthur.

"Isn't Joanna a darling?"

He confessed how little he knew his cousin. Elizabeth looked at him. Her eyes were earnest, beautifully sincere.

"Oh, she is. You have no idea what I owe that girl. I worked my way through college. My father is a Campbellite preacher—a perfect saint, but poor as Job's turkey, of course. I had the hay seed in my hair when I came to New

York." She was involuntarily wistful, wistful because her soul, shining through, was so. "Yes, I owe a great deal to Joanna."

"Are you a writer, too?" he asked.

She shook her head. He caught sight of the naughty little girl again. "I'm just a journalist and rather overcome by all these famous people, though I confess they don't make a very agreeable impression."

He nodded. "I'm seeing this for the first time. My immediate impression is that the greater the name the more I get a whiff of something morbid, almost corrupt—"

"M-hum. Maybe art is a morbid by-product."

"Compensation for physical or psychical or sexual inferiority. That's one theory, as you know."

"Do you believe," she asked, "that it applies to the great masters, too?"

He nodded. But he didn't want to pursue the subject. He didn't want to talk shop. "Tell me more about yourself," he said.

She grinned with a touch of mischief. "Not much to tell. I'm active in the suffrage movement. I'm on the *Clarion*. Father loves me, but knows I'm a lost soul. I'd like to write fiction, but I've got to make my living. Eugene believes I have talent and has offered to subsidize me. But I can't see myself *having* to write because I owed money and had thrown up my job. I'd do nothing but get my fingers inky."

They both laughed.

"And you?" she said.

He told her the story of his recent adventures. He found himself adopting her humorous, self-deprecatory tone. "I haven't a single patient, nor any present idea how I'll get one. But I have a charming office. You ought to come to see it."

"I will," she promised.

"Truly?" A sudden fear shot through him.

"Cross my heart and hope to die."

He gave her his card, which she tucked away in a little bag. She couldn't find one of her own. But she had a pencil and he wrote down her address. . . . A shadow arose before them—a lank, towering emaciated red-headed man with a quaint triangular profile. He was very drunk. He leaned over unsteadily and put his hands on Elizabeth's shoulders.

"Dearie, you ought to do as 'Gene says. Write. You ought to take a lover, too. How the hell can a virgin be productive?" He kissed her.

Arthur felt sick. This was an unknown pang. He saw Elizabeth push the man back a little.

"Don't love me any more? You c'n go to hell." He lurched off.

"Who was that?" Arthur asked.

"Bertrand Jones, the novelist. Isn't it funny how such a brilliant person can be such a swine?"

Joanna came to them. "I didn't mean that you two should stay together the whole evening. That isn't fair to the rest of us."

The party became more and more of a slightly sodden bacchanal. There was no real conversation. The personalities grew broader and broader, the gossip franker. There was a great deal of kissing and cuddling. Arthur imagined that, if he knew these people better and were a little drunker, he too might enjoy this throwing off for an hour of the usual inhibitions. But tonight he couldn't have done so in any event because he found himself peering into the crowd for Elizabeth and with feeble little rages—feeble because what right had he and how foolish it was!—resenting the obvious fact that she was a great favorite and that men kept touching her, putting an arm about her, leaning their lips against her hair. . . . When, at two o'clock in the morning, the party broke up, he tried to lie in wait for Elizabeth; he tried to do it unobtrusively. But unobtrusiveness being no part of the manners that obtained here, he had to see her bundled, as he thought, into a taxicab with a man and driving off. He walked home with a little gnawing in his belly, knowing what had happened to him and hoping to God that it wasn't as he feared.

3

HE knew that the war had loosened the taut strain of Puritan morals. He knew it and approved it as a man and, above all, as a scientist. But he discovered that he wanted Elizabeth Knight excepted from this loosening, that he resented bitterly the thought that at other parties men would touch and handle her again and perhaps discuss with her whether she should remain a virgin or not. . . . He persuaded himself that he wanted to test out the situation and that for this reason alone he called her up at her apartment only two days after the Adams party. It was in the evening and he said that he hadn't been able to get her out of his mind and wanted to see her. She accused him laughingly of using a condescending tone and said that she was tired and in her dressing-gown; she needed to sleep; she needed a great deal of sleep. Always. But if he really cared about it so much he should drop in after dinner on the next day. Why not have dinner together first, he asked. He didn't like her voice at all when she answered that she wasn't a young lady who could be asked out hit and miss, but a working-woman. She had a late assignment next day. He could come if he chose. But the fact that he hadn't liked her tone didn't help him at all. He found, on the contrary, that he longed all the more for the morrow in order to have the impression which blurred the image of her in his mind obliterated. . . .

He went precisely at nine. She was lying on a chaise-longue in her little drawing-room, smoking a cigarette out of an enormously long holder of onyx. There was a tired strained look about her eyes. Behind that look hovered the look of the naughty little girl. Again she had on a black evening frock, simpler than the one she had worn at the party, a little shabby in fact, and again Arthur was stirred by her pale arms and throat and by the proud yet pathetic way she held her head as she sat up to give him her hand.

"Today was worse than I feared. I'll be dull as ditch water."

"What's the difference?" he said. "As I told you, I've

been thinking about you. I simply wanted to see you again."

"You are a nice man. You'll find cigarettes over there. Have you got any patients yet?"

He laughed. "No, but Eugene called me up to tell me that a very distinguished friend of his was coming to see me."

"Wonder who it'll be. I have a hunch it'll be Prout, the author of *Hills of Morning.*"

"What makes you think so?"

"Oh; his actions the other night. I have these hunches about sexual things."

He looked into space. He had a silly sense that she was besmirching herself. "How can you have these hunches without any experience of your own?"

She insisted that that didn't seem to matter. Besides, there was experience and experience. He felt his cheeks and lips tingle; he wanted to know and dared not ask what these experiences were; he was evidently retroactively jealous of her. He tried to guide their talk in other directions, but she came back again and again to the question of the relations of men and women, especially of their physical relations and of the effects of these physical relations upon life and character. Her virginity was evidently an ache to her, an ache at least as much of the mind as of the body, and she resented this troubling wound and lack at the core of her and had cultivated a harsh, almost petulant hostility to men. She said things that seemed foolish to Arthur; she denied the bearing on life of fundamental biological facts; yet all her talk, even at its most wrong-headed, had an engaging quality, a blending of fine, precise speech with warmth. He stopped arguing. He came over and sat down beside her. Into her face came suddenly the frightened expression of a child, and he took her in his arms and kissed her. . . . He was amazed and thrilled and infinitely flattered at the intensity of her response. Her lips clung to his and her pupils dilated until her eyes looked black and she clutched her hands together around his neck. . . . Then suddenly she pushed him away with a peremptory, almost angry gesture and told him to go. He asked her when he would see her.

"I don't know," she said and her mouth quivered a little like the mouth of a child. "I don't know. But I want you to go."

Two days later, toward sunset of a spring day, she came to see him. She had on a black suit with very straight lines and a little hat that accentuated the boyishness of her profile; she was exquisitely gloved and shod. She walked about his apartment like a strange, elegant lady who had come to see it; then she lightly touched things here and there. A faint perfume of heliotrope breathed from her. She seemed ethereal and aloof and more desirable than ever. She would not even sit down, as though that would be a fatal concession, but consented to go out with him for a bite of dinner. The air was very clear and the sky edged with deep rose and fading orange and a faint tinge of green. From every tree set in the pavement here and there, from every tiny square of city-grass, came the fresh, sharp fragrance of life. Elizabeth said she wasn't hungry; she didn't care where they went. The world was so beautiful, so beautiful. That was enough. She could see the fields and ragged groves about her father's shabby parsonage; she could see herself as a little girl, hot and tired from play, hearing her mother calling her in for supper and stopping for a minute quite still, all by herself, a tiny mite of a girl in a terribly plain frock, overcome by the loveliness of earth and sky and the trees darkening against the afterglow. . . . There was something liquid in her eye as she evoked this vision of her childish self for him, and something free and noble and wistful. . . . They went to a small restaurant and she hardly touched the food, in spite of his urging, and went on talking about her childhood: how poor they had been and how her father was in his narrow way a perfect saint who had to be kept from giving his money and his clothes to any chance beggar, and how her mother, frail and burdened by poverty and children, had died early. It was an aunt, an intelligent but unlovable person, who had helped Elizabeth go to high school and then, even more half-heartedly, to college. At Barnard the girl had early been swept into the suffrage movement and had been for several years a paid agitator and organizer and had then been offered a newspaper job. "I never had a single nice thing—just plain, serviceable ones—until I brought them for myself. I love nice things." About all her talk there was something fresh and lyrical and sad. She talked dreamily as though to herself. . . .

They walked back in the direction of Arthur's apartment. The stars were out now and Arthur could feel the throbbing of his heart and he heard himself say—distinctly heard his own voice—"I love you, Elizabeth." And the intoxication of those words was like no other intoxication he had ever felt; it was an intoxication in which one saw things as clearly and as intensely and as visionarily as in a dream. . . . The world of reality was drowned for the hour in another world that was magical and mad and overwhelmingly tangible, too. . . . He was not surprised that she went back to his apartment with him, nor that she entered, nor at her white, scared face, nor at her utter yielding, nor at her straining to him, nor at her sweet ways or beauty of body. . . . Then the magic snapped. . . . She sat on the edge of the bed, wrapping a silk coverlet about her, her face haggard with pain and a touch of brooding horror. "Is that all?" She stifled a sob in her throat.

Arthur slipped into a dressing-gown. He tried to touch her, but she drew away from him. "Is that all?" There was something despairing in her level tone. He gave her a cigarette and lit it for her and took one himself. He begged her to listen to him. He told her that, from a medical point of view, a good deal of nonsense was talked in so-called radical circles about the freedom of love. He hadn't himself the slightest respect for laws and conventions; it didn't matter what seasoned people did with their lives. But the necessity for marriage, not in law but in spirit, and for the intention of fidelity, was founded on the fact that in all but the rarest cases a woman who gave up her virginity found no pleasure in the act of love, only pain and disillusion, and that it required the continuous care and tenderness of a man who loved her to induce in her that subtle psychical and physical

coördination of attention and consent and freedom from
unconscious inhibition which would gradually ripen her for
love. She looked at him with wide, hurt, hostile eyes.

"But a man always—"

He nodded. "Yes, always."

She asked him to go out so that she could dress. Fifteen
minutes later she appeared quite as she had come. A faintly
humorous apologetic smile was on her lips.

"You must think me an awful fool."

He shook his head. "You're sweet and adorable."

She pressed his hand. "You're a nice, nice man. I'm terribly glad it was you." For the first time they kissed each
other tenderly. She asked him not to bother about her for a
few days. She wanted to think. She would be heard from.

4

PROUT came, as Elizabeth had predicted. Short and fat
and fifty-five. He had on a very English suit and a silken
waistcoat and dangled a monocle. He said that Arthur's
apartment was charming, that his new book was already in
its sixty-ninth thousand, that he hadn't really taken much
stock in psychoanalysis. He had told 'Gene Adams nothing.
But having met Dr. Levy the other night, he thought he'd
drop in. There must be, no doubt there would be, the
completest discretion. Arthur asked him to sit down. Prout
hummed. Arthur looked out of the window and waited.
Prout began again to talk irrelevantly.

Arthur said, gently, "Anything to do with sex?"

Prout looked up. "How did you know?"

"I didn't, but it's not uncommon."

Prout leaned forward and groaned. Well, yes. Yes. He
wanted to marry again. A lovely young actress of less than
thirty. Not conventional, of course—neither one of them.
They had gone off for a week-end together. He had been
most frightfully humiliated—oh, most frightfully. A thing
unheard of. God! what an experience! At the very recollection sweat gathered on the fat man's forehead. The thing
was indescribably ghastly, he said, indescribably.

"Complete physical impotence?" Arthur asked.

Prout barked. "Yes, damn it, yes."

"I suppose," Arthur said, slowly, "that we can dismiss at the outset any physical factors, such as venereal infection in youth!"

"Absolutely, Doctor, absolutely. Christ, yes!" He leaned forward, breathed heavily.

Arthur spoke with firm yet gentle decision. It was his first important case. If he could use the Adler short-cut here and avoid a long psycho-therapeutic process it might be the beginning of a practice. . . . He explained to Mr. Prout that the phenomenon he deplored was in nearly all cases psychical in origin and hence curable. There is something in his relation to a woman, let us say, that the patient will not admit to himself, will not permit to rise into the field of consciousness at all. Then the organs of the body will take up the cause of this suppressed truth and speak for it by functioning wrongly or refusing to function. This speech of the organs of the body can be silenced by the expression of the cause of their speech through another channel. . . .

Prout sat up. His eyes were wide open. "Very interesting; very plausible. Go ahead, Doctor."

"When you were alone with that young woman in the country did her conduct in that intimacy disappoint you and jar on you?"

Prout gasped.

"Understand, Doctor, she's a wonder. But—"

Arthur went to the other end of the room. He heard Prout breathing hard.

"She's so disorderly. Never could find anything. Left her brushes and combs on the mantelpiece, couldn't find stockings that matched. Ugh! if there's anything—"

"And has that sort of thing played a part in your life before?"

Prout got up. He roared in unconscious joyous liberation: "Has it? For eleven years I was married to a sloven. It nearly killed me. I'm paying the bitch alimony yet!"

Arthur came back. "For a man of your insight I need hardly say more. You were afraid you were making a desperate mistake a second time. You didn't want to admit it to yourself. So your body made the admission for you. You're probably cured now. If not, come back to me."

Prout got up, happy but sheepish. He had evidently nursed the most desperate fears. "What do I owe you, Doctor?"

"I'll send you a bill by and by."

Jauntily the novelist departed. Arthur could almost have prayed that the method he had employed would succeed. The case seemed clear enough; he had read of not a few like it in the journals. But no record approached the vividness of experience. The moral benefit to himself of a successful cure would be inestimable.

The afternoon sunlight made his apartment seem forlorn. That brilliancy ought to be peopled. He thought of Elizabeth, of course, but he could never reach her until evening. Also, ought he not to wait for a sign from her? The vision of her gave him a faint sense of guilt. He hadn't been home in nearly a week. His mother must be lonely. Hazel and her husband were living in Boston, and since his sister was expecting a baby she rarely came now.

He found his mother crocheting in a seat by the window of her drawing-room. She pointed to her work with a smile. "For Hazel's baby."

He nodded. "Everything going nicely in Boston?"

His mother's face grew grave. "Between them, yes. He's a fine boy. And maybe Hazel's condition makes her see black. But she's terribly lonely. I'm going over to stay with her next week. She has no friends."

"Why do you suppose that is?" he asked.

She shrugged her shoulders. "People don't like Jews in Boston. Especially in Brookline where the children live. They don't know a single one of their neighbors."

"But there must be plenty of Jews in Boston?"

"Of course. But Hazel doesn't like the ones she's met. You know the Sinzheimers are from Posen themselves." She lowered her voice slightly.

"But didn't our grandfather Levy come from Poland, too?"

"Yes. But those were other days. And he was from a fine rabbinical family. But Hazel says she thinks Mrs. Sinzheimer was a *dienst*, a servant, in the old country."

About all this there seemed something dreadfully wrong and even corrupt to Arthur. But he could not say so to his mother who sat there with her graying hair, elegant, composed, with that touch of dignity which she never lost.

"Stay to dinner, sonny. Papa'll be glad to see you."

He agreed to stay very gladly. He suddenly had the feeling that he wanted very much to have a talk with his father, as though, in truth, his father was the repository of some neglected wisdom.

When they were sitting at table he told, by discreet indications, the story of his first patient.

"A *goy?*" his father asked.

"Why, yes!"

"I'm surprised."

"Why?"

"You esk me vy? De vay tings are going in dis country I never vould have believed possible. Vy, a Chewish boy or girl can't get a chob any more. Dey come to our office every day. Ve say ve heve no opening. Dey beg us for anythig. Vy? No Christian will take dem. Dere are more ent more apartment houses going up every day vere a Chew can't get in; in de country dey heve restricted residential parks. Same reason. To keep us out. In de colleges— But don't you read nor hear notting?"

Arthur bowed his head. He knew his father's old faith in America. He thought of Elizabeth.

"What do you think we ought to do, Papa?"

"Stick togedder, I suppose."

"But we don't, do we?" Arthur asked. "The Freefields think they're a little better than we are and Mamma tells me that Hazel thinks she's a little better than her mother-in-law and *her* friends."

"That's always been so among people," Mrs. Levy said. "You can't change that."

Mr. Levy was stern. "It vill heve to be changed. Oderwise ve vill heve conditions like in de old country. I give only to Chewish charities now ent I vish, my son, dat you vould offer to vork for notting for a Chewish hospital. Dere is plenty of money; business is immense. Dere never vas a country vere people had so much money to spend as in America today."

The talk ebbed back and forth. With his mind Arthur agreed to all that his father said. But in order to embody thought in action one needs the emotional impulse. Whence was that to come? All his Jewish experiences from the days of Georgie Fleming on had been negative. All he wanted was to be left alone and function freely within the society into which he had been born. He couldn't do that; he wasn't, upon the whole, permitted to do that. So much he knew now. He had heard his older colleagues talk, too. If you were an Ehrlich or a Freud you wouldn't get a full professorship in any medical college within reach; Jewish students were discouraged. There was no profession today in which Jewish competition wasn't fought. His father's explanation of the situation in business completed the case. Well, one could, as his father said, make common cause with one's fellow Jews. But that outward action would proceed from no inner urgency; it would be an action of quiet despair. It would be like shrinking from a disease, not like embracing one's beloved. . . . No wonder people changed their names and tried to escape so cruel and absurd a dilemma. . . . No wonder. . . . He walked to his apartment. He stood in front of the house in the mild spring night. . . . He needed forgetfulness and ecstasy. . . . He hailed a passing taxi and drove to Elizabeth.

5

THEY became steady friends and lovers. Better friends than lovers. She adored kissing and touching him; she adored his physical nearness. Her ultimate inhibitions were never quite broken down.

"I suppose I can't get out of being a parson's daughter

and granddaughter," she said, wistfully. "The repudiation of the body and its instincts is rooted deep."

He put the entire distance of a room between them and asked her if she felt any strangeness in him because he was a Jew.

"Silly," she said. "Look at Joanna, look at most of my best and kindest friends. I love your Jewish darkness and ardor. I wouldn't have you different on any account."

They were spending a brief week-end in a little inn near Peekskill. They walked along the hill roads under the fresh green trees. He begged her to stay over until Tuesday. She said she couldn't; she might lose her job.

"And haven't you a patient coming?"

"I'd put her off. I think I'll send her packing, anyhow. She's a faded elderly woman who can't get over her loss of sexual importance."

"Did Prout send her, too?"

"Prout has sent no one directly. He's only gone about saying that, to judge from the experience of a friend of his, I'm next door to a miracle-worker. I'd be doing well if I had the cheek to charge what some of my colleagues do."

"Why don't you?"

"I don't believe I'm worth it. I haven't been to Vienna; I haven't yet been analyzed myself. I ought to be, you know. I can't see myself charging twenty-five dollars the half-hour."

It was marvelous to talk oneself out to some one. Elizabeth was a delightful listener; she was a delightful talker, too. That unconscious lyrical touch brightened and softened all that she said, especially her favorite stories of her childhood. Arthur came, through her anecdotes, to know that penurious Protestant life with its hardships and repressions and its faint cool breath of poetry. All summer her father would take an axe and cut the wood for the coming winter. He believed that a preacher should not be divided from his parishioners by any avoidance of hardship or any cloistered ease. He set little store by such slender learning as he had. He was great in brotherly love; great in humility.

His pay was pitifully small and the farmers knew it. Their wives gave the parson pound-parties; they brought a pound of coffee and one of tea and three pounds of sugar and a peck of potatoes and sometimes a chicken. Elizabeth thought that the humiliation of these parties had helped to kill her mother. She remembered one fat tall farmer's wife who would seem to fill the little parlor. The woman had bitter lines about her mouth and great red rough hands and a booming voice. She would say: "I think there ought to be a prayer of thanks here for what the good neighbors has brought." And Elizabeth's father would kneel down and pray. Afterward her mother would be almost hysterical. But her father would say: "No, Sister Tompkins has no humility. But that is no reason why we should forsake our Lord by not having any." Little Elizabeth used to lie awake at nights inventing strange and grotesque tortures for Sister Tompkins. . . . Elizabeth would ask Arthur to tell her about his childhood and adolescence. He tried. He stopped. He had so little to tell. He was inhibited from telling her about Georgie Fleming and about the rough boys at the corner whom he feared so and about the scene in the gymnasium in High School. He found that he couldn't break down the inner resistance that kept him from telling her these things, and that resistance evidently communicated itself to much else, so that his words came slowly and conventionally. He tried to communicate to Elizabeth something of the quality of his mother and father and sister and the atmosphere of his home. She shook her head. "I don't get the feeling. I don't seem to see clear." He groped his way as along a psychical wall of glass. He saw that, somehow, there was very little that was salient about his home or his people, that there was something curiously flat about his past. Yet he could have sworn that essentially his father and mother were very much more salient, emphatic, peculiar personalities than Elizabeth's were or could have been. He shied at the thought that his family lived at the cost of constant suppressions and exclusions: the suppressions and exclusions had become habitual, had become, in that expressive phrase, a second nature, at all events. Of that he was sure for a moment. And then again unsure as he suddenly remembered his father at certain moments of high excitement, in that hour, for instance, now far in the past, when the question of Hazel's marrying Henry Fleming had arisen. He found that that scene had burned itself for all time into his mind, and that, in retrospect at least, the figure of his father in that scene assumed something of nobility, something almost of grandeur. An elemental or, at least, an historic instinct had burned in his father on that evening and Arthur suddenly thought of that instinct as venerable and even beautiful. He started to try to communicate a sense of that hour and scene to Elizabeth, and then, remembering that she was a Gentile and might be estranged or even hurt by the story, closed his lips. . . . Her father evidently had not come in contact with Jews; none of her anecdotes concerned a Jew. It was amusing and contrary to common experience that one of his anecdotes should touch on race prejudice and none of hers, that he should be in danger of wounding her with his past and not she him with hers. . . . And that simply showed how intricate and subtle and infinitely vexing the whole problem was. . . . He tried once to imitate his father's English and phraseology for Elizabeth. She laughed a kindly, tolerant, amused laugh. Her laugh appealed to him for comradeship, took it for granted that his attitude to his father—like her attitude to hers—was, despite an element of true admiration, kindly, tolerant, and amused. He found, a little to his own astonishment, that what she took for granted violated a strong primitive feeling within himself. He saw his father clearly enough as a human being with very definite limitations. Yet he discovered now that somehow he revered him. In his character as procreator merely? Absurd. And equally surely not as an intellectual being. As what then? Under what guise? He meditated long upon this point. He went over the past. He discovered that, upon the whole, all the Jews he knew had something of that same reverence for their parents coupled with a perfectly sane and objective view of them as human beings. It seemed to him, too, that

169

Charles Dawson's attitude toward his father was not as wholly unlike the Jewish attitude as Elizabeth's was. Dawson felt his father to be the representative of his people and his family and the historic tradition of his race and house—the Scottish Dawsons of Inverness. . . . Jews, even Jews who had wholly lost their traditions and their pride, evidently still had that instinctive feeling for their parents as mothers and elders in Israel. . . . Funny, Arthur thought, almost fantastic. . . . He must be mistaken in his analysis. . . . Yet he knew that he could never share Elizabeth's affectionate but wholly detached attitude to her father as to a lovable, muddle-headed, funny little man with a brown beard with whom her connection was more or less accidental—a biological accident, say—but to whom she was allied by no deep-rooted and subconscious instincts. . . . He said one day that she had better meet his people and she said that she would love to, of course. But somehow the time and opportunity didn't come and wasn't sought. She failed to seek it, however, not because she was in the least unwilling, but because it did not seem important to her. Not in the least. He, on the other hand, did not press the point because he had a secret dread of the meeting, though he hadn't the least definite idea of what discomforts it might involve. And he was so happy with Elizabeth and felt so much at home in the world whenever he was with her and listened to her talk, which was clear and lyrical and blithe despite her undertones of sadness, and saw the free lifting of her head and kissed her hair, that he was tempted to pray that time might stand still and leave him and her forever in their sweet and secret isolation.

6

IT was on toward the middle of September that she came to his apartment on an evening of breathless dusty heat. She threw down her hat and shook her hair, which was slightly moist.

"What weather!"

"Yes," he said, "and I suppose you've been in the heat all day." He looked at her as she drooped and cuddled into a chair, and she looked so lovely and child-like and he felt so united to her, that he said, with a sudden lifting of the heart: "You'd better marry me and throw up your ghastly job." He was amazed when he saw her hide her face against the back of the tall chair and suddenly cry quietly but deeply with little hushed, continued sobs. He took her hand and laid his own on her head. "What is it, dearest?"

She recovered herself gradually and wiped her eyes with a moist, funny little handkerchief and turned to him. "Why did you say that just tonight, Arthur?"

"Because I felt it, quite simply."

"I'm glad," she said. "And yet I'm horror-stricken at the position of woman—wholly without decency or dignity."

He sat down opposite her. "How come?" He had caught amusing little American folk-phrases from her.

She sat up flushed, spirited, her eyes dark with indignation. "I came here tonight to beg you or, like all women, wheedle you to give me something which I don't want, in which I don't believe, but which—which is forced on us by our slave status." Her face hardened. "I came to ask you whether you wouldn't marry me, because we're going to have a child."

A tangible substance seemed to melt in his breast. He went to her with outstretched arms, with moist eyes. But she protested.

"I thought, by the way, that you had taken proper precautions."

He couldn't help laughing, though he knew at once that the note of happiness in his laugh seemed silly and sentimental to her. "I have, you know. But there are, unluckily, no unfailing precautions. One has always to reckon with the off-chance."

She still warded him off. "I see. But suppose you hadn't condescended to me, could nothing have been done?"

He was angry. "You're talking nonsense, Elizabeth, damned nonsense. I can conceive of cases in which an illegal operation might be morally justified. This isn't one of them. In my sense of the word we've been married for months. The child is mine as much as yours. It doesn't particularly interest me, except as a social convenience, whether we go through a ceremony or not. I want the child. And since you're the child's mother and human infancy is a long process, you belong to me, too. Such are the biological and the moral facts."

She bit her lip. "It's loathsome."

He felt himself grow pale with anger. "What? Our having a child?"

"No, Arthur. I don't mean that. I mean your attitude of taking possession of me, mastering me, reducing me on account of this accident to the status of a nurse and a slave."

He put his two hands to the side of his head for a moment. Then he arose and strode up and down with his hands behind him and realized dimly beneath his stormy preoccupation of 'the moment that he was walking up and down, like his father, in the characteristic way of Jewish men when agitated. But that perception faded. He turned and stopped before Elizabeth.

"I swear to you, Elizabeth, I had no idea how you feminists had gotten warped and crazed on fundamentals. The use of contraceptives is the accident, the abnormality—a useful and beneficent accident and abnormality, I grant you. Motherhood is the eternally normal thing for a woman. You might as well criticize the rising of the sun and the growing of the grass. And as for your being reduced—reduced"—he couldn't help almost shouting the word—"to the status of a nurse and a slave, well, the length of human infancy is the thing that makes man human. A kitten can fend for itself at the end of a few weeks, a child in modern civilization at the end of from seventeen to twenty-five years. Certainly parenthood 'reduces' both the man and the woman to the fulfillment of certain duties. You have no more right, there's no more sense in criticizing that fact than in complaining, for instance, that we live by food. You remind me of someone who would say: it's so slavish to eat two or three times a day. Let's live on air. Such fool talk!"

Elizabeth had arisen now. She stood straight and had a haughty, girlish sternness in her posture and aspect. Something of the eternal Diana, maiden and huntress. "I shall go on with my work. Understand that. I won't be kept by a man. I shall retain my name, like most of my friends. I'll go through with this thing. I agree that it's the decent thing to do. But you will never see me become the exclusive mother-animal that you'd like to see me."

He couldn't help laughing. "Mother-animal—such verbiage. As for your going on with your work—it's much better for a pregnant woman to be active. But that can be overdone. I'll take you to a friend of mine, a gynecologist, and he'll tell you what's best for both you and the child. I—"

She went brusquely to the table for her hat and gloves. "You'll do nothing of the kind. I'll see a woman physician by and by." She stopped suddenly with outstretched hand. "Pregnant woman! Good God!"

He joined her and put his arms around her. "Elizabeth," he pleaded.

She drooped toward him for a moment and rested her head lightly on his shoulder. She smiled sadly. "You've scolded me like a husband already. I won't have it. Since I discovered this thing I'm not even sure that I love you any longer. I only feel trapped and caged. I'm sorry. But it's so."

He let her go. "I think you'll find that a readjustment will come about and with that you'll hear the voice of normal instincts. Don't be so unyielding, Elizabeth. You're so taut. A woman gets her truest self-fulfillment when she is broken by love and motherhood."

She smiled bitterly. "I had no idea you were so mid-Victorian."

He shrugged his shoulders. "I am strictly scientific and up-to-date. There are a few facts, my dearest, that have not changed, so far as we know, within historic time."

"Well, then, we'll change them now." She kissed him lightly on the forehead and went out, slim, proud, erect. . . .

7

ELIZABETH didn't want fellow reporters to run into them at City Hall. So they were married by a magistrate in Jersey. Arthur asked Elizabeth why all this secrecy, since the fact of their being married would have to be announced quite soon in any event. She shook her head; she would give no clear reasons; she seemed to be fighting for every day and hour of time. He asked her at least to take a key to his apartment, so that she could come and go as she liked. She refused. She clung to her own little apartment with an icy, desperate passion. Actually he saw less of her than he had done before. She looked pale and peaked and refused to take any meals with him. He watched her closely one day and concluded that she was probably suffering from hyperemesis and was dragging herself wretchedly through her work. He took her by surprise.

"What's your woman doctor giving you to help you keep your food down, Elizabeth?" Her eyes filled with tears. "All sorts of stuff. It doesn't help."

He mentioned the name of a new German remedy. Elizabeth hadn't heard of it. He promised to get her some. But he told her at the same time that even this might give her only partial relief.

"Why don't you come here and live with me and let me take care of you? We'll hire a good maid. We'll be ever so comfortable and happy."

She looked at him steadily through her tears. "Maybe it would be best, Arthur. But wait just a little while."

He went to see his mother. It was a difficult errand which he had put off from day to day. He hadn't spoken of this matter to Elizabeth. He had asked her whether she had told her father that she was married. She had answered casually:

"Not yet. I'll write him one of these days soon."

She wouldn't have understood the sense of responsibility to his parents which he felt and to which his emotions consented. She would probably not have understood the fact, either, that he knew of his mother's awareness of some secret that had slipped between his parents and himself. But he could precisely visualize his father and mother wondering what was the character of this secret and he could hear his father saying he hoped it wasn't a love entanglement with a Gentile. Hence no preliminaries were needed. He simply said: "Mamma, I want to tell you something."

She answered, quietly. "Yes, sonny. Tell me."

He took some pains to explain to her the type of modern woman to which Elizabeth belonged.

She smiled. "Never mind all that. You think your mother doesn't read and observe a little. I don't agree with all these modern notions. But the position of woman was not right. I would like to have taken up some work myself, maybe. I don't think anybody would have objected. But there was no opportunity. No, that's all right."

Then came the hardest moment. He had carefully not mentioned Elizabeth's name. Now he had to. His mother clasped her hands.

"I didn't think you'd do it. What will Papa say?"

Arthur had, of course, anticipated that point. So now he confessed that Elizabeth and he were already married and that a child was on the way. His mother put her hands on his shoulders.

"A child? Then there is no more to say. We must hope for the best. I shall tell Papa. Could you get along now if he gave you no more money?"

"Modestly, yes."

"All right. That makes it easier for me." She promised to let him know as soon as she had talked to his father. He thanked her. Her smile was profoundly sad. "What can a mother do? I'm sorry for Papa. And for myself a little. She'll be no daughter to us. Her child won't— But, no, I mustn't talk that way. I promise you this: we'll all do our best." Her sadness had a very special quality. It was an elemental sadness, a sadness as of the earth, the patient sadness of those who are accustomed to bear burdens. It communicated itself to Arthur and he went out of the room and out of the house strangely warmed by his absorption into that sadness, strangely at home in that simple, gigantic patience that consented to the bearing of burdens. . . .

A few days later his mother asked him to come to dinner. He smiled quietly at his own nervousness. He had been psychoanalyzed in the last months and it had been found that his infantile entanglement with his parents was as small as possible. The slight original ambivalence of feeling toward his father had evidently been corrected by the normal maturing of his psyche and the normal fixation of his love-life upon strangers. It was evident, therefore, that somewhere in his mind lurked an agreement with his father's and mother's disapproval of exogamic marriage. He grinned to himself at the use of the term. But wasn't it exact enough! Marriage outside of the clan— a crime among many primitive peoples. And among just as many primitive peoples marriage within the clan was an equally heinous offense. So how could a modern scientifically trained man take seriously any of these taboos in regard to sexual selection? If he could only explain a few of these things to his father. Out of the question, of course. . . .

Dinner was a little strained. Arthur didn't see why he should touch upon the burning subject first. They talked superficially. At last, with a little rude gesture which his mother had always deprecated, his father pushed away his plate.

"So you're married, Arthur?"

Arthur shrugged his shoulders a little. What, since his father knew the whole story, was there to answer? In spite of his slight irritation, however, he got a feeling of pathos from his father's gray face.

"Ent to a *shikse!* No, don't enswer me yet—please. I have no doubt det she is a fine, educated girl, chust as goot as anybody ent maybe better. I mean det. Dere's chust as meny fine *goyim* in de world as dere're Chews. I vant you to know I'm not a narrow-mindet old men."

"Well, then?" Arthur interrupted, cheerfully.

"Vait, vait! Ent I'm not so troublet as I vas ven I t'ought Hazel vas going to marry det *shegetz*. You're nearly tirty ent a doctor ent dere's no danger of your disgracing us by becoming *geshmatt* or such t'ings. You're my only son ent you cen go on heving all de money you need—more den I gif you now. You'll hev a vife ent a child. She shen't be able to say det de old Chew is stingy. No, no! But you von't be heppy and she von't be heppy and ven you heve children you'll be more miserable den ever. Now you can bring her here ven you like ent ve vill treat her like a daughter. Ent it vill do no goot."

Arthur laughed with relief. He had feared a passionate and tragic scene.

"You say you're not narrow-minded. Now what do you call all your predictions? Why shouldn't Elizabeth and I be happy?"

His father leaned his elbows on the table and supported his chin upon folded hands. "I don't know, my son. I've seen a lot in de last years ent I've heard a lot in business ent elsevere. I've het to face conditions det you heven't het to face. Ve sold a large bill of goots to a firm in Texas. Dey het a very goot rating. Ve didn't get de money. Ve vaited nearly a year. Ve alvays do in such cases. Tenk Gott ve cen afford it ent it's better to keep customers solvent, even et a temporary loss. Y'understent? Finally ve vas forced to soo. Vell, Freefield got a letter from de lawyer of det firm in Texas telling us ve could go to hell, because no court in det county would render a chutchment in favor of a kike firm represented by a kike lawyer. Now vat do you tink?"

"I think it's unspeakably loathsome. And if I were you I'd fight that case to the Supreme Court. But, for heaven's sake, what has a thing like that to do with Elizabeth and me?"

"It hes dis to do vit it. Dey hate us. Dey all hate us. Now, as I heard Doctor Katzmann say et a meeting de odder day, it vould be all right if dey vere bet people. But some det hate us most are fine ent honest people in every odder vay. Ent it vould be all right if ve vere bet people ent deserved to be hated. But ve are a goot people, honest ent hart-vorking ent kint ent charitable ent en educated people. Nobody is bet—neider dey nor ve. Ent dey hate us. Now, understent, I'm not comparing your younk vife to fellows like dose Texas t'ieves. But every *goy* in de vorld hes a little bit of det hate in him. He cen't help it. It isn't his fault. But det little bit of hate betveen men ent vife— Vell, I said too much already. You know vere Mamma ent I stent. Ve vill be chust es goot to your vife as dough she vas a Chewish daughter. But I'm glet I said vat I said."

They looked into each other's eyes, father and son. Arthur shook his head slowly.

"Who is this Doctor Katzmann and where did you hear him?"

His father suddenly looked a little embarrassed. "He's a great Chewish t'inker ent I heard him at a *B'nei Brith* meeting. Goldmann ent I choined de order last year."

"Yes, yes."

"You ought to choin, too. It vould bring you prectice. All de great Chews are members."

Arthur got up slowly. He walked over to the mantelpiece. He looked upon this familiar scene brimming for him with a thousand intimate and precious memories. The light fell upon his mother's hair and he noticed for the first time how white it had been growing. She had sat in her sweet, dignified silence all through the talk. He turned to her now.

"Do you agree with what Papa has been saying?"

She nodded gravely. "Yes, Arthur, I do."

He drew a deep breath. "It's not a case for agrument. But I want to tell you this as a doctor: all universal generalizations about people are false—all."

His father pursed his lips tolerantly. "Maybe, maybe."

"Anyway," he went on, "such arguments can't be refuted by talk. Only by life. Isn't that so?"

"Exectly. Ent your mudder ent I don't vant you not to hef a chence to do det. So you bring your vife here Sunday for dinner."

He walked back to his own apartment in a profoundly reflective mood. One didn't know one's nearest. One's vision of life remained, despite thought and reading and observation and even digging professionally into other people's souls, intensely personal, governed by inner fears, avoidances, predilections, tastes, escapes. What his father had said was, within its limits, crystal clear. He himself hadn't wanted to think such thoughts and so simply hadn't permitted himself to think them. He didn't know what to do with them now. He didn't know how to fit them into his life. He was tempted to curse the whole business. Couldn't one help to destroy all these remnants of man's barbarous past by living as though they had no real existence, by living in the light of reason? . . . While his key was still in the outer door of his apartment he heard the violent ringing of his telephone. He hastened in and took up the receiver. It was Elizabeth's voice. She had been trying to get him all evening. She was sick, she was lonely, she ached for him. Would he come and take her home with him?

BOOK VII

1

IT was, you remember, in the days of King Ahasuerus who may have been Xerxes, and of the Persian Empire which was cast down at Salamis, that a certain prince and councillor named Haman sought to destroy the Jews. It may be, as the legend of Esther declares, that Haman was affronted because Mordecai the Jew would not do him reverence. But Haman was a political philosopher with quite modern tendencies. He was far too subtle to ground his enmity toward the Jews upon a personal hurt or discomfiture. He expatiated, as the Egyptians had done aforetime, and as reactionary Germans and Fascist Italians and American Protestant hundred-per-centers were to do afterward, upon the theory of the necessary cultural solidarity of the slaves of the state. "There is a certain people scattered abroad," said he, "and dispersed among the peoples in all the provinces of thy kingdom; and their laws are diverse from those of every other people; neither keep they the king's laws: therefore it is not for the king's profit to suffer them." So far Haman remained upon the ground of political theory. But since the king, like all kings and actual rulers, was given to *Real-politik* and was probably, after the fashion of his kind, a dunce to boot, Haman added the eternal master stroke: "If it please the king, let it be written that they be destroyed: and I will pay ten thousand talents of silver into the hands of those that have charge of the king's business to bring it into the king's treasuries." He knew, oily and astute financier that he was, with some precision the wealth of the Persian Jews. And one notes, for instance, that there has never been felt an equal necessity to destroy, say, the Gypsies in a given country because their laws were diverse from those of other people or because they did not keep the king's laws. The Gypsies were never suspected of having the ten thousand talents of silver. Haman's point was well made. The king gave him his seal. Messengers and letters went forth into all the provinces with the command "to destroy, to slay, and to cause to perish, all Jews, both young and old, little children and women, in one day, and to take the spoil of them for a prey." The pogrom, physical or psychical, has always, you see, been in the end a cash transaction. . . . Big business and the theory of cultural solidarity, Henry Ford and Nordic supremacy, have always been united on the ground of practical politics. . . .

Now it is evidently not pleasant to be killed and robbed nor to live under the threat of murder and robbery or of exclusion and humiliation and insult and persecution. And luckily all Jews have not been heroes and martyrs. For if they had been, there would be no Jews left. So the Jews, being upon the whole, and contrary to common opinion, more passionate about thought than about action, have tried, especially in recent centuries, to persuade their fellow men to believe, on the one hand, that their laws are not diverse from those of other people in the sense of hostility or spiritual divergence, and, on the other hand, that they themselves do keep the king's laws. They have, wrongly, to my way of thinking, accepted the theory of the state as propounded by Haman and others not only to escape injury, but to have a home in the world. No wonder that many of them have kept the king's laws so rigidly and passionately that they have forgotten their own laws. And this process has always revenged itself bitterly in the end because their own laws are an outgrowth of their historic character and experience and the king's laws remain laws imposed upon them from without. But since they had actually forgotten their own laws they had no refuge anywhere and were homeless and didn't know why, and became wanderers without a goal. . . .

The Viennese garden, the precise eighteenth-century garden of a former imperial villa. A Hungarian baron—tall, straight, elegant, a scholar, a writer, a man of the world. Christian for two generations. Keeping, you see, the king's laws. But he protested against the White Terror. Being a Jew, he could not but protest against the White Terror. He is a fugitive and an exile. Hungary is lost to him, lost more profoundly to him than to his Gentile fellow exiles. He hoped for more, loved more, needed more for his self-affirmation as an Hungarian. Other exiles will return some day. Not he. It was necessary for him that the cry *Saujud* be silenced forever. . . . He has forgotten his own laws. Whither is he to turn? To Zion? His smile was ironic, a typical self-ironic Jewish smile. . . .

Keepers of the king's laws: A very fat man reading his poems to a Jewish audience in a Jewish hall. A brilliant poet and his poems are all magnificent pæans to the landscape, history, art, traditions of his native step-fatherland. Next day the Jewish press is enthusiastic, the Nordic press sneers. . . . Or our friend Victor Goldmann, a brilliantly successful young architect now, building Jewish temples and theaters for Jewish managers and factories for Jewish business men and shouting at the top of his voice that there is no Jewish problem, that it is the Jews who want to be treated like the only children of God. . . . Or Joe, his brother, a very successful lawyer now, his office full of Jewish clients, hoping for the world revolution and always in love with some blonde Gentile girl in order to transcend vicariously in conquest of her his Jewish feeling of inferiority. . . . Or the great critic and scholar who has built himself this defense theory that the Jew has always achieved greatness only when he has assumed some foreign guise—Persian, Greek, Spanish, German, American. . . . Or the French man of letters who writes with a mild picturesqueness of Jewish matters: Behold, say his works, how quaint and moral and charming we are! A banquet is given in his honor. The minister of war is toastmaster. Of war: *"Un brave homme,"* say the orators. True. True. Then: *"un homme brave!"* And no one laughs. . . .

2

ELIZABETH Knight and Arthur Levy had been married for two years. After the birth of John, Elizabeth had taken up her work again. She had not gone back to her old position. Through the influence of Eugene and Joanna Adams, as well as of other friends, she had been given a chance to write feature articles for the Sunday papers as well as for certain spectacular magazines. Browsing in Arthur's library, getting him to translate for her extracts from German books—case histories more especially from the psychoanalytical journals—she had very vividly and agreeably put together a series of articles which she called "The Cure of Souls." She had a pleasant fluidity in her writing and a frank, simple way of stating things. It was around 1921 and the American interest in psychoanalysis was at its height. Everywhere in the country a few individuals among the younger generation were beginning to resist neo-Puritan pressure, if only in the inwardness of their minds. Elizabeth sold her articles to a woman's magazine of national circulation at a price that staggered Arthur. He was doing reasonably well himself now. Patients were not too many and he labored with them conscientiously. But they would not have trusted him had he not charged them as much as other practitioners of very high standing. Nevertheless, Elizabeth's single check for seventy-five hundred dollars took his breath away. She had been very sweet about it. She had pursed her lips, and the little girl in her which at rare intervals made his father call her *shiksele* had come out. "Really, you know, I owe it all to you." Arthur had tenderly deprecated his part in her undertaking.

"What shall we do with all that money?" Elizabeth had asked. "Jiminy, I didn't know there was that much money in the world."

"Invest it for John," Arthur had said.

"Oh, bother. John'll have half of your father's money some day. Let's have a good time."

"It's your money, darling."

Elizabeth had bought herself two new fur coats and a fur coat for Arthur and half a dozen frocks specially designed for her by the studios of Baron de Meyer, and had sent a check for a thousand dollars to her father, and had then borrowed money from Arthur that she might send his mother flowers for her birthday.

"Never mind," she said. "I've got a lovely notion for some more articles. And I'm going to write some stories, too—stories about my childhood and the upstate farmers. So be a nice husband and give me a check." She had written both the articles and the stories. She sold everything she wrote. In her stories she had a blending of precision and naïveté, a childlike earnestness with moments of sudden bubbling humor that had true charm and yet managed to hit the taste of a very large public. Checks poured in. Also invitations poured in. Miss Knight became more and more of a figure in that literary New York which is so tremendously in the public eye, is, in fact, one of the sights of the town and sustains so fragile and precarious a connection with literature, after all. That world took to Elizabeth with a kind of passion. There are very many Jews in it, Jews who never speak of themselves as Jews and try hard not to think of themselves as such. Elizabeth being a Gentile, but being married to a Jew, was bound, aside from her personal charm and talent, to be much-beloved. One invited Miss Knight; one had luncheon at the Algonquin with Miss Knight. One was supremely comfortable with Miss Knight. She could have no subtle reserves, no hidden judgments upon one. She was, in the end, Mrs. Levy; she was the mother of John Levy. She was an out-and-out Gentile, and yet (far was it from these ladies and gentlemen to use such a phrase except in the innermost privacies of thought) "one of our own people." The postman groaned under the morning mail for Miss Knight, whose name was duly, under that of Arthur Levy, M.D., on the door of the apartment; the telephone rang all day and voices asked for Miss Knight. Elizabeth enjoyed herself hugely. Of the precise character of the situation she was wholly unaware. So great was her naïveté in this matter that once, being at an all-Gentile editorial conference and hearing for the first time since her marriage the stereotyped remarks about the business acuteness of Jewish writers and the hospitality of Jewish publishers to radical and immoral books, she not only said with a glowing sense of doing the right thing: "Remember, please, that my husband is a Jew!" She not only did that in all sweetness and purity of motive, but came home and told Arthur about it and assumed her little-girl air and expected to be praised for her loyalty and frankness. And Arthur, violently uncomfortable but unable to analyze his own discomfort at the moment, praised her in the expected sense.

They went to parties almost every night. One couldn't, Elizabeth pleaded, go to So-and-so and slight So-and-so. Moreover, one met a terribly useful crowd. She picked up commissions and he picked up patients. One made no effort, but the thing happened. It was undeniably true. Arthur was asked to treat more and more members of the literary or editorial set. His patients were nearly all Jews. He found that their psychical aches and inhibitions and discomforts were all flights from an obscure reality. They substituted; they interposed the barriers of phobias between themselves and reality; they were in pepetual flight. There was no earth under their feet, no heaven over their heads. There was an apartment and the Algonquin at noon and a party at night and the gnawing of a mystic tooth at the soul. . . . They railed and jeered at the neo-Puritan obsession, at the Fundamentalists. They made common cause with Bertrand Jones in his famous fictional attacks on the nation's brutal and massive attempts to draw its traditional forces together and extrude the people and the influences that seemed to it to threaten its fierce loyalties and ignorances and solidarities. . . . They did this, overlooking, feigning to themselves not to have observed, the fact that Jones, more drunk than usual one day, had told his partner at dinner that *he* belonged, and that she had better go back to the ghetto where *she* belonged. . . . Arthur had a curious feeling about these Jewish intellectuals one day—a curious and prophetic feeling. He could not imagine them growing old. What would they do when they could no longer hurry hither and thither and write witty articles and columns and go to luncheons and meetings and support all good negative causes and protest and huddle together for warmth against one another in the meeting-places of New York? What busy souls they were! And how drained of anything of their own! How essentially poor, poorer than the poorest Gentile who, from fraternizing and protesting and jeering with them, could withdraw to his hearthstone built on his bit of earth and trust in the long historic process of his people. But he had the haunting conviction that with these Jews movement of the nimble mind and body was identical with life. They had no center to which to retire; when they could no longer whir about the periphery they would drop and die. . . . Tentatively he said these things to Elizabeth. She listened with that earnest attentive air she had.

" 'Gene Adams said to me one day that the Jews are the worst anti-Semites. What you say, Arthur, almost makes me think he's right. Why, it doesn't seem to me that our Jewish friends are any different from anybody else! Why should you, of all people, judge them so funnily and so harshly?"

He laughed and kissed her hair. "You're a dear," he said. "I suppose I would be hurt and disappointed if you took any other attitude."

He left her. She was busy. He, too, was expecting a patient. That night there was a party at the house of a Jewish playwright, an extremely brilliant and gifted man whose plays were a concentrated bitterness of protest against the hardness and dulness, against the inconceivable (to him inconceivable) life of the American masses. Arthur and Elizabeth did not get to bed till nearly three o'clock in the morning. He had to get up at eight and left her asleep, and saw her pile of mail, and answered the telephone which angrily demanded Miss Knight, and went through the empty rooms to his study.

3

VERY often during the two years of his married life he remembered that scene with his father and mother, that last scene before he had brought Elizabeth to visit them. He saw them at the table in the old dining-room which still had in it the furnishings of his childhood. The scene had not impressed him greatly at the time. Later it seemed stamped and graven upon his mind.

It had been upon the following Sunday that Arthur and Elizabeth had gone to his father's house. In the hall Elizabeth had suddenly reminded him of Georgie Fleming. There had been a vague shrinking and distrust in her eyes, and, had she not lifted her fine straight nose in the ghost of a sniff? To have taxed her with that attitude would, of course, have been monstrous. She was utterly unconscious and innocent. Why would she, under the circumstances, not be a little shy? The older generation always has its conservative moral reserves. And Arthur, convinced in some obscure inner region, blamed himself for attributing to that momentary shyness and shrinking of hers any quality that it would not normally and universally—granting the circumstances— have had.

The door had opened. His mother had appeared and at once folded Elizabeth to her bosom. The old amethyst ring with the tiny diamond flower in it had glowed on Elizabeth's shoulder. Elizabeth had tried hard to yield; she had had no conscious impulse against yielding. Arthur took all that in with his psychical antennæ. But she had simply not been able to soften suddenly and unexpectedly under this thing that was to Mrs. Levy a mere matter of course and had to her the quality, even though beautiful, of an unforeseen emotional attack. She had felt in that embrace more than a gesture of affection and good will. She had felt in it a subtle reaching out after her and possessing of her and drawing her irrevocably in. And against that assumption of her no longer belonging wholly to herself or her kind, but of being, by a gesture that was also a ceremonial, absorbed into a community of fact and feeling and interests the very existence of which she had not suspected—against that her instincts rebelled. She and Arthur had met freely in a free world of more or less detached human beings. One was nice, to be sure, as nice as one could be, to the relations of one's husband. But one wasn't, at least nowadays and in America, sucked into a clan. . . . Arthur and Elizabeth had never discussed this matter. Arthur knew that Elizabeth would have denied, and very honestly and sincerely denied, these various emotional imputations. Honestly, because any formulation in words made the whole thing intolerably gross—the thing which, in itself, was the shadow of a shadow in the twilight of the mind.

The embrace, which had lasted but a moment, had been crucial. Arthur's mother had experienced the subtle rebuff which she had expected. She would have been happy not to have felt it. But she was not, being human and a woman, wholly dissatisfied to have her foregone conclusions proved and to be able to assume the generous, unweariedly giving and slightly tragic maternal rôle which, ever since Arthur's announcement, she had been prepared to assume. She put her arm through that of her strange new daughter and drew her into the living-room. Arthur was suddenly aware of the fact—he hadn't ever noticed it before—that the furnishings were somber and old-fashioned. He also saw that the watch-chain across the chest of his father, who stood there with arms outstretched, was too thick and showy. Slowly the outstretched arms dropped. Mr. Levy came up to Elizabeth and kissed her lightly on the forehead. They all sat down.

The moment had weighed upon them. Stones seemed to lie upon their hearts. Arthur's father had said: "Our son tells us det you write." Elizabeth did not, of course, realize the terribleness of this remark. How it showed a blending of hopeless estrangedness with a self-tormented desire to propitiate. A Jewish daughter-in-law—well, if she had written, he would have teased her about it later. First he would have asked her quite other questions. Or, rather, there would have been no need to ask questions. All that would long ago have been eliminated. They would be, they would have been from the beginning, on some bit of common ground. But Arthur, shivering a little at his father's question, knew suddenly why Jews were sometimes psychically unmannerly. On different grounds, emotionally out of touch, aiming wildly, one aims amiss. One is, for all practical purposes, blind and bungles and stumbles and crashes. He remembered the story that had been told him of a colleague introduced into the Gentile milieu of his betrothed and behaving abominably. Poor Dr. Bergmann, afraid of seeming distant and a stranger, had, out of the depth of his Jewish conception of the family, been overintimate. He had asked questions which would in Jewish circles have been taken as a warm and gracious sign of interest on the part of so new a member of the clan, but which here sounded and, in truth, were excessively prying and rude. He had been glad that, upon the whole, his father and mother were not expansive people. He could imagine Elizabeth with the elder Goldmanns. She had, at all events, regarded his father's words as natural and kindly and had turned to him with relief. She had been in those early days quite deprecatory about her writing. She had joked about it, in fact. His father had smiled and something of the heaviness of the moment had been lifted from them all. . . . But during the dinner it had descended upon them again. Arthur saw that his mother was burning to speak, almost to cry out, to assault Elizabeth and break something in her, break down the invisible barrier which she felt. But it was precisely the intangibleness of the barrier that made the situation so hopeless. Elizabeth was friendly and even cordial. No fault could be found with her. But she was cordial as with people of whom she wanted to make friends. He could hear his father, had his father's articulateness in English extended so far: "Frients! De vife of my only son sits dere like a strange lady vanting to make frients wit me! Better she shoult begin by hating me ent I could show her det I hef for her de heart of a fadder!" Oh, it was hopeless! Elizabeth pulled herself together. Elizabeth was charming in a way that seemed to Arthur's mother unbearably casual and detached. As a last resort Mrs. Levy brought out photographs of Arthur taken from year to year all through his childhood and boyhood, and the two women, going toward the window, seemed to have a moment that drew them together. Then, alas, Mrs. Levy offered to part with some of these treasures and Elizabeth said: "They're awfully sweet and I love them. But you'd better not give me any. I lose things so easily."

At last it had been over and Arthur and Elizabeth had been walking home along West End Avenue. He took off his hat and let a cool wind of early autumn blow through his thick hair. They had not spoken. Arthur had wondered vaguely what Elizabeth's thoughts had been. He felt utterly dispirited. Intellectually he was entirely on Elizabeth's side. No fault could be found with her. She had, in all sincerity, done her best. On the other hand, there tugged and gnawed at him the profound sense of his parents' grief. He felt this so strongly that he rebelled against its irrational causes. Why the deuce did one have to be so sentimental about family matters? Why did one have at a first meeting of this kind to melt? What function did this immense Jewish sense of family solidarity have in modern life? Of course Elizabeth couldn't even comprehend what had been expected of her. . . . And all the while below these thoughts he knew how happy he would have been, how instinctively and completely happy, if his wife could have assumed the part of a Jewish daughter and he could have come out of his father's house on that day with the conviction that the bonds of solidarity and love had been sustained and strengthened.

4

IN the many succeeding months the inevitable results of the life that Arthur and Elizabeth led and of the character of that first meeting had become more and more emphatic. They had quite literally no time for any social life that was not part of the life of the circle in which they moved. Had Elizabeth been strongly drawn to Arthur's parents, a distinct effort would no doubt have been made. On the other hand, Arthur felt morally certain that, had Elizabeth's own father lived in New York, she would have seen very little of him, too, and that her conscience would not have troubled her at all. Then how could he, except at very rare intervals, ask her to add another burden to her already overburdened professional and social life? On Sunday she was usually quite tired. He, too, valued their Sundays alone together. They were so rarely alone together, anyhow. Hence he drifted into the habit of going home alone on occasional afternoons, on occasional early evenings. But these visits were of no comfort to him. His father and mother took it for granted that Elizabeth did not want to come in an actively negative sense which was utterly unjust to the real state of her feelings. If he reported her words exactly: "Darling, I know it's shabby of me not to have been to see your people in all these weeks or to have asked them. But you know they'd disapprove of our friends, just as much as Dad would in another way. And I'm just broken today. Do go and give them my love and tell them I'm not as low as they think!"—if he repeated these words exactly, he was believed. But under those words his parents felt something which was not there. For the casualness of that attitude was inconceivable to them, the security of belonging instinctively into one's world and not wanting to belong, not feeling the need of belonging to one's given group. They understood attraction or repulsion. They did not understand the specific detachments of the children of a soil. . . .

Those had been weeks of great comfort to his mother when Elizabeth had been in the Sloane Maternity Hospital. She had gone there daily with fresh flowers and had been able to be tender and protective a little in her attitude to her daughter and to her grandson. But the two women had not fundamentally drawn closer together even then. And next had come the burning issue of the child's circumcision. Arthur knew that his parents had taken counsel together when his father had called him up and had asked him not whether but when the ceremony would take place. Arthur had put his father off and gone to Elizabeth.

"Father's just called up. I know from his tone that he's scared to death you won't permit the baby to be circumcised."

Elizabeth, still weak, had smiled rather wanly. "All modern doctors recommend it as a matter of health. I needn't tell you that. And John's name is Levy. So I have nothing against it, Arthur. How do you feel about it?"

He had stopped in front of her and reflected. "It's more troublesome to me than it is to you, dear. It opens the whole problem for me. I know you think there isn't any. But I think I'll just be guided by my father's feeling, if you don't mind."

"Not a bit," she answered.

So Arthur was able to invite his parents for a certain date on which a more or less religiously-minded Jewish surgeon of his acquaintance introduced little John into the company of Israel. Arthur was astonished at his own satisfaction. He interpreted it as relief in his parents' relief and as a result of the very rational consideration that a boy named John Levy and uncircumcised might find himself from the start in a puzzling situation. But Elizabeth had one of her flashes of insight.

"I didn't know you were so Jewish in your feelings."

"Do you mind?" he asked.

She smiled. "I have atavistic attacks myself when I hear Gospel Hymns."

He shook his head. Somehow it was different, different. . . . Life was becoming more confusing for him from day to day. It had never been clear. There had never been in it a fundamental order. Now he often grasped his head. It seemed to spin. Aside from the strange alienation from his parents, from the friends of his youth, aside from the restlessness of his life with Elizabeth, there was another factor which had become more and more acute and to which, both as a man and as a psychologist, he could not but allow great weight. . . . It was a subtle and difficult and delicate matter. . . . One could not cope with it by either words or action. . . . It was there . . . Elizabeth was very busy. She was always tired at night. . . . She was desperately afraid of having another baby. . . . When they had been out to a party Elizabeth almost fell asleep in the taxi home. When they spent an evening at home, she begged to be allowed to go to bed early in a sweet and child-like manner. . . . Once Arthur had said:

"But, darling, we might as well not be married."

She had pouted. "Is *that* what marriage means to you?"

He had smiled. "You are a little Puritan, just the same."

She had grown grave. "Not in my opinions, Arthur. But I don't really think that that side of life means much to me personally." After that she was careful to create occasions once in a while and to give herself to him. But it was a weary and deliberate and joyless process. . . .

He wondered afterward why he had not rebelled long before. But Elizabeth was disarming in her sweetness, her reasonableness, her instinctiveness. She was that sort of a woman. The sort that keeps her name, goes on working, thinks of marriage rather as a pleasant companionship than as a deeper and more tragic union. She was without blame within her ethical universe. Moreover, all modern ideas were on her side. She was entirely in the right. For opposed to her conception of marriage was the old sex-slavery of the Puritans with its cruel subjection of woman, its denial of divorce, its fierce and ugly repressions. No wonder that the women of her race and her tradition had rebelled and were now at times tempted into extremes. No wonder. And Arthur knew that if he protested she would take immediate fright; she would think that he was protesting from the point of view of that old Puritan notion of marriage which had crushed her mother, from the point of view of the dominant Gentile male. And how was he to tell her and, above all, to convince her, that what he had in mind was something different, was a third kind of condition or estate which he felt to exist but which he himself could neither precisely define nor describe? All he knew was this, that, except in imitation of their Gentile sisters and more or less from the lips outward, Jewish women were not dissatisfied with their position and did not protest against the dominance of the male. He knew of none that did not rule unquestioned in her sphere nor of any that was not her husband's most valued councillor in his. He knew no Jewish

196

home in which the children were not brought up in equal obedience and respect for both parents and in which the equality of the parents in function, wisdom, worth, was not silently and fundamentally taken for granted. But that was not all. There was an indefinable element. As women grew older among Jews they were instinctively treated with a touch of unquestioning reverence as though they were the repositories of some special grace or wisdom. And this thing went so far that he had seen grave and learned men listen dutifully and even cheerfully to the inconsequential babble of old ladies, because these old ladies were their mothers. No, he couldn't explain it; he didn't know enough; he had to rely solely on instinct and casual observation. But he knew with the utmost certainty, just the same, that if he felt cheated in his marriage with Elizabeth, it wasn't because he wanted to be like the older generation of Anglo-Saxon men; he wanted to exercise neither the male arrogance combined with chivalry of the upper classes among them, nor the brutalities of the lower. But in any male resistance to her present theory or method Elizabeth immediately scented, with a touch of hot terror or rebellion, either the one attitude or the other.

5

IT was toward the end of their third summer. Elizabeth and the child had been visiting the Adamses, who had a large bungalow in Atlantic Highlands. Arthur had been kept in town by two patients who were afraid of interrupting their treatment. He could perhaps have soothed them and put them off. He didn't because there was no place for him to go. He had suggested to Elizabeth that they should buy a place in the hills or by the seashore. But Elizabeth had a terror of possessions, of material entanglements. She liked to feel free, unbound, unrooted. She felt at home everywhere and so had no need to localize the feeling of home. The problem of the summer was one of several unspoken problems between them. Places where people named Jones and people named Levy could dwell together in amity were rapidly disappearing from the land. Wherever the Levys came the Joneses withdrew. From their refuge to which they withdrew the Levys were sternly excluded. So the Joneses lived alone with their kind, and the Levys with theirs. Arthur had gathered, quite unintentionally, a little library of prospectuses of places of summer sojourn, in each of which it was stated, in forms of varying emphasis, that Hebrew guests were not wanted. . . . He couldn't possibly "see" Elizabeth in the hotel at Far Rockaway where his father and mother were old and happy and comfortable guests. He couldn't "see" her in any place to which they would have access. Had his name been Cone or Freefield—he smiled at the recollection of his sister's old miseries—he and Elizabeth might, as the Negroes put it, have "passed" in the summer. But the name of Levy is an indelible stamp. Just once the year before Elizabeth had said to Joanna Adams:

"I don't care, but I'd like to see them keep me out."

"Not if you register as Elizabeth Knight, of course," Joanna had answered.

Elizabeth, in one of her sudden adventurous moods, had taken the baby and his nurse and had gone to a fashionable hotel in the Adirondacks. The clerk had assured her that there was a suite vacant before she had registered. Afterward the manager had informed Mrs. Levy that a mistake had been made. The suite was bespoken. Would she forgive him for changing her quarters. She had been assigned a small, hot room over the kitchens. She had fled. It was Eugene Adams who had told Arthur of this incident. The two men had looked at each other. Then Adams had said, awkwardly: "It's a passing phase, a post-war reaction." Arthur had changed the subject. He disagreed wholly with Eugene. But he had no arguments. He had dropped in to see Joe Goldmann, a thing he rarely did in these later days, and had told him the story. Joe had chuckled.

"A hell of a passing phase. That passing phase has managed to turn up with the regularity of clockwork for a good bit over two thousand years. It's the contrary that is a passing phase when it occurs."

Arthur had barely listened to Joe's economic interpretation of the causes. "Look here, Joe," he had said, "you're always chasing some Gentile girl, just the same."

Joe's golden-brown eyes had their old quenchless melancholy. "The thorn is in my flesh. But they're not ladies. I'm not marrying one, you observe."

Now the heat of early September rose over the city like a burning tower and Elizabeth had written that she was coming home. She loved Joanna, but she was tired of 'Gene and of other guests who were in the bungalow. It was too bad for the baby, of course. She supposed it was hot in town. But she thought she would come home, just the same. It was, he supposed later, her casualness about the baby that had wounded and angered him. It was also a way she had of never telling him precisely when she was going or coming, as though she feared that exact knowledge on his part would assign to him a quality of authority. She called his solicitude "bossiness." With a smile. But the misunderstanding rankled.

She now came in, as was her wont, unexpectedly, with the child and its nurse on an evening of still, great heat. She kissed him lightly. "Ooh, isn't it just sticky!" He could not bring himself to answer. He went in and looked at his little son. The child was hot and fretting. He came back. Elizabeth had thrown her hat on the floor. She lay back in a chair and fanned herself with a newspaper.

"You can't keep John in town in this weather."

His tone stung her.

"Can't, Arthur? Well, suppose you provide a place for us."

"I've been anxious to build or buy a place. You haven't wanted me to."

"Because you know, yourself, it would be a nuisance."

Her tone was conciliatory now. There was nothing angry or ugly in Elizabeth. Only, it seemed to him, a little ultimate core of hardness that nothing could reach. It was he who burst through the repressions of the long months.

"It wouldn't be a nuisance if you had any time for your duties as a wife and a mother instead of scribbling inutilities. I want both a house in town and a house in the country. I'm sick to the soul of this casual existence and these silly parties and these everlasting engagements. I'm amazed that John has pulled through as well as he has. I love you as much as ever, Elizabeth, but I feel with the utmost seriousness that you are not a wife to me at all."

She drew herself up. Her eyes were very dark. "The old Adam."

He raised his hand in protest.

She nodded. "You're right, Arthur. This is really our first quarrel, isn't it? But of course I've seen how you've held in. You are nice. There's no doubt about that. And I'm dreadfully sorry. But I can't do what you want me to do."

"Why not?"

"I'm not fit for it and all my instincts rebel against it. If I gave up my work and just kept house for you and took care of John, I should feel unutterably useless and degraded."

He was walking up and down. "Then why did you marry at all?"

"Can't a woman have a love-life without becoming so disgustingly domesticated?"

"Love-life!" He couldn't keep the irony out of his voice. "It's precisely because you have no real love-life that the normal instincts of womanhood don't function in you. I personally have no warmer desire than to become domesticated. I want a home with all the responsibilities that it entails. I want another child—"

She jumped up. "And if I give up my work and my connections and my friends—I know you've never really liked them—and spend myself on taking care of a house or two and children, what will become of us?"

"I don't understand you, Elizabeth."

"Do you expect me to be satisfied with the society of the Goldmanns and the Bergmanns and of some of your—ugh—colleagues and their wives?"

"Jewish colleagues, you meant to say."

"No, I didn't, Arthur. I give you my word. At least it wasn't in any derogatory sense."

He bit his lips. There was no use going on with that question. It opened abysses unexplored, deliberately unexplored by himself. He stopped. He took her hand.

"Are you happy, Elizabeth?"

Tears came into her eyes. She shook her head.

"Then why not try my plan of living?"

"Because it would mean becoming more hopelessly involved." Her voice was hard and yet sorrowful.

"What is lacking between us, Elizabeth?"

She withdrew her hand.

"Nothing." She laughed a pathetic, weary little laugh. "Everything. I don't know." She walked to the window. "You'd better send baby and his nurse to your mother at Far Rockaway. She'll be very good to him. I think I'll run away for a week and see Dad. Do you mind?"

"Of course not, Elizabeth. But what then, what afterward?"

"I don't know. I can't tell. You're always generous, Arthur. Leave it just so. Will you?"

He assented. Next morning he telephoned to his mother, who immediately came into the city to fetch her grandchild. By the time Mrs. Levy arrived Elizabeth was already gone. Mother and son avoided any confidences.

"You look tired, sonny. Why don't you run over to Boston? Hazel and Eli have always wanted you to visit them. And they have a fine house and a beautiful car."

"I believe I will," he said, passing his hand over his forehead. "I need a change."

6

THE Sinzheimers lived on a sunny street in Brookline. It was a new street and all the houses in the street were new and handsome and had magnificent mechanical equipment of all sorts and large concrete garages. The trees were young and small and gave no shade, and the concrete sidewalks had no cracks, and the awnings over the verandahs were striped blue and white or orange and white and looked as though they had been bought yesterday, and the patches of well-sprinkled lawn were emerald-green even in this September weather. Each house in the street was a little different in shape from every other. But it was clear to any observer that this outward variety concealed an inner sameness. But that sameness could not be helped because perfection in a special kind is perfection and cannot be changed without becoming less than itself.

Arthur was amazed at the eager joyfulness of his reception. His brother-in-law called for him in his new Apperson car and bubbled with enthusiasm about the car and business and his house and Arthur's scientific distinction and new phonograph records and the brilliancy of Lenore, his and Hazel's only child. Hazel, he said, looked magnificent and was lovelier than ever, but he wasn't a bit satisfied with her nervous health, and for that reason, in addition to all the others, he was delighted to see Arthur. He wanted to do something definite for Hazel. Money was no object. He had cleaned up fifty thousand dollars the previous year in spite of the fact that he had been "stuck" with a large number of women's high shoes, which had gone out of fashion with a completeness that he had not seen equalled. Under all this brave talk Arthur perceived clearly a want of ease and of inner peace, and this perception grew stronger as Eli launched out into the more or less inevitable bragging about the excellence and the reliability of his bootlegger and the "slickness" with which, if you could pay the price, real Scotch from Canada was made to flood New England. . . .

They drew up before the spick and span house and there Hazel stood on the verandah, lovely, as Eli had said, though a little matronly in her contours. But what was gone from her wholly was the tenseness, the something fine and blade-like, which had characterized her girlhood. She embraced Arthur and tears came to her eyes. She struggled with a sob and Eli looked significantly at his brother-in-law. She drew forward her little girl, a dark, beautiful, glowing, very

Jewish-looking child with clear wise eyes. And the child, too, seemed inordinately glad to see her uncle from New York and clung to him with a quiet affection from the first.

Arthur rested and dressed in his airy guest-room with its mahogany furnishings, including a four-poster bed and the charming hooked-rugs on the highly polished floors. The room was a model of all the elegant standardized amenities of modern American life. No last descendant of a Back Bay family could have found a false note either here or in the rest of the house. Arthur became aware of this as, just before dinner, Eli insisted on taking him through all the rooms. Around the walls of Lenore's sweet white room was a Maxfield Parrish frieze; Eli and Hazel had adjoining rooms discreetly and exquisitely furnished and decorated; the bathroom was a marvel; the living-rooms downstairs had spaciousness and dignity; the objects in them were well chosen and not too many. And the entire house had, despite its unemphatic luxury, a touch of austerity and simplicity that blended in with the New England tradition. It was, in brief, a Boston house, and through it, in this mild weather, there went a breath of desolation that blew upon Arthur like a harsh wind from some outer space beyond the habitations of men. . . . The objects of wood and fabric in this house were stiff and recalcitrant to the people who lived here. They had not been broken into any love or even familiarity. No relation had existed and none had been established. The house, so full of life, was an empty house. . . . The Sinzheimers camped here. They had no home; their child had no home. . . .

Dinner began with chilled grapefruit. The silver was Colonial. A neat Irish maid passed softly in and out. Conversation was formal and hesitant. Everything was icily correct and dead. Chicken. French ice-cream. Salted almonds. The food was rather tasteless and rather meager. Both Eli and Hazel had a tendency toward plumpness; so had little Lenore. They all ate this flat American food without pleasure; they seemed impelled by a sense of duty. . . . Once, when the maid was out of the room, Hazel told Arthur that her husband would go every now and then to his mother's house to eat. She couldn't stand those greasy, old-fashioned messes herself. They were so frightfully fattening, anyhow. She had a terrible time preventing Lenore from sneaking over to her grandmother's house and being stuffed with pastry. . . . . All the while she looked critically at her dry bit of roast chicken. And so Arthur knew that poor Hazel suffered perpetual hunger for the sake of her American conformity and an American silhouette.

After dinner they gathered in the drawing-room and Eli played a Wagnerian record on the Victrola, and then a great violinist's performance of the "Kol Nidre," and for a few minutes a human warmth came into the room. But when the instrument was silent that warmth faded again, and suddenly—Arthur never remembered how the subject was broached—they were talking about the more and more intense anti-Jewish feeling in Boston. They had no Gentile friends; their neighbors on both sides ignored their existence. When little Lenore went out into the street the mothers of the other little boys and girls on the block immediately called their children in. It was terrible. Arthur asked Eli whether his parents felt the same way. Eli smiled. "Well, no. They live in what is virtually a ghetto and father is president of a congregation and they have a swell time." Suddenly there was something handsome and natural about the man. "They have magnificent Passover celebrations and guests every Friday evening, and Dad still fasts and weeps on the Day of Atonement. They don't give a damn. But" —his voice grew small and cramped—"that's nothing for Hazel and me. I've sometimes thought that it mightn't be a bad thing for Hazel to join the Council of Jewish Women; she might meet some very fine people there. But Hazel has her own ideas on the subject."

Arthur turned to his sister. A pained, dissatisfied, struggling expression was on her face. She was simply inhibited on that subject. Something subtle and terrible of which Arthur was unaware must have happened to her in her childhood or infancy. She had so shattering and crushing and tragic a Jewish inferiority complex that she could not sustain her life psychically at all without nursing a strong sense of superiority to some one, without despising some one. And the only people whom she dared to despise were her own people. Thus, Jewish to the core by every instinct, she lived in misery and loneliness and dread and clung to life and sanity on these tragic terms by despising all that she yearned for, all that she needed. . . . The old story, Arthur thought. A psychic hurt and then flight from reality, flight from that reality through which the hurt had come. A kind of madness. Like all flights from reality. . . . Gently he asked Hazel why she felt as she did.

"I don't like Jews; I want to bring up my child as an American. All that doesn't mean anything to me."

Eli looked sad. "You see how it is, Arthur. I don't know that I blame Hazel. But it doesn't make life very pleasant. I've thought of moving to New York. But I really can't do it. The shoe business is here and it's here to stay."

Once more Hazel asked after Elizabeth. She had done so at once, of course, when she had seen Arthur. He had made a conventional reply. Now he got up and went over to Hazel.

"I'm not at all sure that Elizabeth and I will go on living together."

"Why, Arthur, I'm shocked! I've so wanted to meet her and know her."

Eli looked concerned. "What's wrong?"

"Nothing," Arthur said. He felt a sudden sense of liberation. "Nothing except that she's a Gentile and I am a Jew. We're fond of each other and we understand each other intellectually, but at the emotional basis of life there is—no, no opposition—there's a divergence. You've heard of the parallel lines that can never meet? It isn't very clear to me yet—the whole thing; I haven't probed it. But I feel as though I'd never been married at all. Maybe I'm wrong and it's just because Elizabeth is a very modern woman and I am, by instincts, an old-fashioned man. But I don't think

205

that that explanation suffices. There's something deeper. Elizabeth has, in my special sense which I'm forced to believe a Jewish sense, no heart. Mind you, only in that sense. She's a splendid woman and I hope she finds her true happiness sooner or later."

Eli got up. "How about your boy, Arthur?"

Arthur lowered his head and he felt the corners of his lids burning. "I don't know . . . I don't know."

They gathered about him after that first evening, his sister and his brother and even their child, as though to protect him from the blows of untoward circumstance. Something streamed from them that was deeper than affection. An immemorial solidarity? Creatures always exposed to the storms of earth and having to cling together for protection? He could not tell. He only knew it warmed him—this attitude of his kinspeople—warmed him and cleared his brain. It warmed them, too, in their desolateness. They begged him to stay another day and another. But patients were clamoring in New York and he had a wistful tragic longing for Elizabeth—a longing like the longing one feels for autumn, for leave-takings, for the end of a feast in its midst, for night at high noon, for the ache of loneliness. . . .

7

ELIZABETH was already at home when he returned. She seemed rested and softened. She clung to him for a moment when they met and he blamed himself for feeling even in that clinging the presage of farewell. The child was still in Far Rockaway and so Arthur and Elizabeth were alone together as they had been during the early days of their union. The memories of those early days were here to haunt them with their pathos in the bright, tense, perishing autumnal days. . . . They had dinners out and Elizabeth told Arthur of the renewed impressions she had received of the countryside and the people of her childhood. She thought she would like to spend a rather quiet winter and try to do a novel, a slightly new kind of novel for a contemporary

American of their set. Not a book of implicit and explicit criticism and protest, but a sort of idyll, recounting those simple lives of the Protestant farmers from within, from their own point of view. The center and pivot of the story would be a full-length portrait of a man like her father. She lifted her head in that proud, sweet, girlish way which had never lost its magic for Arthur and said:

"Dad was too dear and pathetic for words. He asked me whether you and I were quite happy. I told him that I was afraid that I wasn't altogether the right kind of a wife for you. Do you know what he answered?" Arthur shook his head. " 'You must try to obey and please your husband in every way—especially in this case.' I was curious and asked: 'Why especially in this case?' 'Because,' Dad said—and you should have seen the utter innocence and conviction in his eyes—'because you might bring him to Christ.' " She played with a spoon in front of her and looked down at the table. "Does that seem very ridiculous to you?"

"Not at all. It was beautifully in character, of course."

She looked up. "Isn't life funny? Father is quite Christ-like. So, in the sense of patience and kindness and not judging, are you. Oh yes, you are! It came all over me—I hadn't seen Dad in three years, you know—how alike you and he are. It's conviction with him and instinct with you. I'm the rebel and the pagan. But I can't help it."

They were silent for a while. He put his hand over hers.

"What are we going to do, Elizabeth?"

"Don't know yet, darling. Do you mind this uncertainty terribly? Of course, it depends a little or, rather, more than a little, on you."

He withdrew his hand. "It's not for me to be impatient or intolerant, Elizabeth. I only know that I seem to be living in a void. And it seems to me more and more as though many Jews are living in a void. Now what they do is to settle down and establish a real home in the quite old-fashioned sense and cling to that and so shut out the sense of emptiness and of not belonging anywhere. I have the same impulse, but it seems that this complete settling down is repugnant to your instincts. You don't need it. You're not living in a void. You belong somewhere and in fact everywhere. Even if you forced yourself to do outwardly as I wish, I doubt whether that would solve the problem. I'm on the edge of perceptions that I dare not admit even to myself. They are so extreme that you would laugh at them. They are so extreme that my father and mother would think that I'd lost my mind; my Jewish colleagues would be quite sure of it. So, you see, I have no more certitude than you have. I have less, in fact, far less. Who am I to be impatient?"

She looked at him earnestly. "I'm a fairly intelligent human being, Arthur. Why don't you tell me what's really in your mind?"

"I will as soon as it is clear and so articulate. Today it isn't. I don't know enough. I'd like to spend a quiet winter, too, and take up some studies that have nothing to do with either medicine or psychiatry. But I want to raise a practical problem that cuts into the root of the matter: How are we going to bring up John?"

She nodded. "Dad raised the same question. But I put him off. He is afraid, of course, that John's soul won't be saved. Well, we're not."

"I am." He saw her utterly astonished look. "You're saved, Elizabeth, because you live in a stream of tradition that is native to you. The stream changes. You don't believe what your father believes. The intellectual processes and assents are different. But the stream is the same. You are an American Protestant. Your divergences from your ancestors are normal divergences within the native tradition of your race and blood and historic experience. But I and many like me have tried to live as though we were American Protestants or, at least, the next best thing to that. And we're not. And the real American Protestants know we're not. And so we live in a void, in a spiritual vacuum. The devil of it is we don't know exactly what we are. Now, to come back to John. I'd be perfectly willing to have him brought up as a partaker in your tradition and have him feel at home in his country and its life as a Protestant American. But I can't help to bring him up that way. And, what's worse, his name *is* Levy and the more of a Protestant American he were in his heart and soul the more disastrous to him would be the things which in a Protestant American civilization are bound to happen to someòne named Levy. I don't see all that clearly enough yet. But I see it."

Her eyes were wide. "I think I see what you mean, Arthur. But don't you think you overestimate the prejudice?"

"No, I'm afraid not. Your international literary crowd in New York is no criterion."

A look of fear, instinctive and unavertable, came into Elizabeth's eyes. "You don't mean to say, Arthur, that you would think of having John brought up as a religious Jew?"

He did not answer at once.

"Tell me, Arthur," she repeated. "Is that what you mean?"

"I'm not prepared to go as far as that. I told you that I was only on the edge of perceptions. But your instinctive terror at the very thought is enormously instructive."

She drew herself up. "It's all a nightmare. Can't we all just be human?"

Arthur smiled. "What is it to be human? Nothing abstract. Show me a human being who isn't outwardly and inwardly some *kind* of a human being, dependent, though he were the most austere philosopher, in his human life on others of more or less the same *kind*. There is no place of *kindless* people in the world. And if you established a colony of extra-religious and supra-national philosophers and sages, male and female, their extra-religiousness and supra-nationalism would establish their kind and their inner kinship, and, far from having broken up the families of mankind, we would have added but another family—a magnificent one, I grant you—to those that already exist. In a word, this vague cry, let us be human—it's a favorite cry among Jews—means nothing and gets you nowhere."

Elizabeth smiled. "How brilliant you are, Arthur. You ought to write something about that. It would make a gorgeous article."

They laughed together.

"You know I don't write. And, anyhow, what good would that do John?"

"Poor little John," she teased. "Don't let's be so solemn and intellectual about it all. I have a notion that it will all take care of itself in some natural way. As Dad always says, God is good."

A few days later the elder Levys returned to the city and the child with its nurse came home. The summer had done the little fellow good. He was sturdier and more vivid. He looked more and more like Hazel. His nose was almost as straight as Elizabeth's. But he was, in coloring and expression, a Jewish child. He had never been continuously with his grandparents before. He had taken a tremendous fancy to them. He wanted his grandpa and his grandma. Elizabeth said with a tang of bitterness:

"Of course he's spoiled. Your mother bettied around after him all day long. I can't quite do that." John was on Arthur's lap. Elizabeth looked at them. "I suppose you think that's what I ought to do."

"No, I don't think *you* ought to do it."

"Which is to say that you wish John had a mother who would and could and wanted to."

Arthur put the child down. "It isn't like you, Elizabeth, to try to pick that sort of a female quarrel."

"I suppose not. But don't be so terribly superior. I must say, Arthur, I do think that that is a Jewish characteristic. It's probably an excellent thing for John that the world doesn't rotate about him when he's at home. Run along to nurse, John. No, you must obey mother. Run along. You see, Arthur, he's very nearly unmanageable." Her face was slightly red.

"What's irritated you so, Elizabeth?" Arthur asked, quietly.

"I don't know. I'm sorry."

"Is it that John struck you as looking particularly Jewish today?"

She tugged at a little handkerchief which she was holding. "I think you're trying to goad and nag today, Arthur. That isn't like you, either. The best thing for me to do will be to go out. Don't wait dinner for me. I'll be late."

He sat beside the child's crib until late that night. He sent the nurse to bed and watched the sleeping child hour after hour.

He did not think; he did not reason. Neither can it be said that he indulged in vivid emotion. He brooded over the child, over himself. He recalled his own childhood and boyhood and its difficulties and he wondered how this boy of his would adjust himself, by what inner means of adaptation or resistance he would adjust himself to a hostile and complicated world. . . . He remembered his own clinging to his father's house, later to streets and squares. John did not even have a house to cling to, only an apartment, an office, a passageway. . . . But perhaps he would not need that sense of protection and refuge; perhaps, like his mother, he would be at home in the world. . . . At home in the world . . . at home in the world. . . . How did one achieve that? His father and mother had it upon some terms that Arthur could not quite make clear to himself. His generation had lost it—he and Hazel and Joe; and even Eugene and Joanna only persuaded themselves and feigned to themselves to have it by a specific kind of refuge in a small and unique society. . . . Where would be the spiritual dwelling-place of his boy? . . . He heard the latch click. Elizabeth was coming. He was glad that she had a little trouble with the key. It gave him time to slip unobserved into his own bedroom. . . .

BOOK VIII

1

THE winter of 1921-22 was the quietest that Arthur and
Elizabeth had spent together. Elizabeth was working on her
novel. She worked in the evenings and often late into the
night. Eugene Adams, whose publishing-house had become
one of the most notable in America, encouraged her, begged
her to drop all other work, and told her jestingly to draw on
him for money if Arthur was stingy. Arthur, closely ex-
amining his conscience, discovered that he would be genu-
inely pleased if Elizabeth were to be as successful as Eugene
hoped and believed. What was it, then, that irritated and
chilled him during those long evenings on which his wife
was working? Had he not asked for quietude? Had he not
wanted time to contemplate himself and his world? It
would not be the result of Elizabeth's labor that would
annoy him; no, it was the process, it was the labor itself.
First his home had been a gate and a roadway. Now it was a
workshop. But was it not his workshop, too? That is what
Elizabeth would immediately and crushingly have replied.
Very true. Had the thing anything to do with marriage or
with the fact that Elizabeth was a woman and he a man?
Perhaps not. Perhaps no two people could comfortably
work so closely side by side, the weather and tempo and
aims of whose minds and tempers were so different. Two
friends, wholly independent of each other, might leave such
a situation still tolerable. But married people were not independent of each other and could not be. Even in the
loosest and most modern union, if there had ever been any
deep feeling, an emotional interdependence had been established. Fine psychical threads led from one to the other.
Fine but firm. One or the other could tug at these threads.
Arthur came to the conclusion that for his home and for his
work he needed either a wife in the traditional sense or no
one. A working colleague in the house, and a working colleague, above all, on whom his emotions and his nerves were
dependent—ah, that was another matter. He sat there and
the door between the rooms was open and the slight scrib-

ble of Elizabeth's pen or the rustle of her movements or her sigh constituted a continuous small rumor that brought him a sense of her absorption and detachment. Was he not, when engaged in his scientific work, equally absorbed and detached? No, not equally detached. His heart was more vigilant. It might not always be speaking; it was never asleep. He worked for the sake, first of science, secondly of his wife and child, thirdly to satisfy the pride of his parents. He never worked for the sake of what Elizabeth called ambition. Not that she was not a conscientious and deeply feeling craftswoman. But what impelled her ultimately, impelled her even to perfect herself in her craft, was neither the craft itself nor any human love or kinship, but something which it would be harsh to call mere self-assertion, but which had in it an element of mere vanity in the sense that it was utterly unaware of the vanity of things. What ailed Elizabeth, as it ailed many women of her type and precise period, was not wholly unlike the thing that ailed so many Jews. She had an inferiority complex as a woman. She needed to compensate. She must vote, write, succeed, be active—never permit herself to lapse for a moment into the immemorial moods and occupations of her sex. She was not racially or historically used to this feeling. It made her hard. Jews were so used to it that the hardness it induced was tempered. They might be ruthless to competitors; they did not forget father and mother and wife and child. Because beneath their hardness was an old, old knowledge of the ultimate vanity of all things except a few fundamental and very simple human things. No, Arthur was quite sure that he was not jealous of Elizabeth's work as work. He was simply aware of the fact that her work shut him out— him and the child—and that his work never shut her out. Thence arose an unnatural inequality, a fatal disturbance of the necessary equilibrium of life. . . . He sat there with his nerves ever so slightly on edge. But when, her evening's work done, she came in to see him for a while, he gave no sign of the exact character of his thoughts and feelings, because he knew that to do so would change nothing and only irritate her and perhaps impede her work. . . . There is no use in demanding what is not given one freely. Pressure never produces a gift, only a tribute. . . .

He himself had ordered for the evenings of this winter some books on Jewish subjects. He had done so with a curious touch of inner shame. It was shame partly of his own ignorance. He had looked over book catalogues and ordered almost at random. He wanted to know, and yet felt, deeply ingrained in him by all the forces of his environment, a doubt whether there was anything profoundly worth knowing. He passed over the few books he saw that dealt with Talmudic lore. That, of course, was mere unhistorical and unscientific trash. Worse than mediæval. It never occurred to him to reëxamine the Old Testament. It was hopelessly connected in his mind with—*kosher* cooking, not a bad thing hygienically, perhaps, but unimportant. He finally selected the English translation of Graetz's *History of the Jews*. He found the heavy red volumes—physically heavy and unmanageable—hard reading. A German professorial style of the worst type, he thought, graceless and unctuous at the same time. The book also seemed to him confused in narrative structure. So little, it seemed to him, was known of the earlier periods and Graetz tried to make that little big and important with mountains of words. Gleams came to him from the later volumes, gleams of a dim grandeur. But nothing took on life or meaning. Old, unhappy, far-off things. . . . He hadn't even read Zangwill hitherto. He now read the amusing Ghetto stories, but he was afraid that his amusement had in it an element of condescension. Then he read the same writer's book *Dreamers of the Ghetto* and, though he perceived that it was romantic and had touches of both rhetoric and pretentiousness, yet he got at last the sense of something greatly and richly alive. So there had been Jewish heroes and philosophers and saints in the more recent centuries? So that was the countenance of Uriel Acosta and such the legend of the founder of the despised *Chassidim?* . . . He remembered how once, many years ago, his father had told a story of his early days and had said contemptuously: "Dere vas a little town dere, full of *Chassidim*. . . ." Arthur, who was then a child, had taken it for granted that these were poor and degraded people of some outlandish locality. . . . He now saw that, faintly enough, his father was the bearer of a great tradition, the tradition of a long and profound battle over what did in truth constitute the spiritual life of mankind—a battle with its martyrs and saints and legends and gospels. And all that had happened no longer ago than the middle of the eighteenth century. . . . And Arthur wondered whether any of his own ancestors had met the Master of the Name. . . . An ancestor of Elizabeth's father had fled and preached and been wounded by the stones of villagers in the early days of John and Charles Wesley. . . . Was it sentimental to feel, as he had felt more and more, the ache of kinlessness and kindlessness? But he had seen the security and, yes, the human dignity, that a tradition lent to the freest minds. There had been Dawson with his Scotch tradition; there was Elizabeth with hers. She wasn't a Methodist, of course. Her immediate ancestors had even left that particular communion. But she was rooted; she continued something alive; she had something to rebel against. To rebel with pain. The rebellion still cost her something; it still had a touch of the heroic, for what she rebelled against was her father's faith and the tradition in her blood. . . . Jews of his generation had nothing even left to rebel against. Oh, it was easy enough for them to join the Christian rebels. And no doubt they thus fulfilled a very useful function. But what they rebelled against was not their own and hence there was no true virtue in their acts. . . . They were terribly poverty-stricken, the Jewish men and women of thirty. . . . Unconsciously they clung and allied themselves to anything Jewish in the world or anything that seemed of Jewish origin: the new psychotherapeutics, like himself, the doctrine of salvation through economic reorganization like Joe Goldmann. . . . Neither he nor Joe had been conscious of the fact that his choice of a profession and a philosophy had been a Jewish choice or, rather, a profoundly human choice in that it is human to share the vision and the appetences of one's own kind. . . . Of course. And the mentalities of Marx and Freud were, after all, Jewish mentalities. . . . Following this strain of thought one got into deep waters. . . . The ultimate conclusion was that Jews like himself who denied any tradition or character of their own were really trying to do a thing that was unhuman, that no one else was trying to do. . . . No one. . . . Not the freest minds. Not the most exalted. . . . Men like Bertrand Russell and Henri Barbusse were pacifists and internationalists and revolutionaries, political and moral, and on a merely conceptual basis one might express their fundamental thoughts in the same formulæ. But those formulæ would be mathematical, unpersuasive, stripped and dead. What made these men splendid and prophetic was the flesh, blood, substance of their work and vision and these were everlastingly English in the one case, indescribably French in the other. And just as the artist must express himself through some medium—words, sounds, paint, marble—even so in the larger sense human expression is effected through the medium of some national culture. . . . There is no expression in a void. . . . But was not the assumption of his friends, Arthur reflected, that they were Americans? . . . Elizabeth came in, as usual, after her work, as he had been passionately struggling with these thoughts. He took her unawares:

"Elizabeth, am I an American?"

She was still warm and preoccupied with her work. She wiped an inky finger on her hair. "What did you say? Are you an American? No, of course not." She wandered about the room. Suddenly she stopped. "What were we talking about, Arthur? I really was not thinking. I was full of my story. It's going fine. Did you ask me whether you were an American?"

"Yes."

"What a quaint question! And did I say you weren't?"

"You did."

"Oh well, I wasn't thinking. Certainly you are. Oh, but I'm tired. I'll drop right to sleep. Good night."

2

IMMEDIATELY he had no more time either to read or to reflect. New patients announced themselves daily. They were all Jews and Jewesses of the younger generation. A young woman who loved her husband passionately but was utterly unable to respond to him. . . . A young man who had started out to be a not unpromising writer and had suddenly been no longer able to compose an intelligible sentence. . . . A somewhat older man very near despair and suicide through the dry-rot of a hopeless marriage and so inhibited by the conventional American notions of marriage (which no longer had any force among liberal Americans) that he hoped for a word of liberation and release from a psychiatrist of his own race. . . . A girl who hated her mother and yet, being an only child, was riveted to that mother by a chain of compassion. . . . In each of these cases Arthur saw or thought he saw at once the specifically Jewish element: a Gentile fixation, the breakdown of a compensatory mechanism that corresponded to no native gift, the terror of an alien law and morality, the problem of the social isolation of Jews who didn't want to be Jews. . . . He worked with his patients nearly all day. He spent many evenings at the house of his parents, whither he had been summoned to help in a painful and disastrous complication.

Suddenly, on a dark day in the middle of winter, Hazel and her little daughter had arrived unannounced at her parents' house. She had asked in a choked voice whether her father and mother would take her in—her and her poor child. She was never going back to Boston. She had left her bags and her small daughter downstairs and had rushed up to her old room and gone to bed and drawn the coverlet over her face. Mrs. Levy had carefully not tried to get information out of her little granddaughter, whose dark, sad, prematurely wise glances followed her movements. She had waited and had then gone up to Hazel and sat down beside her on the bed. Hazel had held herself rigid, and compressed her lips till nothing but a thin white line showed her mouth. Thus she had lain for hours, and Mrs. Levy, helpless and at last frightened, had telephoned for Arthur. He had at once recognized the fact that his sister was deliberately and volitionally heightening half-hysterical symptoms in order to be protected against the necessity for explanation, against the responsibility involved in the step which she had taken and concerning which doubts were already gnawing at her mind. He quietly told her that he saw through her manœuvre without in the least blaming her for it, that it was a frequent and natural refuge for sensitive and impulsive women; he begged her to try to relax and talk and be sensible since, whatever the state of affairs, she had nothing to fear from anyone. He would personally promise her that no one would blame her. She sat up suddenly. Her eyes were wild, her hair streamed. She clenched her hands. A torrent of words came from her. Blamed? Oh, she didn't think she would or could be blamed. And she would rather beg in the streets than be sent back home. Home? It was no home of hers. That horrible house in which she had sat alone evening after evening—utterly alone after she had put the child to bed. Eli had had business engagements downtown. He had taken the car—she couldn't even have that—and had gone off. As if the day weren't long enough for business. But at first she had believed him that he had to meet buyers at dinner and give dinners to buyers and show them the city. Suddenly, however, she had felt a knife entering her very heart. She didn't know why. On an impulse she had called up the Copley Plaza hotel where Eli had said that he was dining with some men. He had been there, too, oh yes, but his voice had been tipsy and she could not help hearing faintly but distinctly the ribald laughter of women. . . . He had come home and had explained. Two buyers from the Middle West had had women with them. Their wives? No. That's why he hadn't asked her to come. These men had a habit of picking up fancy ladies and registering with them as their wives. Well, she had wanted to know whether he was so poor as to have to associate with such people on such terms. He had said that business was not so good as last year and that these men bought merchandise to the extent of many thousands of dollars for big department stores. Anyhow, he had asserted that all the manufacturers and big jobbers did the same thing. His father couldn't do it and he was the only other member of the firm. Now Hazel wept. She had believed him, fool that she had been, she had believed him. But last Saturday night he had again come home late. Late? Oh, at three o'clock in the morning. Naturally he had been snoring Sunday until noon. And she had gone around to the garage for the car to have a little spin with Lenore. And in the car, right on the seat, there had been a woman's vanity bag—an enormous, evil smelling vanity bag, soaked with patchouli, containing a huge lip-stick and a powder-puff and a—a—no, she couldn't bring herself to name the name of such an object. She had rushed home and shaken Eli and held up the evidence of her betrayal and his shame. He had said: "Oh, go to the devil!" She had packed her bags quietly and taken her child and caught the first train to New York. Here she was. If they didn't want her, she would go into the streets with her child. That was a decenter place than the house in Boston. She fell back among her pillows and hid her face and sobbed.

Arthur and his mother exchanged glances and left the room together. They went downstairs.

"What do you think, sonny?"

"It's not so simple as Hazel tries to make out."

"Do you think that Eli was unfaithful to her?"

"It's possible." He saw his mother's face grow tense and pale. "Don't take it so hard." He put his arm about her shoulder. "The important thing is not whether he was unfaithful to her, but why."

Mrs. Levy smiled wanly. "You with your modern scientific notions! Did you notice anything wrong when you were in Boston last summer?"

Arthur nodded. "Not this kind of thing. But I think we should hear Eli's side. I'm pretty sure he'll be heard from. In the meantime tell Papa I advise him not to be indignant. Just let the whole thing slide for a day or two and treat her simply and naturally. She's hysterical, of course."

He was summoned again that night. His father had evidently not heeded the warning and Hazel was violently hysterical. He gave her a strong sedative. He warned his father to treat the girl gently.

"Vy dese shameful doings? In de first place I don't believe it ent in de secont place vy not vait ent talk ent see. It isn't de first time in de history of de vorld, you know. I don't want a divorce in my femily. A Chewish divorce, like in de old times—all right. But a scandal in dese *goyish* courts ent papers. No." Arthur asked him to have patience. Things would probably reach no such extreme. Eli would be heard from.

Sinzheimer was, in fact, heard from two days later. He telephoned from the Grand Central Station, saying that he would be at the house that evening and specifically asking that Arthur be present. Arthur's mother immediately informed him and added that Hazel declared she would meet her husband under no circumstances. He dismissed his last patient early and told Elizabeth the character of his errand. She said: "Poor girl. But why carry on so? She can divorce him and you people all have lots of money."

It took Arthur nearly an hour to persuade Hazel that as a matter both of duty and of justice she must see her husband. He had finally to be curt.

"If you don't I shall be more convinced than ever that in the last analysis it's your fault."

She sneered: "Your lovely old habit of siding with everybody against me."

They waited for Eli in the dining-room. No one had really eaten. The bell rang and in a moment Sinzheimer appeared. He looked crestfallen and determined at the same time. He tried to kiss Hazel. Indignantly she turned from him. He shook hands with his mother-in-law and Arthur. Mr. Levy's face was gray and forbidding. Eli sat down and sighed and muttered irritatedly to himself. Arthur gave him a cigar and lit one himself.

223

"Let's not be too terribly solemn. Tell us, if you want to, what's on your mind, Eli."

Sinzheimer struggled for words. The expression of subtleties was not, as he would have said, in his line. He burst out: "I don't think that Hazel was properly brought up."

Mr. Levy's face grew a little red. Arthur saved the moment.

"None of us were," he said with finality.

Sinzheimer looked at him gratefully. "Anyhow," he went on, "I've made up my mind not to say whether what Hazel thinks is true or not. I don't even think it's anybody's business whether I always went to dine at the Copley Plaza on business or not. You see? But I will say this: I've been lonely and miserable and driven to things I don't like and don't approve of. And I don't think Hazel has had any too good a time, herself. Well, she can divorce me if she likes. I love her just the same. But there's no use our trying to live together unless Hazel agrees to sell the house in Brookline and move to a Jewish neighborhood and associate with my friends and—and—have some more children—I'd like a son—and—and oh well, be a Jewish wife same as her mother or mine. That's all. If she'll do that, I'll promise that she'll never have anything to complain of again. Never. I love her."

His voice broke a little. He sucked manfully at his cigar. They all turned to Hazel. She looked small and girlish. Eli walked over to her and put his arm around her and she rubbed her cheek against his coat.

"And I want my children to be brought up as observant Jews, same as I was, no matter what they believe. I don't believe much myself." Suddenly they all melted toward one another and drew together around the table, and Mr. Levy went downstairs into the basement for one of his last bottles of pre-war Rhine wine. Hazel snuggled against her husband. When the glasses were filled she stopped a moment before clinking her own to Eli's. "But we'll join a nice congregation, won't we? I don't like these Russians and Poles."

3

A faint fear stole into Arthur's heart. He found himself surreptitiously touching objects on his desk with the half-conscious intention of warding off ill-luck. It was amusing that he, of all people, should nurse a compulsion neurosis. He must break himself of it promptly. The causes of his difficulty were not far to seek. He and Elizabeth had become friends. Since he no longer even by a gesture, even by a waiting attitude, asked her to be his wife, their relations had become less strained and more natural. Another man might have sought that specific consolation elsewhere. It didn't seem to Arthur that he wanted to do that. Society was so constituted that if you lived with one woman and had relations with another, that second relationship was certain to be tinged with vulgarity, with something hard and ugly and surreptitious both from within and from without. The thing had nothing to do with legality, but with the subtler, including the interior sources of social control. Legality didn't matter and divorce didn't matter. Fidelity, as a free act, did matter. One man living with one woman, the right man with the right woman—that was the only thing. At least for him. He knew too much about the inconceivable complications in contemporary life to judge anyone. But he knew, too, from the miseries of his patients, that a good deal of suffering and disease could be avoided if people would respect legal marriage less and harmonious mating more. Especially Jews. For Jews had nothing in their blood and tradition with which inwardly to consent to the Christian notion of marriage as a sacrament; hence they were never resigned. They pretended to be Americans, but they could never, just the same, bring themselves to see why they couldn't get divorces quietly and for the asking.... Always the same thing. . . . Always the same discoveries in whatever direction. . . . It was the same thing with Prohibition. Oh, Gentiles didn't like it, either, and many thousands broke the law and many of the more enlightened resisted it, whether they broke it or not. But even in this breaking and resistance there was understanding. Jews, whatever they might pretend, were quite blank in the face of the whole thing. They had to say to themselves deliberately: Alcohol *has* been a danger . . . the barroom *was* an evil thing for the American people. It is necessary to realize that to understand. . . . But it was an external and alien matter. Neither alcohol nor the barroom had ever been a danger to them. There were no memories of drunkenness in their families, no tradition of So-and-so having been ruined by drink. . . . Arthur would violently have repudiated the notion that Jews were better than other people. . . . Of course they weren't. But they were different and a thousand ills arose for them from not living clear-eyed within that immemorial differentness of theirs. . . . He couldn't, at all events, see himself being untrue to Elizabeth so long as socially and morally they were man and wife. Elizabeth, he knew, took a quite different view of the matter. Things being as they were, she wouldn't have blamed him at all for having an affair of some kind. She hated the thought of divorce. . . . She rather resented Arthur's faithfulness. . . .

He was pulled out of these preoccupations by an occurrence of an obscure and tragic sort. A rather restrained paragraph in the *World* stabbed him one morning at breakfast with the information that the brilliant young architect, Victor Goldmann, had committed suicide the night before. He had left his studio on Fifty-ninth Street at nine o'clock in the evening. The colored elevator boy had seen him and remarked nothing unusual in his demeanor. At nine-forty he had appeared at the house of his father, Mr. Nathan Goldmann. He had seemed rather absent-minded then and had a little surprised the family by saying that his studio was noisy; he could get no sleep. He had been urged to go upstairs to one of the bedrooms in the house and rest. He had gone to his old room and at eleven the report of a revolver had been heard. The family had found him dead. The bullet had gone through both temples. He had left no explanation and had been—so far as anyone knew—in no

226

difficulties. His father and mother were prostrated with grief. . . .

Arthur flung down the paper, caught a cab in front of his house, and drove to the Goldmanns. He was in a state more of excitement than of grief. He was terribly sorry for Victor's parents. Victor himself had always been indifferent to him. But he felt as though he must come upon Victor's secret, as though that secret held some profound and personal meaning for him. A silence seemed to wrap the house and the very block. The maid who had been with the Goldmanns many years recognized and admitted him. In the drawing-room he found Joe all by himself, sitting at a table, hunched up, brooding. He didn't look up.

"Hallo, Arthur." His voice was perfectly expressionless. "The folks are upstairs; Mother's in bed with a nurse. Your father's walking up and down with mine."

"And Victor?"

"He's lying in his old room. Nothing to see except the wound. You can go up if you like."

Arthur sat down. "What was it, Joe? What was it?"

At last Joe looked up. Both the irony and the fear had gone out of his golden-brown eyes. "I've been trying to figure it out. He had plenty of money. There was no woman, either. Victor was always so scared of women that he managed to get along with burlesque girls and that sort. I think it was self-disgust."

Arthur was tense. "What makes you think that?"

"Well, do you suppose that Victor didn't know that everybody disliked him and that people almost fled from him? And yet he couldn't help shouting them down and antagonizing them. He quarreled with the people who gave him commissions; he quarreled with his colleagues; he had a feud with the very janitor and the attendants in his house. There was something in him that he wanted to shout down, that he had to shout down. What was it?"

Arthur put his hand on Joe's arm. "What do you think it was?"

Joe shrugged his shoulders. "He came to my apartment

about ten days ago and said he thought he'd go to Europe for the spring and summer. 'All right,' I said. 'Why don't you?' He sort of snarled: 'I don't know that it's worth while. You meet the same damned Jews there that you leave here.' " Joe was silent for a moment. Then he asked: "Well?"

"He was trying to shout down his Jewish soul," Arthur said.

Joe got up. "You and your Jewish soul! What is a Jewish soul? And, anyhow, why did he have to shout down his Jewish soul? Except for occasional parties and luncheons he worked for Jews, met Jews, associated with Jews. There are enough of 'em in New York, you know. Oh, I know what you are going to say: they are all Jews who are trying to suppress their Jewishness. But does that get you anywhere?"

"I think it does." Arthur spoke slowly. "Yes, I think it does. Of course the thing works differently in different people. Victor was madly intense and pronouncedly Jewish. He even looked like a handsome, sultry Arab, didn't he?"

Joe nodded and now his eyes were moist.

"Very well. And from his very infancy on he was somehow made to feel from the very air about him that to be happy and successful and acceptable in the world he must be something that he wasn't, something that he didn't even clearly grasp or understand, namely, an Anglo-American gentleman. Well, he had no gift for mimicry. He was confused. He was maddened. He shouted. He began to hate himself and his own kind. You said yourself it was self-disgust."

"Oh, maybe so, maybe so," Joe said, wearily. "We're an accursed generation, certainly. Look at me. I'm tangled up in a love-affair again that makes me suffer like a dog. Why? The woman isn't worth it. I know she isn't. I know she's a gold-digger. I know everything anyone can tell me. And yet, and yet . . ."

"Marry a Jewish girl," Arthur said.

Joe almost recovered his old grin. "Fine advice for you to give."

"Just for me, Joe. The wheels are running down. I don't believe that Elizabeth and I will be together many more years."

They were both silent for a while. Then they heard footsteps coming down the stairs. The door to the hall had been left open. The footsteps came nearer. Joe and Arthur turned to the door and saw Nathan Goldmann and Jacob Levy, two old gray men now, walking deeply bowed but arm in arm. They did not see their sons. Leaning upon each other, they went out into the street. Joe held up clenched, trembling hands.

"Two old Jews. It's *Shabbes*, you know. They're going to *shul* to pray." For a moment he wept. But he recovered himself almost at once. "Let's go somewhere, Arthur, and have a cup of coffee." They walked along the streets together without many words. "I loathe restaurants today," Joe said. "Come over to my place and I'll brew some coffee there." Joe's little apartment, when they reached it, had a tumbled look. Joe busied himself at once with his Turkish coffee outfit. But he talked during this occupation. "I don't get sleep enough, Arthur. I never do. I'm haunted by a feeling of loneliness—terrible, bitter loneliness. That's why I go in for these women. Oh yes, I'm a damned sight more on to myself than you think. That's why I go in for communism. Great masses of comrades, men and women. No chance to be lonely. O God, I'm lonely." A nervous shiver ran through his small, spare form. He turned around and faced Arthur. "Hell! we can't go to *shul*, you and I, can we?"

"No," Arthur admitted, "we can't."

"Then what are we to do? What?"

"That reminds me of Elizabeth," Arthur said, slightly to his own surprise. "She mocks her father a little and says: 'What shall we do to be saved?' "

"Not such a damned bad way of putting it. Well, what shall we do?"

But all that Arthur could answer was that he had offered his services to a Jewish hospital and that his work there would begin next month and that he could but wait and see.

4

THE Beth Yehuda Hospital was a white building set on a hill. Twice a week Arthur went there for some hours in his capacity of consulting psychiatrist. The nurses, doctors, officials, patients were, of course, all Jews. It was the first time in his life that, except in some small family circle, Arthur was wholly surrounded by Jews. For two or three times something within him—something which he was experienced enough to watch carefully—drew back. What was it? The old, old fear of danger through the act of being openly identified with those who were through all ages exposed to danger. The feeling was as crude as that and as strong as that in its origin. Modern Jews veiled it sincerely in various ways. They pretended to themselves that they didn't like Jews or, at least, certain specific Jewish qualities. And there was no doubt that in the mass Jews had their unlovely qualities. Like all people in the mass. Only these Jewish qualities seemed and, in fact, were, more salient because they were not the qualities that one expected in an overwhelmingly non-Jewish world. Also, and this was the sharpest prick, one was afraid of sharing these qualities, of being thus hatefully salient, grimily emphatic in an unsympathetic world. . . . Dr. Herz, the chief of the hospital, was accustomed to talk in parables during the staff meetings. A very young physician, fresh from the Harvard Medical School, asked whether one couldn't stop the women from wailing so noisily. It created a bad impression in the neighborhood. Dr. Herz swung his head about slowly as though to disengage his beard from some obstacle.

"Call it 'keening,' Dr. Gerson, and see how much better you feel about it at once. Do you know the experience of the American Jewish gentleman in the subway? An Irish lady of forty-five came in, the wife, let us say, of a prosperous contractor. Very fat. Very bumptious and very, very heavily hung with diamonds. Her ungloved fingers glittered. Within him the American Jewish gentleman smiled a tolerant and amused smile. Next a Jewish lady came in. A description of her, except for color, would be identical with that of the Irish lady. The Jewish lady's husband was in cloaks and suits. A flush of rage darkened the face of the American Jewish gentleman and he said in his heart: 'Christ, how vulgar!'" Dr. Herz got up. "Ponder that anecdote, Dr. Gerson. It holds the key to all your difficulties. But under no circumstances"—his face grew stern—"is the wailing of the old ladies to be interfered with. Our Mother Rachel also wailed."

Gradually Arthur came to look forward to his visits to the hospital. He lingered and prolonged his stay each time. A peace stole into his heart, a sense of ease and of being sheltered. He remembered, of course, the extreme Freudian theory that no human being ever got over the shock of birth and that all our seeking of human or physical shelter is an obscure urge back to the security of the womb. . . . Nor did he forget his own dislike of all gregariousness, his conviction of the danger of all herd-instincts. . . . No, in his ease and comfort in the hospital there was a finer element, a residuum of something more nobly human. . . . If a dispute broke out in staff meeting it was still a dispute upon common human grounds. One didn't first have to consider and weigh and twist one's words and attitudes because So-and-so was a Gentile and didn't understand, or because So-and-so was a Jew and would be hurt. . . . One could deal with an equal freedom with the patients. There were no obscure misunderstandings or hidden grudges or subtle indelicacies. . . . Here, among Jews, one could be most human, most personal, least herd-minded—least torn between the instincts of one herd and those of another, most—if one liked to put it so—un-Jewish in the traditional sense of the dispersion because the planes of psychical friction—how that phrase came back to Arthur—were reduced to the normal and natural and human ones. The freedom of this Jewish community for a Jew lay in its uncomplicatedness, in the reduction of the complications within it to the ordinary complications inherent in the life of man. . . . The more freely Jewish one was, the less consciously and agonizedly Jewish one was forced to be. . . . Arthur was astonished at the comparative simplicity of these perceptions. . . . Why the devil were they not more general? Wasn't it, if one permitted oneself to think, clear as the noonday sun that a Negro could be more freely and nobly human in a world of Negroes where he didn't have to spend the better part of his time in warding off slights, in cruel and difficult inner and outer adjustments, in the mere physical trouble and discomfort of having to go miles out of his way for a restaurant or be diplomatic about a Pullman berth or a seat in a theater? If Jews were reduced to no such gross adjustments in a Gentile world, they were still subject to a thousand subtle and wounding ones that warped and bitterly complicated the whole of life? . . .

He had not been going to the hospital long when he began to feel two dark, strangely clear and half-whimsical-looking eyes upon him. They were the very eyes, it seemed to him, that he was not yet prepared to encounter if, in truth, he ever would be. For they belonged to the representative of a great world-wide orthodox association which had a very strong financial and administrative interest in the hospital. They were the eyes, then, of Reb Moshe Hacohen, who went about in an elegant silk *caftan* with a velvet collar, the glossy blackness of which was always set off by the most gleaming linen, who never, by any chance, took off his hat and whom even the dapper New York nurses, although he spoke almost faultless and rather elaborate English, called Reb Hacohen. . . . Arthur rather avoided the man. But one day coming down the steps of the hospital he was caught. Reb Hacohen was beside him.

"Dr. Levy?" Arthur bowed. "I have been watching you. There is something in your face. I believe we are *mishpoche*—kinfolk; do you know the expression?" There was something mild yet authoritative about Hacohen's voice.

Arthur nodded. "Yes, I'm picking up a good many of the more familiar terms."

"You never heard them at home?"

"Very few."

Hacohen hummed a little to himself. "Yes, yes."

They were walking along the street now. Arthur had a strong impulse to excuse himself and go home. But he didn't somehow see his way clear to doing that without being obviously discourteous to Hacohen. And that seemed suddenly an inconceivable action to him. Hacohen hummed again.

"Will you tell me the name of your grandfather?"

"Efraim."

"And where did he live?"

"In a German town named Insterburg." Arthur felt a hand upon his arm.

"Then your father is Jacob, the youngest son of Reb Efraim, the one who emigrated to America?"

Arthur looked at the face beside him. It was a grave and sensitive and strong face. The skin was very fair and the small beard very black and the lips very red. It was really a stern face. Yet through its sternness there shone a loving-kindness. Arthur felt a touch of humility before that face.

"You are very well informed, Reb Hacohen."

His companion nodded. "I met the young Krakauers in Breslau last year. You have heard of them?"

"I heard my father say long ago that a sister of his lived in Breslau. And I believe that Krakauer was her married name."

"It is so, then, as I thought. Good. Your grandfather's mother was named Braine and her father was Reb Eliezer Hacohen, a very great and learned man. You are Reb Eliezer's great-great-grandson. Now this Reb Eliezer had a younger brother whose name was Moshe, like my own, and I am the great-grandson of Reb Moshe—peace be upon them all, peace!"

233

What flashed into Arthur's mind was a scene of years ago. He had been standing on the Columbia campus with Charles Dawson, and Charles Dawson had lightly and humorously and yet with an earnest undertone explained about the Dawsons of Inverness and the clan from which they came and the tartan which they had the right to wear, and Arthur had felt naked and an outcast and shivering in the world. He turned to Reb Hacohen and held out his hand.

"What you tell me interests me extremely. I am very glad to know it."

The other took his hand and pressed it lightly but warmly. "Now I must tell you, too, of an old division in our house. My great-grandfather joined the *Chassidim*. His older brother, Reb Eliezer, a learned Talmudist who traced the descent of the family from great scholars and pious men of the Middle Ages, considered this a disgrace. Do you know what *Chassidim* are?"

"Dimly; I've been reading up a bit lately."

Reb Hacohen wagged his head a little. "Let me tell you a story. The *Chassidim*, the pious or holy ones, called their Talmudic adversaries *Mithnagedim*. And a man came to a *Chassidic* rabbi and asked: When the Messiah comes, will he be a *Chassid* or a *Mithnaged?* And the rabbi answered at once: A *Mithnaged*. For were he a *Chassid*, the *Mithnagedim* would not believe in him. But the *Chassidim* will accept him whatever his origin."

Arthur looked at the grave intellectual face beside him. "Are you a *Chassid*, too, Reb Hacohen?"

A very winning smile stole slowly over Hacohen's face. "I am, my son. And next you will ask me in your American way whether I believe in the coming of the Messiah?"

"Exactly."

"I believe that active love will gradually build a better world, a world of brotherhood and peace. When that world is completed, the Messiah will be among us. Do you doubt that?"

Arthur laughed and shook his head. "No, I suppose not, Reb Moshe."

"That is it. We must love and not be afraid. There is an old *Chassidic* saying: It is the fear in men's hearts that builds walls against the light. But I must not keep you."

"Oh, but you're not. Please!"

The grave head wagged a little. "Good-bye. And *Shalom* —peace."

5

THEY met again a number of times and conversed briefly. Their talk was not as serious as it had been on the first occasion. Reb Moshe told Arthur something about his travels, which had been very wide. He had visited Jewish communities in Persia, in the Caucasus, in North Africa. His last long journey had been to Rumania, where the Jews were sore beset. Arthur had been reading of pogroms and threats of pogroms in that country and he was a little astonished at Reb Moshe's sorrowful but quite calm and almost businesslike attitude. He spoke of this. Reb Moshe said. "Most Western Jews take the attitude of benevolent Gentiles. They are astonished that their pretty sentiments have not been more effectual. They almost begin to forget their World War. But we from the East always knew that we were living in a barbarous world, a world without love, a world unsaved. What do you expect?"

They were walking side by side once more as on that first occasion. A sharp wind was blowing and made speech difficult. Dark was falling and the street lamps were lit. Arthur should have taken the subway to go home. But he kept within the grave rhythm of their silent striding. It almost seemed to him as though he were companioned for the first time in his life and also as though for the first time he was beside some one who, in the deepest sense of life itself, held some instruction for him. In all this there was nothing mystical. On many points Reb Moshe was an uninstructed man. Nor did Arthur for a moment repudiate his own points of view as a modern man and a man of science. But through Reb Moshe even when Reb Moshe did not speak, he reached a source of spiritual rectification, of readjustment in those depths that lie below the reason and its operation. . . . At last he stopped. Elizabeth was probably at home this evening. She never waited for him. She considered that in the manner of a reproach and an unspoken infringement of liberty. For that very reason he was anxious to be punctual. . . . He stopped. Reb Moshe turned to him.

"We have had a wonderful talk." Arthur smiled. Reb Moshe said: "Another old saying: The Way is not communicated by any report or any book but from soul to soul."

Arthur shook his head in wonder. "Why haven't I ever before heard these marvelous things that you're always quoting? Even from my father?"

A subtle look came into Reb Moshe's eyes. "You are probably better acquainted with the sayings of a certain Rabbi Jehoshua of Nazareth. Well, even he said something about the lost sheep of the house of Israel, didn't he?"

Elizabeth was just ready to sit down to dinner when Arthur arrived. She jumped up and kissed him on the cheek. "Arthur, I've finished the book. I'll take it to 'Gene tomorrow." She had not kissed him for weeks. He looked at her. She seemed far away from him, divided from him by a bright and infinitely long corridor. And that feeling smote with a sharp sorrow upon his heart. He forced himself to seem interested and even enthusiastic. But as he spoke Elizabeth seemed curiously enough to withdraw herself again and to remember something she had forgotten and to regret the impulse with which she had greeted him. So silence fell between them, a grievous silence, full of clamorous unspoken thoughts and difficulties. Elizabeth finally said that she was going to a late informal party at Prout's. She had promised to come if her book was done. And, thank God, it was. She asked Arthur whether he wanted to come along. He looked into her eyes.

"Do you really mind, Elizabeth, if I don't?"

She lifted her head in her old way. She was incapable of

dishonesty. "I'm sorry Arthur, but I'm afraid I don't." She got up. "But I honestly don't think it's entirely my fault. You don't seem to take any interest any longer in any of the things you used to. I wonder if you realize yourself, how you've withdrawn yourself."

"I?" he said. "I?"

She shivered. "Can't you think of anything but *that?* Is that—"

"A Jewish trait?" he finished for her.

She leaned her hands on the table. She forced her tone to be gentle. "I don't want to quarrel, dear Arthur. I don't for a moment pretend that I've been a satisfactory wife to you. Isn't it true, just the same, that you too have become estranged from me?"

He leaned back in his chair and looked up at her. "Yes, Elizabeth. I've been preoccupied by things that I couldn't share with you. Perhaps I wouldn't have become so preoccupied if you had made what I call a home for me. On the other hand, I'm not sure even of that. So I'm infinitely willing to call it all square."

She lingered; she wanted apparently to say more; but either the impulse died or the words would not come—the right words. She went out with an involuntarily wounded gesture.

Next evening she stayed at home with a little air of purposefulness and brought a book with her into Arthur's study. She had not done that for many months. They read, each pretending to be more absorbed than was the case, each tingling a little within. Both were relieved when they heard the bell ring and heard the maid go to the door. A moment later, unannounced, stepped in Reb Moshe Hacohen. Arthur jumped up impulsively. Elizabeth's eyes were large and round and almost frightened. Arthur took his friend's hand and led him to Elizabeth. "My wife."

Reb Moshe smiled a very winning smile. He said to Elizabeth: "I have taken the liberty of coming because Dr. Levy and I are kinsmen."

Arthur laughingly explained to Elizabeth the matter of

the kinship. But Elizabeth could not for the life of her take her eyes from Reb Moshe's hat. It was there on his head. Was it glued on? She had never heard of such a thing before. She did not stop to consider that it was a trifle. A trifle under the aspect of eternity, even if the man had merely forgotten. That black hat loomed to her as the sudden symbol of something infinitely alien and dangerous and rancorous and terrible of which her husband was a part. This was a Christ-killer. . . . This black man. . . . Arthur read Elizabeth at this moment, read her sorrowfully, read the very depth of her ancestral consciousness. . . . Suddenly in the silence rose Reb Moshe's voice, rich and mild. He turned to Elizabeth.

"Millions of pious people in the world, my child, keep their heads covered and bare their feet in holy places." Then very slowly he took off his hat and revealed his head still covered by a round little cap of black silk.

Arthur urged him to sit down. Elizabeth had relaxed and smiled faintly. But there was still a remnant of terror in her eyes. Reb Moshe had sat down beside her and was watching her.

"All day long," he said, "I have been thinking of a story that happened not long ago in a Jewish village in Poland."

"Please tell it," Arthur urged him.

"The son of one of our orthodox rabbis"—Reb Moshe turned to Elizabeth—"was stricken with a dangerous and very infectious illness. The boy had to be taken to the hospital and in the confusion and grief the rabbi and his wife forgot to lock the door of the house. In the night thieves stole in. The rabbi's wife heard them and alarmed the rabbi. He went down and found the thieves and said to them: 'Whatever you have taken, good people, I freely give you in order to release you from the sin of theft. But be careful not to drink from the silver cup you have taken, for it has been used by a person ill of a dangerous and infectious illness.' "

Reb Moshe leaned back in his chair. Elizabeth's eyes sought Arthur's. They were moist.

"You know, Arthur, I can see my father doing that?"

"My wife's father," Arthur explained, "is a Christian clergyman."

Reb Moshe nodded. "Real Christians are capable of Jewish actions."

Elizabeth stiffened again. Arthur himself thought that Reb Moshe should have struck another note. But he knew that under his friend's mildness there was a stern and uncompromising conviction. To break the strain Arthur said with a smile:

"You didn't come, Reb Moshe, to tell us *maasses*"—he saw Elizabeth wince ever so slightly at his use of the Yiddish expression—"you have something on your mind."

Reb Moshe nodded. "Our brethren in Rumania are permitted neither to live nor to die. We are sending an American commission to investigate. One member of the commission should be a physician and, if possible, a psychiatrist. Will you go?"

Arthur got up. The thought agitated him. He walked over to the mantelpiece. "Why have you thought of me? I can scarcely understand Yiddish."

Reb Moshe slipped his hands into the sleeves of his *caftan*. "There are three reasons. You are not poor. You can afford to miss your practice for two months. We both belong to a family that has always sought to serve all Israel and to sanctify the Name. The last reason is that it will do you good."

Arthur looked at his wife. "What do you think, Elizabeth?"

She was prim and crisp, a rare attitude for her. "It might be a very interesting experience for you. You've certainly gone stale on New York and all our friends and interests."

Reb Moshe followed Arthur with his eyes. "Well, Doctor?"

Arthur shrugged his shoulders. "I can't tell you tonight, Reb Moshe, whether I'm going. I have to think it over. It involves more for me than just the trip and the work."

Reb Moshe got up. "Don't go unless the thought gives

you joy. There is no good in gloom. There is no virtue in forcing yourself. But I would like to know soon."

"Can I have a week to decide in?" Arthur asked.

"A week. But no more."

He took Reb Moshe to the door. When he came back Elizabeth was still sitting in the study, leaning forward with folded hands.

"Do you think you will go, Arthur?"

A little flame seemed to be burning in him. But he looked upon Elizabeth and she recalled to him earlier years and love and brought streaming into his consciousness the bright busy American world of which he had so wanted to be a part. And the flame flickered and died and a revulsion of feeling came over him against the thought of Rumanian ghettos and *caftaned* Jews and Reb Moshe himself.

"I don't know," he said. "I doubt it." He went to her and touched her hair. "Elizabeth," he said, softly.

She looked up at him. "You did love me once, Arthur, didn't you?"

"Yes," he said, "yes. And today, if—" He stopped. It was only, was it not, his starved passion and the pathos of the past that brought that warmth, that strange and, after all, only autumnal warmth, into his heart?

Elizabeth got up. "I think you will go, Arthur. I think that in reality you went months ago."

6

HE was, of course, aware, beyond the wont of ordinary men, of the infinitely complicated processes that go to make up what is called a decision. There is no fiat issued by the will, since there is no such abstract organ or even function. Simple men follow an instinct, an inner monition, an ancestral trend, and haltingly though passionately supply reasons later. All that differentiates such men from savages or even animals in their conviction, which again has become instinctive, that man is a rational animal and ought to be able to produce reasons. The growth of that conviction is a handsome and encouraging thing, a thing that seems to lend a dignity to human nature. Its practical uses are still far to seek. When a Negro has been burned at the stake it helps him little that his tormentors are honestly convinced that all black men have evil designs on all white women. Rationalization helps rather to hide than to curb the evil that is under the sun. . . . Arthur Levy came almost to doubt whether men would ever be able to use their reason, whether our only hope was not to refine and humanize the instincts under the millennial discipline of civilization. . . . He tried to disengage the various elements that would contribute to a decision in his case—a decision that obviously involved far more than a two months' trip to the Balkans. He found that these elements were largely, if not wholly, emotional in their character. He found his strongest emotion to be a revulsion against the thought of turning back upon the road that he had so indifferently at first, so accidentally and yet so definitely, taken. He knew all the stock arguments against the taking of that road. They amounted essentially to this: did one not, by reidentifying oneself with one's own people or group or clan, play into the hands of the very group and clan spirit by protesting against which one had set out? That was an argument the strength of which it was idle to deny. One couldn't, in fact, reply to it except by observing that human life was, to say the least, not wholly rational and that at the end of this, as at the end of every train of thought, one came upon an irreconcilable contradiction. Meanwhile was the command to live! One could shirk that as poor Victor Goldmann had done. But if one went on living one had, according to the old Latin tag, to find some mode of living. Now Arthur could very easily imagine his future if he turned back. His practice was growing; it would probably continue to grow. By and by his father would die and he would inherit the half of a modest but considerable fortune. He would be very distinguished and very prosperous. Nearly all his patients and nearly all his friends would be Jews. He and his patients and his friends would be united by their Jewishness, but they would all strip that Jewishness to its minimum. They would be busy impoverishing the most powerful factor in their spiritual and social life. And hence that life itself would be thin and cold and comfortless. . . . About the very homes and interiors of such Jews he had often observed something chill and, despite elegance and taste, haphazard and homeless and temporary. . . . Wasn't it a self-stultification, since one had to and did in the end live Jewishly, to live Jewishly on as poor and stripped and ignorant a basis as possible? Why? So as not to emphasize one's Jewishness in the eyes of purely theoretical *goyim*. Purely theoretical, since one's Gentile friends would not fail to respect one for being richly and heartily what one was, and as for the mob, —the mob instinctively disliked and hated Jews anyhow, and invented reasons for that hatred afterward, which were wholly unconnected with anything that actual Jews were or were not, did, or left undone. So that the thin and icy and careful and drab life of Americanized Jewry was a vain oblation to a blind idol. . . . How could such very clever people be so foolish? . . . Why not, since one was a Jew and had to live Jewishly, get—in vulgar but sensible parlance— the maximum of good out of one's Jewishness, out of one's traditions, one's racial poetry, one's ancestral history? All other people did so and throve in spirituality and self-respect and richness of the texture of their lives thereby. That was it—the texture of the life of the Americanized Jew was poor and colorless and thin. . . . No, he could not go back to that kind of life. It didn't, on the simplest principle, suit his temperament. He wanted more. . . . Perhaps if Elizabeth had been a different kind of a woman. . . . But then she hadn't been! And perhaps his inability to choose a mate with wiser instincts was again due to the fact that he and his kind had deliberately let their instincts wither. . . . Of course he was arguing in the direction of his desire. But the existence of the desire was in itself a profoundly significant factor, especially as a similar desire was announcing itself, as he faintly but definitely knew, in this generation in very, very many Jewish breasts. . . .

242

He could not turn back. He must not, on that account, deceive himself as to the difficulty of going forward. Barriers of ignorance, of inhibition, of fear were to be overcome. Such moments of revulsion as he had had the other day in the presence of Elizabeth might come again, would come again. They were part of the price one had to pay. The withdrawal of one's earlier self and of one's immediate ancestors from Judaism—a phenomenon which doubtless had had its legitimate function in the historic process—this withdrawal created inevitable difficulties. These one must try to overcome. He had at least one certain staff to lean upon: his scientific cognition that all flight from reality is strictly akin to madness, that every effort to reintegrate with reality is a sign of sanity and health. . . .

It was the afternoon of the seventh day from Reb Moshe's visit. Arthur came home, and he had no sooner stepped into the hall than he felt a breath of emptiness and disorder blowing subtly into his face. He stood in the dim hallway for a full minute. A great and hollow silence was about him. His heart began to accelerate its beating. He went into the rooms nowise astonished at their silence. He saw that Elizabeth's tall wardrobe trunk was gone; he saw that his child was no longer here. He went thereafter straight to his desk and found the expected letter from Elizabeth and in it almost the expected words. She had taken John and gone temporarily to Eugene and Joanna Adams. She did not want to embarrass him or influence his decision. She thought she knew how far-reaching that decision was. She had taken John, since the child was so young and Arthur was going away. But she would, of course, whatever happened, respect his wishes in regard to the child and the child's education. She wanted no money for herself; he would, of course, want to contribute suitably to the expenses of his child. She would always think of him with respect and deep affection, and she hoped that he would come to see her before he left. . . .

He sat down at his desk. He held Elizabeth's letter in his hand. How difficult all farewells are! How they partake of

death and admonish us of our mortality! How admirable
and loyal to her own principles of living Elizabeth was! At
such a moment—he had always known it—she would be
fine and straight and honorable. Fine and honorable as the
best type of American gentleman. . . . He sat there ponder-
ing for many minutes. . . . When the bell rang in his ears he
realized at once that it had rung before. He switched on a
single light and went to the door, and silently let Reb
Moshe in. Together they came back into Arthur's study and
Reb Moshe sat down. He peered into the dimness of the
room. He laid a roll of paper on a little table beside him. He
hummed softly.

"Do you know the word *Shechinah*—the spirit of the
glory of God?"

"I have heard it recently."

Reb Moshe had a singing undertone as he spoke again.
"Why do our sages say that greater is hospitality than waiting for the *Shechinah*, the breath of the Eternal? Why is it
so written? Is that not excessive? No. Because in a house that
dispenses true hospitality you know that the *Shechinah*
dwells even now between the man and the wife. Why then
wait for it?"

Arthur bowed his head a little.

"Are you going?" Reb Moshe asked.

"I think so."

"Here," Reb Moshe tapped the roll of paper, "I have
brought you something. When the Russians sacked the
house of your great-great-grandfather, Reb Eliezer Hacohen, he gave an old chest that contained family papers to
my great-grandfather, his brother, the *Chassid*. Have you
heard the story?"

Arthur shook his head.

"One of the documents was an account of events that
he had witnessed and heard of, written by Reb Efraim ben
Reb Jacob, the direct ancestor of Reb Eliezer and Reb
Moshe and therefore of you and of myself in the eleventh
century of the Christian era. It has come down to me and
a young friend of mine has translated it from Hebrew

into English. Here it is. Read it." Reb Moshe got up. "It is written," he said, "that a man must be reborn every day in order to become perfect. It is also written: How do we know when a sin has been forgiven us? When we no longer desire to commit it. . . . No, don't get up. I can find my way alone." He lifted his hands in a curious gesture of priestly blessing and walked out.

BOOK IX

ALONE, at night, in the strangely desolate apartment whence his wife and his child had fled he took up the pages written nearly a thousand years ago by Reb Efraim ben Reb Jacob whose blood was his, whose bone was his, whose very gestures and mannerisms—the shrug of the shoulders, the outstretching of the hands, the biting of the lip, the pacing in agitation up and down—were his own. He sat at his desk and read. The room was dark except for the orange light upon the pages. A voice came to him, unutterably remote, terribly familiar, far away and as close to him as his own hands and feet.

"And now I shall begin to relate how destruction came upon the congregations who let themselves be slain for the sake of the name of the Eternal, and how with their whole souls they clung to the Eternal, the God of their fathers, and acknowledged Him, the One, with their last breath.

"It came to pass in the year 4856, which is the year 1096 according to the calendar of the nations. In that year, trusting the prophecies of Jeremiah, we were expecting consolation and help in our exile. Joy was turned into sorrow and into mourning and lamentation. All the terrors with which we are threatened in the books of the Torah descended upon us, all that is written came to pass with much that is not written; over us and our sons and our daughters, our old men and boys, the great among us and the humble, came desolation.

"It was the impious Pope of Rome who arose and issued a call to all the peoples, the sons of Edom, who believe in the Christ, bidding them to gather and fare forth toward Yerushelaim and conquer the city in order that they might freely go on pilgrimage to the grave of Him whom they have made their God. The command was obeyed; the nations gathered. Their numbers were as the sands of the shore and their voice like the roar of the storm.

"It was now that there arose that Duke Godfrey of Bouillion—may his bones be crushed!—a ruthless man, driven by the spirit of evil to join him with these dissolute hordes. For he sware a great oath that wherever he came he would revenge the blood of his God upon the blood of Israel and leave of the seed of our people neither remnant nor fugitive.

"Among us was raised up one who sought to stem the danger, one who feared God and was worthy of eternal joy, Rabbi Kalonymos who presided over the congregation of Mainz. Swiftly he despatched messengers to Heinrich, the emperor, who had been lingering in Italy for nine years. The emperor was wroth and sent letters to all the provinces of the empire commanding princes and bishops and viceroys and, above all, Duke Godfrey, to keep the peace and to protect the Jews and to grant them help and refuge against the rabble. The impious Duke sware that it had never been in his soul to so much as pluck a hair from a Jew's head. Moreover, the congregation of Cologne gave him five hundred marks of fine silver and the congregation of Mainz as much again, and he pledged his honor to protect them and to keep the peace. . . . But He whose Name is Peace had departed from us; He hid His eye from His people and delivered it up unto the sword. No prophet nor seer, nor any man however wise or learned, can fathom why the sins of our people weighed so heavily that the holy congregations had to suffer as though blood-guiltiness were upon them. But He is a just Judge; ours, ours must have been the guilt. . . .

"First came an insolent rabble of Christians, a raging mob of Frenchmen and Germans who had taken it into their minds to fare forth to the Holy City and to drive out from thence the sons of Ishmael. They fastened a cross upon their garments, both men and women, and they were numerous as locusts upon the earth. . . .

"Whenever upon their way they came into cities in which Jews had their dwelling, each said to the other: 'Here we are setting out on so long a journey toward the grave of the Lord and meaning to be revenged upon the

Ishmaelites. And behold, in our very midst dwell the Jews who hung Him innocent upon the cross and slew Him. Let us be up and doing and revenge ourselves first upon them; let us stamp them out from among the peoples so that the name of Israel be no more remembered. Or else let them become even as ourselves and accept our faith.'

"When the congregations heard such speech they did after the manner of our fathers, exercising themselves in penitence and prayer and charitable deeds. But the hands of the holy people wearied and their hearts misgave them and their strength went out of them. They hid themselves from the sword in their innermost chambers and mortified themselves with penitential fasts. Three days they fasted, both day and night, until their skin clung to their bones and they were thin as faggots. They cried aloud and wept in the bitterness of their hearts, but their Father heard them not. He rejected the tents of Israel; a cloud was round about His Countenance; for this matter was fated and a punishment for old sins. And He had chosen this generation because it had the strength to bear witness in His temple, to fulfil His word, to sanctify the ineffable Name. It is concerning such that David spoke: Praise the Lord, ye messengers, ye heroes who are mighty to fulfil His word.

"In that year the Passover fell upon a Thursday and the first day of the new moon of the month of Ijar on a Friday. It was on the Sabbath, on the eighth of Ijar, that the judgment came upon us. The Crusaders, joining themselves with the townsfolk, arose first against the holy and pious congregation of Speyer, thinking to catch them all in the house of prayer. But the Jews, getting word of this, rose early on the morning of the Sabbath, prayed hurriedly, and left the house of prayer. The enemies, seeing that their plan had failed, fell upon the Jews and slew eleven of them. Thus the fatality began.

"When the evil news came to Worms that eleven men of Speyer had been slain, the people of Worms cried to the Lord and raised a great and bitter weeping, for they saw that Heaven had determined their destruction and that there was no way out, neither forward nor backward. The congregation divided itself into two parts: one part fled for refuge into the bishop's castle; the other part remained in their houses because the townsmen had promised them protection. But these promises were false and treacherous and like a broken reed. The townsmen had an understanding with the Crusaders that our name and our remnant was to be obliterated. 'Fear them not,' they spoke to us, 'for whoever slays one of you will have to answer us with his life.' By fair speeches they made all flight impossible. Relying on their faith, the Jews put into their hands all their goods and precious things, for the sake of which the townsmen betrayed them afterward.

"On the tenth day of Ijar these wolves of the desert attacked those who had remained in their houses and exterminated them—men, women, and children, young and old; they hurled them down the stairs and hacked down the houses and plundered and looted; they stole the scrolls of the Torah and stamped them into the mud and shredded and burned them and left death and horror behind them where the children of Israel had dwelled.

"On the twenty-fifth of Ijar the terror came also over those who had taken refuge in the house of the bishop. The enemies tortured them like the others and delivered them over unto the sword. But they had been fortified by the example of their brethren and accepted death and sanctified the Name. They stretched forth their heads to be hewn off in the Name of their Creator; nay, many and many too laid hands of violence upon themselves and their most dear. One slew his brother, another his kinsmen or his wife and his children; bridegrooms slew their brides and tender mothers their little ones. All accepted from the depth of their hearts the judgment of God and, commending their souls to their Maker, cried in a loud voice: Hear O Israel, the Eternal is our God, the Eternal is One. The enemies stripped them naked and dragged and hurled them about; they left none save a few whom they forced to accept baptism. Eight hundred was the number of the slain on these two days; naked they were thrown into a common grave. They fell by the hand of God. He brought them to their rest, to the great light in the Garden of Eden. Behold their souls are in the covenant of life with the Eternal Who made them even unto the end of days.

"Now when the pious men of the great congregation of Mainz, shield and refuge of our exile, famous through many lands—when they heard of the slaughter of the saints in Speyer and in Worms, they were first stricken and their hearts turned to water and they cried to God with a great cry. Thereafter they met together and chose wise men out of their midst to take council how the evil might be averted. These chosen men determined to ransom the lives of the congregation by giving their entire fortunes as bribes to the princes, the governors, the bishops, and the counts. The heads of the congregation who were well seen at the bishop's court went thither and spoke to him and to the officers of his household and asked them what they should do to escape the fate of their brethren in Speyer and Worms. The answer was: 'Take our advice. Bring all your fortunes into our treasuries and do you, with your wives and sons and daughters and all who are with you, come into the house of the bishop and stay there until the Crusaders have passed by. Thus you will be secure.' They spoke thus, but their words were lies. They brought us into their power; they caught us as fishermen catch fishes in a net in order to rob us of our money, as afterward they did. Thus the event explained the beginning. Only the bishop was honestly inclined to put forth his power in our favor. But had we not given great gifts to him and his servitors for their promise to protect us? But neither bribes nor pleas availed in the end nor guarded us when the day of wrath came.

"It came to pass on the day of the new moon of the month of Sivan that Count Emicho, the oppressor of all Jews—may his bones be ground in a mill of iron!—came with mercenaries and Crusaders and villagers and set up his tents outside of the walls of the city, for the gates had been barred. He was our sorest enemy who had mercy neither on old men nor virgins nor suckling babes nor the sick, who was bent on stamping the people of God into the mire and put our youths to the sword and ripped open the bellies of our women who were with child. He wore the Crusaders' cross and was a leader of armies. He feigned that a messenger of the Crucified had appeared to him and set a sign upon his flesh and promised to wait for him in Sicily, there to crown him with the crown of empire in token that all his enemies were overcome. For two days he besieged the city.

"Learning of the arrival of this impious one, the elders of the congregation of Mainz hastened once more to the bishop and bribed him with three hundred marks of fine silver, beseeching him to remain in the city, for it had been his plan to visit the villages of his diocese. He invited all the congregation into the great hall of his palace and vowed to stand by them. The count of the citadel too declared that he would protect the Jews until the Crusaders should have fared onward, but stipulated that the Jews were to bear the costs. To this the Jews agreed and both the bishop and the count declared that they would, if need be, die with them. Furthermore, the congregation determined to give money to the impious Emicho as well, and to assure him in a writing that other congregations upon his way would pay him equal honors. 'Perhaps,' they said, 'God will still show us mercy.' Thus to the bishop and his officers and to divers of the townspeople they gave four hundred marks of silver and to the impious Emicho they sent seven pounds of pure gold. But it was all of no avail.

"It was on that third day of Sivan which once, when the Torah was given us, was a day of sanctification and separateness for Israel; upon this day it was also granted to the saints of the congregation of Mainz, separated and purified, to ascend unto God together. In their death they were not divided. All were in the bishop's great hall when the wrath of God arose against them like a flame. In one place they were gathered together. With them were the Torah and greatness of soul, wealth and honor, wisdom and humility, charity and faith. And all was mown down. They were destroyed as were the sons of Yerushelaim when the temple and the city fell.

"At the hour of noon the cruel Emicho moved against the city with his hordes, and the citizens opened the gates. 'Behold, the gates opened of their own accord,' said our enemies. 'Thus doth the Crucified to be revenged upon the blood of the Jews.' With fluttering banners the army drew up before the bishop's castle. But the sons of the holy covenant knew no trembling in the face of these mighty numbers of the enemy. All of them, strong or weak, put on armor and girded on swords. Rabbi Kalonymos ben Meshullam led them. And Rabbi Menachem ben David Halevi, one of the great men of his age, said: 'Do you sanctify the ineffable Name in perfect devotion!' Thereupon they proceeded toward the gate in order to fight against the Crusaders and the townsmen. Cruelly the combat raged. But by reason of our sins our enemies prevailed against us and streamed into the castle. The bishop's men, pledged to help us, fled and delivered us into the hands of the wicked. The bishop himself fled into his church, for they threatened him because he had spoken in favor of the Jews.

"May darkness devour the memory of that dread day! May God forget the name of that day and let no light shine upon it forever! Why were ye not extinguished, O constellations, ere you lit the earth for our foes?

"When the sons of the holy covenant saw that their fate was about to be fulfilled since their murderers swarmed into the court, they lifted up their voices—old men and youths, virgins and children, men servants and maid servants—and wept. But they submitted to the decrees of the Eternal and urged each the other to take upon him the yoke of Israel's martyrdom. And their one deep fear was that the weakness of the human flesh under the extremity of torture might keep any from sanctifying the ineffable Name. Therefore they all cried, cried even as one man and with a loud voice: 'We dare delay no longer, for the enemy is upon us. Let us hasten and sacrifice ourselves to the Lord. Whoever has a

255

knife, let him see that it has no notch and let him first slay us and then himself.'

"The first upon whom the enemies came in the courtyard were some of the most devout, among them that great scholar, Rabbi Jitzchak ben Moshe. These pious men had disdained to flee into the inner chambers in order to buy one more poor hour of life. Nay, they sat wrapped in their praying-shawls ready to fulfil the will of their Maker. The enemies first overwhelmed them with stones and arrows and then hewed them down with their swords. When those in the inner chambers saw the great patience of these saints they cried: 'The time has come!' The women girded their loins with strength and slew first their sons and their daughters and then themselves. Many men, too, plucked up courage and slew their wives and their children and their servants. Gentle and delicately nurtured women slew each her favorite child. Men and women slew each the other. And girls and young men and women who were betrothed looked out of the windows and cried: 'Behold, O God, what we do to sanctify Thy holy Name and to avoid being forced to acknowledge the Crucified!' Some slew and some were slain; the streams of their blood flowed and the blood of men was commingled with that of their wives, of fathers with that of their children, of brothers with that of their sisters, of teachers with that of their pupils, of children and babes with that of their mothers. All, all were slaughtered upon that day for the sake of the Oneness of the dreadful Name of God. He who hears thereof, is not his very soul shaken? For what has man seen in all ages like unto this thing? Ask whether since the days of Adam there was a martyrdom like this? Eleven hundred were sacrificed on one day. Each was like the sacrifice of Isaac, the son of Abraham which .made to tremble the foundations of the universe. Why then did not the heavens grow dark and the light of the stars go out and the sun and the moon die in their stations on that third day of Sivan when eleven hundred souls were slain in martyrdom—children, among them, oh, so many, and little babes, the poor innocents who had not yet sinned? Canst Thou let such things be, O Lord? Were they not slain for the sake of Thee? Avenge, O Lord, the blood of Thy servants soon, in our days, for our eyes to behold! Amen!

"Has human ear heard a tale like unto that of the deeds of that young woman named Rachel, the daughter of Rabbi Jitzchak ben Asher and the wife of Rabbi Jehudah? 'I have four children,' she said to her friends. 'Spare them not for the Christians to catch them alive and make renegades of them. Let them, too, sanctify the Name!' But when one of her friends took up the knife to slay one of the children the young mother cried aloud and beat her head and breasts. 'Where is thy loving kindness, O Lord?' she cried. And in her despair she spoke to her friend: 'Oh, do not kill Isaac before the eyes of Aaron. He must not see his brother's death!' But when little Aaron ran away, she nevertheless took Isaac, who was the younger and fair to look upon, and killed him and caught his blood in her sleeves as in a ewer. Aaron, seeing this, nevertheless, tried to hide behind a chest. The woman also had two very lovely young daughters, Bella and Madrona. These took up the knife of their own free will and whetted it and brought it to their mother and bent back their whie throats and besought her to sacrifice them. When now she had slain three of her dear children, Rachel called to her last child, to Aaron: 'Where are you, my son? I dare not spare you!' And by his foot she drew him forth from behind the chest where he was hidden and sacrificed him unto God. When her husband saw the death of his four lovely children he went and cast himself upon a sword and his entrails oozed forth from his quivering body. But the mother hid her dead children two in each of her wide sleeves, and sat her down and lamented. When the enemies came into the room they roared: 'Give us the gold, Jew wench, which is doubtless hidden in thy sleeves!' But when they saw the dead children they struck down Rachel, the mother, with one blow, so that she perished without a moan."

He had been reading long, and now for the first time lifted his face. Beneath his intense absorption he had felt a dull impulse. What was it? Yes, he thought he knew. Slowly the impulse rose intelligibly into his consciousness. He got up and walked to his shelves, to the shelf where he kept his favorite non-medical books. There it was, the volume of the great Christian philosopher. And the volume fell open, as Arthur drew it forth, almost at the page and at the penciled passage which he wanted, the eloquent and moving passage in which the philosopher declared that he would rather, in such a life as this, take his station with the Crusaders under the banners of the Cross than with those "Jews and Protestants" who love the world and possess it. He put the book back and began to pace up and down. He had always read that passage with the faintest of protesting twinges. But that twinge had been involuntary and irrational. His waking mind, aware of the historic process as described by Christian writers—and whether they were believers or not did not matter—his waking mind had accepted the legend and the symbol of the Crusades as wars and pilgrimages following a dream, an ideal, of the Crusaders as men who pressed to their bosoms something not made with hands. And his mind had also accepted the legend of the Jews (forced thereto, perhaps, he would have argued, by untoward conditions) as materialists and money-grubbers in that world of the streaming legions of Christ and of the great cathedrals. And he would not be less than just now, he considered, nor deny that above that rabble of murderers and thieves were remote leaders inspired by a sense of high and exotic adventure tinged by a mystic faith. But man for man, woman for woman, child for child, it was his people, it was the Jews who had clung to that which is not made with hands and had engaged, in those mediæval days and years, in an adventure which would draw down to them the everlasting mercy of God, if there was a God, the everlasting reverence of man, if man were not a liar and a special-pleader and wholly blinded by the idols of his tribe and place and tradition. And of course all history had been written from the same point of view and was, therefore, so far as Jews were concerned, a falsehood and a libel from beginning to end. And yet everywhere, or nearly everywhere, Jews not only went to Christian schools and believed what they were taught, but believed it with passion and with romantic yearning and identified themselves spiritually with those who had carried the banners of the West to the Holy Land. And the great lie was still in the making, was being lived day by day, hour by hour, here, as Reb Moshe would have said, in our generation and in our day. Jews were still regarded as money-grubbers and as stripped of spirituality, and the Christian rabble still held itself superior. And the thing had gone on so long and the flail of the ages had been so continuous and the lie had so soaked in that it would be no wonder if in truth so and so many Jews had become subtly or grossly cynical and had set their all upon material things. Nor had the actual slaying, the actual martyrdom, ever ceased. Yesterday in Russia, today in Rumania, tomorrow where?

He went back to his desk and sat down and took up the manuscript once more. The great and tragic tale repeated itself; it repeated itself in Ham and Sully and Carentan in France. Now and again the chronicler wove in some brief laconic human incident that lifted an hour and a day out of that far past into the very nearness of the living heart. "Two men, Rabbi Izchak ben Rabbi Joel, a Levite, and Max Yehudah, were in their vineyard on an autumn day, gathering the grapes. There a malignant Crusader fell upon them who were unarmed and slew them and fled. The dead Jews were buried with their fathers. The Crusader was never seen again. . . ." Somewhere a pious and repentant bishop caused the dead bodies of the slain Jews and the legs and arms and toes and thumbs that had been hacked from living Jewish bodies to be gathered in a wagon and washed and annointed and buried in his garden. "Later," said the chronicler, quietly "later Rabbi Chiskiah ben Rabbenu Eliakim and his wife Judith bought the garden of the bishop and gave it to their brethren as a burial-ground.

Their memory is blessed." The dread tale repeated itself in the towns and hamlets of England, especially in the city of York, where, at their own bidding and behest, Rabbi Jomtov slew sixty of his brethren lest they incur the danger of apostasy under torture. "Many a one who in ordinary life was so luxurious and fearful that he dared hardly set his foot upon the ground now commanded his children to be slain before his eyes. Others jumped into the flames in order thus to bear witness to the Unity of the Eternal. . . . Their houses were demolished, their gold and silver stolen, and their precious books, incomparable in beauty and more costly than jewels, were sent to the Continent and sold to the Jews of Cologne and of other cities."

Arthur put his hands against his temples. Often in other years he had a little resented his father's absorption in business. He thought that he suddenly understood the quality that marked Jewish absorption in business. Money was not success; money was security, weapon, defense, it built a home in the homeless world; it was the only reliance in the evil day. The enemy was never to be reasoned with. He might be bought off. . . . There were the learned to be taken care of and the poor and God's fools. . . . He read on and one passage concerning the happenings in England burned strangely into his mind: "There was a town in which the community consisted of only twenty souls. And they were all proselytes. All these were slain. They would not return to their former faith, but preferred to sanctify the Name by their death." He didn't, of course, care about myth or ritual or dogma. He never would. But he had always taken it for granted that even in the ages of faith the Jewish faith had had no persuasive power, that the spirit of Israel was hard, self-contained, unbending. But in that age one Christian proselyte outweighed ten thousand Jewish ones. For the Jew who became a Christian received in return security and fellowship and honor; the Christian who became a Jew received hatred, torture, death. . . . There were a few more pages.

He could read no more. And had he not read enough? . . .

How still it was about him! Still as the beginning of things. The only pain in the stillness was the absence of his child's voice. He must try to save his son's heritage for him, his incomparable spiritual heritage. His son should not stand before a Gentile friend as he had stood beside Charles Dawson, and wish that he, too, could boast as ancestors tartaned clansmen who had fought at Flodden Field. His son should have too much pride to need to be proud. Too much inner security to be hurt by words or slights. His son should be incapable of feeling excluded; he must possess the knowledge that he stood by birth at the human center of things. For if history has an ethical direction its symbol is not the clansman or the warrior, but he who passively defends an idea and thus sanctifies an ineffable Name. . . .

He made an appointment to see Elizabeth. The Adamses asked him to dine, but he said that he preferred to come in after dinner. He hardly knew whether he wanted to see Eugene and Joanna or not. He left it to chance and was received by his cousin. Eugene talked trivialities. Each knew that a subject burned between them. But Eugene had armored himself in advance. He had chosen his path with the utmost sagacity; he had reached his goal. Neither he nor Joanna ever pretended that they were not Jews; they were sincerely convinced that it mattered neither negatively nor positively. They were more than accepted. They were social and intellectual leaders in the group that was most congenial to them. If there were, in spite of all, whisperers behind their backs—well, there were vulgar and stupid people everywhere. One reckoned with that. How precisely they managed to shut out of their consciousness the needs and sufferings of their people Arthur didn't know. That was, he supposed, a matter of temperament. It was also a carefully and tacitly nursed ignorance. If once one *knew*. . . . One was careful not to know. . . . Finally, Arthur couldn't help saying, "I'm going to Rumania on a commission to investigate the condition of the Jewish communities there."

Eugene flicked the ashes from his cigarette. "Frightfully interesting. You ought to write something about your trip when you come back. I'm thinking seriously of starting a magazine. By the way, Elizabeth's novel will be our first serial. It's charming—charming." Yes, Eugene was armored. He had determined not even to admit the possibility of a discussion.

Elizabeth and Joanna came in together. Joanna couldn't be quite as icy as Eugene. In spite of her husband's frown she teased: "So you're going back to the Jews, Arthur. What a quaint thing to do!" Elizabeth took Arthur's hand and kept it for a moment in her own. Almost immediately—it had evidently been arranged—the Adamses withdrew. Elizabeth sat down on a low chair and leaned her right elbow on her knee and supported her chin in her cupped hand. She was grave and graceful, but a little wan. She asked him first when he was leaving, and he told her.

"I'm going away, too," she said. "If you don't mind on account of John, I'm going to the country with him. I want to be quiet and I think it will do him good, too. Spring is almost here."

"Eugene tells me they've asked you to stay on indefinitely."

"Oh yes. They're very sweet to me. But it's sort of cold and comfortless here. And they quarrel with me about you." She laughed a little.

"About me?"

"Yes. Isn't it funny? I hardly know how to explain it. They think you're making a plain damned fool of yourself. In addition they consider your folly dangerous. They think that any emphasizing of the Jewish question might drag them in and shake their position."

"Well, Elizabeth, and you don't agree with them?"

"Of course not. I'm my father's daughter. I understand the religious and humanitarian temperament instinctively. When I was a kid, long before I knew what suffrage was, I thought I'd like to be a missionary in China and maybe be martyred for the sake of our Lord. Only—" She hesitated.

Arthur leaned forward. "Do go on, Elizabeth, do!"

"Well, you see, we're not suited to each other in a number of ways. I know that, you poor darling. And then can you see me, with the best will in the world, trying to be a Jewess? You can't, can you?"

"No. Things like that can't be learned. I suppose they have to be resurrected out of one's inner self."

"That's it. Of course you did me one injustice."

"What's that?"

"Through your ignorance of yourself. You didn't know you were going to resurrect the Jew in you."

"You're right, Elizabeth, quite right. But really I didn't even have to resurrect the Jew. I just put away a pretense —a stubborn, hard, protective pretense. But no more."

"It's a kind of an argument, isn't it, against mixed marriages?" Her eyes were sad.

"I'm afraid it is," he answered. "One among many others."

She nodded. "You must see John. He's getting to be such a duck. What are we going to do about him?"

They went upstairs. The child was already asleep in his little bed and they moved softly. John's long black lashes were lying on his cheeks; his nose was delicately curved; a slightly careworn look was on his forehead. Arthur kissed the child gently and they went across the hall into Elizabeth's room.

"A Jewish child," he said.

She nodded. "I'll consent to anything reasonable in regard to his education. Are there Jewish boarding-schools?"

"There must be. I'll inquire by and by. There's still plenty of time for that. But you're very dear and splendid, Elizabeth."

Her eyes were moist as she answered: "My life has been hollow, too. I've come to see that recently. Maybe that has helped me to see your point of view. I think I may take a cottage in the country for good."

"Do you think you'll want to marry again, Elizabeth?"

"Can't tell. But you will, Arthur." She laughed a pathetic

263

little laugh. "You'll marry a nice Jewish girl some day. I'll release you whenever you like."

He took her face into his hands. "It's rather a pity about us, isn't it?"

"Rather."

He kissed her and begged her to remember him to the Adamses. He would see her and the child again to say good-bye.

Having listened carefully to his son, old Jacob Levy said: "I knew det story about de old chest and de docooments. My grendmudder Braine—de von who vent to die in Cherusalem—she told it to my fadder ven he vas little. Ent I can see my fadder chust like if it vas today telling us children about it. Of course I vas de youngest ent I didn't understent so vell. But I remember. I remember a great deal, come to t'ink about it, det I t'ought I hed forgot. Vy do ve forget? De olt people in de olt chenerations didn't use to forget. Maybe in de olt country dey forget less den ve do in America. I don't know. I don't know. . . . But in de early years here I chust forgot everyting ent your dear mudder—*her* mudder had already forgotten—ent so ve told you notting. It's funny, too. In our business, you know, ve come in contact wid de people det manoofacture reel Colonial antiques. Every family wid a New England name vants reel Colonial antiques ent den dey tell deir frients—some of dem, anyhow—det dey inherited de t'ings from deir ancestors. Deir proud of deir ancestors. Vell, of course, some of dem are foolish about it. But it's natural for people to be proud of deir ancestors. Vy did ve forget so? Maybe because America used to say: Dis is no place vere ancestors count. Only individooal vorth. . . . But det didn't last long. It hes changed in my time. . . . Yes, in my time. Vell, I'm glet to see my son remembering. I hear of odder young people remembering. My cheneration tried to pull down de house of Israel; maybe yours vill build it up again. . . ."

Hollsworthy Brown, D.S.M., joined Dr. Charles Dawson at luncheon in their club. Brown spoke with a perceptible

British accent: "You used to know Arthur Levy at Columbia?" he asked.

"Very well. We were great friends at one time. Sort of drifted apart later. A fine chap—quiet, thoughtful, very able."

"Well," Brown said with pursed, ironical lips, "I hear that he's abandoned his wife because she was a Christian and has become religious and has gone on a Jewish mission to the Balkans. Isn't that rather curious?"

Dawson's cool, pale eyes took in Brown with a touch of contempt. "That doesn't sound like old Arthur. Thoroughly decent chap. I'd want to know the facts from him or his wife. I wouldn't carry that sort of poisonous gossip if I were you. As to his casting in his lot with his own people —I don't know but what I like that; it's natural and thoroughly honorable to him. If all Jews did it, I for one would respect them the more. I don't think that Jews who try not to be Jews do themselves any good in the eyes of intelligent people. There's something wrong with a man who betrays his own kind. . . . I didn't always take that point of view. But I've changed my mind about a good many things during the years since the war. . . ."

Reb Moshe said to Arthur: "Don't be too enthusiastic. Jews are people. Remember that even our teacher Moses was angry at them. The Jews have always been a difficult people. Avoid two errors—a *goyish* error and a Jewish error."

Arthur smiled. "Now you're going to tell a story."

"I am. Listen! A man came to a Polish magnate and asked him: 'What do you think of the Jews?' The answer was: 'Swine, Christ-killers, usurers, not to be trusted.' 'But what do you think of Isaac?' 'A man after my own heart. An honorable man. A kind man. He saved me from bankruptcy.' 'And what do you think of Berl?' 'I have known Berl all my life. He's one of the best.' 'And of Shmuel?' 'Shmuel is a saint as everyone knows.' The same man went to a rich and pious Jew and asked him: 'What do you think of the Jews?' The pious man answered: 'A kingdom of priests and a holy nation, the elect of the Eternal, blessed be His name.' 'And what do you think of Isaac?' 'That thief? That scoundrel? May his bones be broken. He looks at you and you are robbed!' 'And of Berl?' 'A fellow of the same kind, without truth or justice.' 'And of Shmuel?' 'Do you think I am taken in by his piety? A pretentious idiot.' " Reb Moshe hid his hands in his sleeves. "Avoid both errors." Arthur laughed. He was quite sure that he would fall into a thousand errors. He was equally sure that the sky curved over him like a tent against the outer darkness and that the earth which his foot trod was his natural habitation and his home.

NOTE.—The historical narrative in Book Nine is based upon authentic sources contemporary with the events.